The Heart's Lonely Secret

*Also by Jane Peart
in Large Print:*

The Pattern
The Pledge
The Promise
Thread of Suspicion
Shadow of Fear

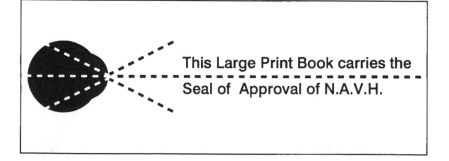

The Heart's Lonely Secret

JANE PEART

Thorndike Press • Waterville, Maine

Published in 2001 by arrangement with
Baker Book House.

Scripture quotations are from the King James Version of the Bible.

Thorndike Press Large Print Christian Fiction Series.

The tree indicium is a trademark of Thorndike Press.

The text of this Large Print edition is unabridged.
Other aspects of the book may vary from the original edition.

Set in 16 pt. Plantin by Al Chase.

Printed in the United States on permanent paper.

Library of Congress Cataloging-in-Publication Data
Peart, Jane.
    The heart's lonely secret / Jane Peart.
      p.   cm.
    ISBN 0-7862-3286-2 (lg. print : hc : alk. paper)
    1. Frontier and pioneer life — Fiction. 2. Orphan trains
— Fiction. 3. Middle West — Fiction. 4. Young women —
Fiction. 5. Orphans — Fiction. 6. Girls — Fiction.
7. Large type books.
I. Title.
PS3566.E238 H38 2001
813'.54—dc21
                                         2001027092

This book is dedicated to Mary Ellen Johnson, Director of the Orphan Train Heritage Society of America, gratefully acknowledging her encouragement, help and support, and to the *real* "riders" of the orphan trains, the over 100,000 children who were transported by train across the country to new homes in the Midwest, from 1854 to the early twentieth century, whose experience and courage inspired this series.

Prologue

"No! No!" The scream pierced the darkness and Ivy Austin came awake with a pounding heart. She sat up, clutching the bedclothes with small clammy hands.

The orphanage dormitory was dark, and none of the children in the other cots had stirred. Slowly, Ivy realized that the scream had echoed only in her mind. It was her old nightmare, the one she had had over and over, time and time again. Shivering, she lay back down, pulled the thin blanket over her shoulders, and curled herself into a ball. Still trembling from the dream, she relived the night it had all *really* happened.

Even though she had been only five then, Ivy still remembered the house where she had lived, especially the little room with its slanted ceiling where she slept in the small white iron bed.

Something had awakened her that night. For a few minutes she lay there listening to the rain pebbling on the tin roof. Then she realized she was thirsty.

For some reason, she wasn't sure why, instead of calling out for Mama to bring her a drink, Ivy had decided to go downstairs to ask for one. Her mother would be in the kitchen, maybe ironing or sewing, and would probably pretend to be provoked. She might put her hands on her hips and say, "What are you doing up, young lady?" Then she'd smile, take a glass tumbler down from the shelf, and fill it with water from the black cast-iron pump on the counter by the sink.

But when Ivy crept down the narrow stairway, the floor cold to her bare feet, she became aware of movement and hushed voices. She felt a chilly draft as the front door opened, shut, then opened again.

Then she heard her mother's broken sobs. "It can't be true! It just can't. Will can't be dead!"

That night was indelibly imprinted in Ivy's memory. It came back to her in recurrent nightmares — that night she had learned that her father was dead. Much later, she was told he had been killed in the line of duty as a fireman.

As hard as she tried to remember her father, all she could bring back were images of a tall man with twinkling blue eyes and reddish-brown whiskers, tossing her up in the air or cuddling her against his rough, blue serge jacket, two rows of shiny brass buttons pressing against her cheek.

When she thought of him, it seemed always to be Christmas — all of them together in the kitchen, warm and cozy, with the fire crackling in the black pot-bellied stove and the smells of peeled apples and baking pumpkin pies filling the room with spicy fragrance.

Her mother was in that picture, too, a slim, dark-haired woman, her face flushed with happiness and excitement as she stirred something on the stove, laughing over her shoulder, "Oh, Will!"

But after that terrible night, Ivy's memory of her mother became blurred, seemed to fade, and finally disappeared altogether. It was not long afterward that she recalled sitting at the kitchen table, spooning oatmeal into her mouth, while a group of the neighbor ladies huddled in the kitchen, whispering and giving her strange looks. Then they told Ivy that her mother had "gone to heaven." Gone to heaven and left Ivy here alone? She had screamed with rage at being left behind and had to be carried upstairs, kicking and crying.

The only other clear memory Ivy had of that time was being bundled up and brought to Greystone Orphanage. That was three years ago. Now Ivy was eight.

To bring back any of these scenes into her mind required tremendous effort. For as much as the nightmares upset her, Ivy clung to them fiercely, so terrified that, without them, she would forget completely. Forget that she had ever had a father or mother or a real home.

Squeezing her eyes tightly shut, Ivy wished she could go back to sleep even if it meant having the scary dream again.

As she lay huddled under the blanket, she heard, from somewhere out there in the night, the mournful wail of a train whistle. The sound made the hair on Ivy's head prickle. She shuddered. It made her feel even more alone. And yet, there was something about its wavering notes . . . as if somewhere — a long way off — there was something calling, beckoning. Could there be something unknown just ahead . . . another life than the orphanage?

Part 1

A Strange New World

Chapter One

Greystone Orphanage
March 1887

The shrill whistle signaling the end of the rec-
reation hour split the chilly March air. All
games stopped, and the children reluctantly
straggled into line. The older ones gathered
up balls and beanbags and jump ropes and
deposited them in the large wood storage
bins.

Ivy gave one longing glance over her
shoulder at the chalked hopscotch layout on
the cracked cement playground. She
dreaded the hour stretching ahead, hated
the thought of going back inside to the
drafty assembly room for the study period
before supper at five-thirty. Greystone followed the prevailing wisdom of the day —
that rigid discipline was necessary to control
large numbers of children. Unless the orphans were in the schoolroom, at meals, or
at their assigned duties, they were to remain
seated on long benches along the walls.

For Ivy, this was often agony. Her small,
wiry body needed the constant motion of

vigorous exercise to keep her muscles from twitching restlessly. Two daily forty-five-minute periods of playtime were simply not enough.

She sighed heavily and took her place in line with the rest of the children. At least today she would only have to stay until the bell summoning her to her chores released her. At five o'clock she had to report to the dining room for duty because this week was her turn to set tables. When the clapper banged three sharp clicks, she marched back into the gray stone building.

Just as they came inside, Ivy felt a hand grip her thin shoulder, and she was yanked out of line by Miss Preston, the hall monitor, who was standing at the door. "Ivy, you're wanted in the front office. But first go to your dormitory and put your clothes and other things in this." Miss Preston handed Ivy a canvas valise. "And hurry!"

Puzzled, but knowing better than to ask questions, Ivy obeyed. She ran up the two flights of steps, down the linoleum-floored corridor to the long room lined on either side with narrow iron cots. At her own cubicle she began stuffing her few meager belongings into the little case. All the while her mind whirled. What was this all about? Was she going somewhere? A flutter of hope stirred in her small chest — the hope of all the children at Greystone.

Miss Preston was waiting for her at the bottom of the stairway, impatiently drumming her fingers on the newel post. When Ivy reached the last step, Miss Preston put her hand under Ivy's chin, scrutinizing her. "Your hair's all tangled. You should have brushed it." Frowning crossly, she tugged at the regulation braids from which Ivy's unruly curls had escaped and straightened the collar of her coarse cotton uniform, sighing. "Not that it will matter, I daresay." She sniffed, wrinkling her nose distastefully. "Hmmph! Circus people!"

Ivy had no idea what that meant. But no explanation was forthcoming from Miss Preston, who simply gave her a little shove. "Go on. Miss Clinock's waiting for you."

Gripping the handle of the valise tightly, Ivy proceeded down the long corridor to the Matron's office. She knocked timidly and waited until she heard the invitation. "Come in."

She had only been in Miss Clinock's office a few times, usually to deliver a message from one of the other supervisors. It was only when you had done something very bad, had broken one of the big rules, or were going to be adopted that Miss Clinock

15

sent for you. That thought sent a little shiver all through Ivy. Was she going to be adopted?

As Ivy stepped over the threshold and then hesitated, Miss Clinock, seated behind her desk, glanced up over her nose glasses. "Hello, Ivy. Come in and shut the door, please," she said and went on with her writing.

Ivy did as she was told, then stood, feet close together. Sitting in the chair opposite the Matron was a swarthy, dark-haired man. Ivy darted a shy look at him. To her dismay she found him staring at *her* from under heavy black brows. She felt a quick, sharp fear. There was something menacing in those opaque eyes.

The sound of Miss Clinock's pen scratching on paper was the only sound in the office. Finally she finished writing, placed some papers into a folder, and handed them to the man. "Well, Mr. Tarantino, everything seems to be in order — all the papers on which our signatures are required. As I pointed out, with no living relatives, we have the authority to release the minor child, Ivy Austin, into your custody with your agreement to provide shelter, food, and an elementary education up to and through the eighth grade, until she is fifteen years of age. As far as we know, there is no impediment to this adoption."

Adoption? Ivy swallowed hard. Then she *was* being adopted!

Adoption was constantly discussed at Greystone. Among themselves, the children often imagined what it would be like to be picked out from the others and taken to a home where they would be cared for and loved. But *this,* Ivy realized with a nervous little tremor, was hardly the adoption she had daydreamed about.

"Ivy, this is Mr. Paulo Tarantino," Miss Clinock was saying. "You will be going with him. He wants you to be part of his family."

Ivy's heart began to thrum fast. What kind of family would it be? Where was the mother? Were there other children? Where was their home?

Miss Clinock came from behind her desk, bent down, and tucked a tiny, black imitation leather New Testament into the pocket of Ivy's jacket. "Good-bye, Ivy, be a good child and do as you're told. Try to remember the things you were taught here."

The next thing Ivy knew she was following Mr. Tarantino down the hall to the front door. Her shoulders and neck felt stiff. She wanted to look around to see if Miss Clinock was watching them, but somehow she didn't dare.

The March wind penetrated Ivy's thin jacket as they went outside and down the steps. At the sidewalk, something compelled Ivy to turn and look up at Greystone. Somehow she knew she was seeing it for the last time. She didn't know whether to be happy or sad, for she had no idea whether what was ahead of her was better or worse.

Mr. Tarantino walked over to a horse and wagon, hitched to the post across the street. "Get in, kid," he said, jerking his head in its direction. She clambered up. Mr. Tarantino climbed up on the other side, giving her a sidelong glance. "You like animals?"

Ivy nodded.

"Well, you gonna see lotsa animals where we're goin'." He picked up the reins. "Horses — you like?"

Again Ivy nodded. "Yes, sir."

He gave a short, harsh laugh. "You betta like horses."

It seemed to Ivy that they rode for a long time after they left the city streets, crowded with delivery carts, tram cars, carriages, and drays. Driving the rig well out into the country, Mr. Tarantino turned into a rutted lot. There, parked in haphazard fashion, Ivy saw a long line of painted wagons circling a number of gaily striped tents.

This must be a circus, she thought with a mingling of excitement and alarm. She'd seen pictures in one of the battered books in Greystone's limited library. But she'd never seen a *real* circus.

Skillfully Mr. Tarantino manipulated the wagon through the maze of vehicles, coming to a stop in front of a small tent.

"Hey, Angela!" he shouted. "I'm back. I got the kid."

A minute later, the tent flap was pulled back and a woman in a flowered robe looked out. She might have been pretty, Ivy thought, if it weren't for the sour expression on her face.

The woman surveyed Ivy with dark shadowed eyes. Then her lips curled unpleasantly. "I thought you wuz gettin' a *boy!*"

Mr. Tarantino let go a torrent of words that Ivy figured must be in a foreign language, for she couldn't understand a word of it. But from the tone of his voice, he sounded angry.

The woman did not flinch, only retorted, "And this is the kid you've been watchin'?"

Another rapid spate of unintelligible words tumbled out.

The woman shrugged. "Well, I hope you

know what you're doin'." Then she stepped back inside the tent, letting the flap fall shut behind her.

Mr. Tarantino muttered something under his breath, slapped the reins on the horse's back, and they moved forward again with a jerk. After a minute's silence he said, "You'll be sleepin' in Sophia's wagon. She used to be one of us before she got too old and fat. Now she tells fortunes. She's got an extra bunk in her caravan." He fixed Ivy with a look that made her shrink inside. "You'll sleep dere. But you take orders from *me*. Nobody else." He jabbed his finger first at her, then tapped his chest with his thumb. "Unnerstan'?"

Ivy nodded.

Mr. Tarantino turned the wagon into a scrubby plot beside the tent into which the woman had disappeared. Then he jumped down from the driver's seat and looped the reins over a tent pole. "Come on, I'll take ya over dere."

Ivy scrambled down from the wagon and, gripping her valise tightly, followed him as he threaded his way through the maze of tents and wagons. She tried to keep up with his brisk stride, but it was almost impossible. Besides, she was constantly distracted by all the new and interesting things she was seeing.

She wanted to stop and look all around, but she was afraid to for fear she'd lose sight of Mr. Tarantino and not be able to find her way. If she was going to live here, there would be other times to explore.

All at once a terrifying roar startled Ivy so that she dropped her little suitcase. "Oh, my goodness!" she gasped. Turning to see where the frightening noise was coming from, she stood, rooted to the spot. When she caught her breath, she saw just ahead, a line of wagons. Inside, animals she had only seen in picture books paced restlessly.

Ivy resumed walking, her eyes widening in fascination as she slowly went past, peering into the cages. There was a sleek black panther, a tawny-maned lion, and a gold and bronze tiger, pawing at the bars of its cage, his jagged, white fangs exposed in a snarl.

An ear-splitting whistle jolted her. Ivy spun around and saw Mr. Tarantino standing several yards ahead, his hands on his hips. "Hey, you kid, stop gawkin'!" he yelled at her, motioning her forward with an impatient wave. "Come on! I ain't got all day."

Ivy hurried forward, shifting her valise to the other hand. As she did, the flimsy clasp sprung open and the contents spilled out. Hastily she poked everything back in and ran to catch up with him.

Breathless from running and afraid that Mr. Tarantino would get cross again, Ivy stayed close behind as he weaved in and out between the randomly parked caravans and wagons. Finally they reached a brightly painted wagon with a curved roof. Every square inch of the sides was embellished with clouds, stars, circled moons, curlicues of gilt, and exotic flowers, floating on a blue background.

Mr. Tarantino rapped sharply on the little arched door. "Sophia! Hey, you in dere? It's Paulo!"

Did he ever talk in a normal voice? Ivy wondered.

After a short wait, Paulo knocked again, louder.

A querulous voice called, "Whatcha want?"

"The kid I brung from the orphanage today . . . can she sleep here tonight? We ain't got no room in the tent."

The door inched open and a pale, moon-shaped face peered out. It was framed in a halo of brilliant orange corkscrew curls. Ivy had never seen such astonishing hair. The head came out farther, swiveled to the right and left and then, spotting Ivy, speared her with small, bright eyes. "Why, she's a *girl!*"

Intimidated, Ivy took a step back.

"I thought you wuz gettin' a boy, Paulo."

"So?" He shrugged. "What's the difference if I think she's got the stuff?"

"Huh!" The woman made a derisive grunt. "And do *my* old stunts? No girl equestrian's been able to do them since I quit."

"Sure, sure, Sophia." Paulo made a dismissing gesture. "Well, we'll see. Maybe yes, maybe no." He lifted his shoulders, "And if not . . ."

The "if not" hung in the misty air, taunting Ivy. If not, what then?

"So, Sophia, what will it be? Will you put her up or not?"

"I said I would, didn't I?"

Paulo seemed satisfied. "You stay here with Sophia tonight," he told Ivy. "Tomorrow we'll start your trainin' — ridin' a horse. You'll like that. All kids like ponies." He gave Ivy a pat on the head with his knuckles — though it felt more like a rap — and walked away.

Ivy looked uncertainly at Sophia who was staring after his departing figure, a curious expression on her face. Then, as if remembering Ivy was there, Sophia gave her a smile that revealed several missing teeth. Beckoning to her, the belligerent tone she had used with Paulo softened. "Come on in, little lady."

Feeling chilled and a bit disoriented, Ivy was glad to be invited into the caravan. Outside, it had seemed garish but inside it was like a dollhouse. Ivy looked around with wonder and pleasure. Dainty ruffled curtains hung at the tiny windows. Paper flowers filled colored glass bottles, pottery mugs, and vases. Shelves built around the room held a collection of costumed dolls. Japanese fans were hung on the walls. Plump flowered pillows — some, embroidered with "Sarasota, Florida" or "Do unto Others" — were piled on a narrow bunk. There was so much to see that Ivy was momentarily speechless.

"You hungry?" Sophia asked.

The strange woman's question reminded Ivy of her empty stomach. It was past the early suppertime at Greystone. "Yes, ma'am."

"Oh, don't call me ma'am. Call me Sophia. Everyone else does. Although my *professional* name was Sophrania Tarantino, not that I'm any relation to *them*. I was hired by Paulo's father, Lorenzo. He used to be the head of the troupe and he wanted to bill us as a family act." Sophia shook her head. "He

24

was a lot different from Paulo. Stern, yes, but kind . . . patient." She made a clucking sound with her tongue. Ivy got the feeling Sophia must not care much for Paulo.

Ivy put down her suitcase, which had become quite heavy, and sat down on the edge of a chair, watching Sophia move around in the tiny chamber. Sophia was huge, taking up most of the room in the small space. She went over to the stove where something delicious-smelling bubbled in a pot. Picking up a long wooden spoon, she pointed it at Ivy. "So they're going to make you an equestrian, eh?"

Ivy didn't know what *equestrian* meant. But Sophia didn't seem to need an answer. She went on talking, one hand on her ample hip, as she stirred with the other. "I was a headliner in my day." She sighed, remembering. "My act used to be a real show-stopper. I'd enter the ring, driving Venus in a painted two-wheel cart decorated with garlands of roses. I'd be in a gown — all flounces and flowers — and a hat trimmed with ribbons. I'd put Venus through a routine of fancy steps and a series of gaits, then we'd end the number by having her rear up on her hind legs again and again before the exit. It took real skill, I don't mind tellin' you, and lots of practice so as not to overturn the cart."

While Sophia talked on, adding herbs and seasonings to the simmering pot, Ivy listened to her stories about her days as a performer. To look at her now, though, it was hard for Ivy to imagine her as a graceful horseback acrobat.

Sophia paused for a moment to take a sip from her spoon. "Ummm, that's good, if I do say so!" She shut her eyes in ecstasy, then opened them. "Ready for the taste treat of your life, little lady?" she asked, chuckling. "Well, sit down over there and we'll have at it." She nodded toward a small table between two of the windows.

Ivy sat down on one of the quaint blue chairs, her mouth watering from the tantalizing smells wafting up from whatever Sophia was dishing into two bowls. When she brought the bowls to the table, the contents turned out to be a thick, savory stew of meat, vegetables, and potatoes.

With some effort, Sophia wedged her bulk into the other chair and sat down. Clasping her pudgy, heavily-ringed fingers together, she glanced across at Ivy. "Do you know a grace to say?"

Ivy only knew the blessing they said in chorus at the orphanage at every meal, but at Sophia's question, her mind went blank.

Sophia waited only a second, then spoke up. "Never mind. I'll say it tonight." She bowed her head, squeezed her eyes shut, and murmured, "God be thanked for this food, bless the hands that prepared it, and bless those who partake. Amen."

Ivy joined in on the "Amen" and Sophia smiled approvingly. "We're going to be great friends, I can see that, little lady."

For a few minutes they simply ate, relishing the delicious food. Then Sophia wrinkled her brow. "I forget. What did Paulo say your name was?"

"It's Ivy. Ivy Austin."

"Ivy, huh?" she repeated, then shrugged. "Well, they'll probably change it. Make it something Italian, I expect. But it don't matter. Whatever you are *inside* is what counts." Sophia tapped her bosom. "Don't let anyone ever try to change you *there.*"

They ate in silence for a few minutes, then Sophia asked, "Do you think you're going to like circus life?"

"I . . . don't know."

"Oh, it may seem strange at first, but I 'spect you'll come to like it. Most circus folks are born to it, or come because they've got a yen for it. Maybe the circus passed through their town, and they got a whiff of sawdust and decided that was for them."

Sophia's eyes had a faraway look. "Once you get sawdust in your hair, you never get it out."

Having eaten her fill and, comforted by the coziness of the little caravan and by Sophia's friendliness, Ivy's eyelids began to droop.

"Time for you to turn in, little lady," Sophia told her.

By placing folded quilts and pillows on a ledge under one of the small ruffled windows, a makeshift bed was soon arranged. Gratefully Ivy crawled up into it and snuggled into its extraordinary softness. Tucking her in, Sophia announced, "In the morning you can go to the cookhouse tent for breakfast. I don't make breakfast. I sleep late and don't have anything but my java until noon. But a growing kid needs good, nourishing food. Besides, you gotta get strong enough to be in Paulo's act. Jim and his wife, Bella, are fine cooks. Just tell 'em you're bunkin' with me. They'll treat you real good. And you'll get a chance to meet some of the other circus people . . ."

Sophia's voice droned on, but Ivy heard no more. No matter how strange her new family, at least she had a home. Secure in the thought, she drifted off to sleep.

Chapter Two

Higgins Brothers' Circus

When Ivy awoke the next morning, she lay quite still, unsure of where she was. Slowly the events of the day before filtered back into her mind, and she remembered. Adopted! She'd been adopted by that surly man, Paulo Tarantino, the man with the frighteningly piercing dark eyes. According to Sophia, he was going to teach her to ride a horse. From now on, the circus would be her home.

What kind of life would it be? Ivy had no idea. She knew nothing about circuses. Filled with curiosity, she eased herself up and out of the bed Sophia had fixed her the night before. The sound of rhythmic snoring came from behind the curtains drawn across the alcove at the far end of the caravan. Her hostess must still be asleep.

Not wanting to disturb her, Ivy tiptoed over to where she had put her clothes the night before and quietly got dressed. As she did, she was startled to see the amazing mass of orange curls resting on a wooden stand on top of the bureau. So that wasn't Sophia's *real* hair, but a wig!

Ivy felt hungry. To her question as to the whereabouts of the cookhouse tent, Sophia had replied offhandedly, "Ask anyone. I'm not sure where they set it up this time. It's never in the same place twice."

Knowing she'd have to find her own way, Ivy noiselessly pushed open the caravan door and slipped outside. She stood for a minute in the early-morning mist, wondering which way to go. The few people she saw all seemed busy and preoccupied. Feeling too shy to ask directions, Ivy began walking past wagons and caravans, hoping she would come upon the tent herself.

However, she had taken only a few steps when a cheery voice called out to her, "Hello there! Lookin' for somebody?"

Ivy turned to see a bald-headed man with a stubble of beard on his weathered face. "You're new around here, ain'tcha? Not lost, are you? Or did you run away to join the circus?" As he came toward her, she could see the twinkle in his blue eyes.

Ivy shook her head. "I'm looking for the cookhouse."

"It's breakfast you're wantin', is it? Well, come along then. I'm going over there myself. You can tag along. I'm Timothy

O'Brien, better known as Gyppo."

"I'm Ivy, Ivy Austin."

"Well, now, that's a nice name." As he fell into step beside her, he commented, "I'll bet a dollar to a doughnut, you're to be with the Tarantinos."

Puzzled, Ivy frowned. "How did you know?"

"Ach, the whole circus knew somethin' was brewin'. Not many secrets around here, I can tell ya that much. Paulo and his two younger brothers were a team. All three have tempers and, from time to time, one or the other would blow up. Not too long ago they had a set-to you could've heard two counties over! Since it was all in Italian, no one knew what it was all about. Then Tonio and Luca just up and quit. Left after their last performance and didn't show up when we got ready to move North for the start of the season. You'd think a coupla months apart, they'd have cooled off and come on back. But they didn't." Gyppo shook his head. "And circus performers are supposed to know that whatever happens, *the show must go on.*"

"So what happened?"

"Well, I guess *you* happened is what happened." Gyppo chuckled. "Paulo's been braggin' how he could replace Luca and

31

Tonio, no problem. *He* could train somebody to replace 'em in three weeks.
Someone young and agile, he kept sayin'.
That Paulo's a secretive kinda fellow . . .
except for what he wants people to know.
Lots of rumors was flyin'. Talk was he'd
been scouting around — orphanages,
mostly — looking for someone to train. But
time was gettin' short. The season's about
to open." Gyppo glanced down at Ivy speculatively. "So I guess you're it, kid."

They'd reached a big tent from which
floated the smell of coffee and frying sausage. Ivy felt her stomach tighten. Gyppo
held the flap back for her to enter.

Inside were rows of tables and benches.
At the far end on a longer table were set
large shiny steel cauldrons with steam rising
from them and huge blue coffeepots. Here
in the warmth, the aromas were even more
tantalizing than they had been outside.

"Come along. You can eat at the performers' table with me this marnin', even if you
ain't quite one of us yet." Gyppo smiled
down at her kindly. She followed him over
to the long service table. Behind it stood a
red-faced woman, scooping up generous
portions of fluffy scrambled eggs, links of
sausage, and strips of crisp bacon. Ivy could
hardly believe her eyes. Breakfast at

Greystone had been lumpy oatmeal, one slice of toast, a cup of watery cocoa.

"Marnin', Bella," Gyppo said. "I'd like you to meet my companion here, Ivy, Ivy Austin. She's goin' to be with Paulo."

Bella grimaced. Then glancing at Ivy, she asked him, "Who's she supposed to replace? Tonio or Luca?"

"Who knows?" Gyppo helped himself to several strips of bacon. "I hear he's plannin' a whole new act."

"But she hardly more'n a slip of a little *girl!* Can she do a backward flip on horseback? What's Paulo thinkin' of?" Spatula in one hand, Bella wiped her forehead with the back of one arm, eyeing Ivy sadly. "Poor kid." She put another large dollop of scrambled eggs on Ivy's plate. "Here, honey, you'll need to grow some muscles if you're gonna work with Tarantino."

"She'll do all right, Bella. Ivy'll make a place of her own. She's a plucky one, I can tell."

"Well, good luck then!" Bella's voice trailed after them as Ivy carried her laden tray, following Gyppo to one of the tables. Others were already seated there, eating, talking together, and drinking coffee from large white mugs. They greeted Gyppo, gazed curiously at Ivy, then smiled and nodded as he introduced her. Soon they all went back to their conversation. Glad not to be the center of attention, Ivy dug into her breakfast, enjoying every bite.

She was almost finished when Paulo, accompanied by the same woman who had spoken to him from the tent the evening before, came in. Seeing Ivy, he nodded. After filling his plate, he set it down at another table and came over. "Look kid, soon as I eat, I'll take ya down to the ring and we'll get started. Ever been on a horse?"

Ivy shook her head.

Paulo grunted, "Well, there's always a first time." He frowned, mumbling almost to himself, "Maybe I shoulda got a kid from a farm . . ." Shrugging, he looked at Gyppo as if he had just noticed him. "Can she hang around with you till I'm ready?"

Gyppo grinned. "Glad of the company."

With that, Paulo went back to where his heavy-lidded wife was sipping coffee and staring over at Ivy. He sat down beside her and within minutes an argument had erupted between them. Their quarreling voices soon could be heard all over the tent.

Horrified, Ivy looked at Gyppo.

He gave her a broad wink. "How about you and me goin' to see the elephants?"

"Oh, yes!" she replied, relieved.

"Then come on. Let's get outta here."

They had to pass by the table where the Tarantinos were still going at it, but neither one seemed to notice. It was the first time Ivy had seen grown-ups shouting angrily at each other, and it made her feel uncomfortable.

Outside, the lot was a web of tangled ropes and yards of canvas being unrolled from a giant spool. It seemed impossible, but Gyppo assured Ivy that before the afternoon performance, they would have the big top ready, banners flying, and everything set for the band's opening medley, announcing the beginning of the show.

"They do this nearly every day," he explained, "and tonight, after the final performance, they'll take it all down, be ready to move on to the next town and set it all up again. But we're not due to start for another week. So all this week the performers are puttin' the finishing touches on their acts."

Gyppo took her around back where the elephants were being prepared for their performance that afternoon and introduced her to their caretaker, Harry.

Harry winked at Ivy. "So this here's the kid Paulo's been boasting he can make into an equestrian star in six months?"

"Well, maybe this time he can prove

something he says," said Gyppo. "This here's one smart little lady."

"I think you're right, Gyppo." Harry smiled at Ivy.

"Could she stay with you while I get ready? I'm due at rehearsal in twenty minutes."

"Sure thing."

"See you later then, Ivy." Gyppo waved as he moved off toward his own tent.

Ivy stayed while Harry watered and fed the elephants.

"Some folks might think this kind of job — takin' care of animals — is well . . . beneath 'em . . . know what I mean? For me, though, it's my dream come true. You see, I run away from home when I was fourteen to join the circus," he told Ivy. "I've always loved animals. When I was a little tyke, I wore out a picture book of jungle animals, just lookin' at it. But, to me, the elephants are special." Harry stroked a coarse-skinned trunk. "Big as they are, they're gentle and sensitive. They know if you love 'em, care about 'em."

Ivy watched as Harry went from one to the other of the giant animals, talking softly to them. After all of them had finished eating, Harry said he had to take the elephants to put on their fancy headdresses and capes. "Even though it's just a rehearsal, we have to be sure they know what's expected of them when it's time for the real show."

Just then Paulo swaggered into sight. Although short, he had a trim, muscular build and moved with athletic grace. Giving Harry a brief nod, he addressed Ivy, "Come on down to our tent. Angela'll give you something to wear. Then we'll go down to the corral and get you started."

As she turned to follow Paulo, Harry called after her, "Good luck, Ivy!"

From the expression on his face, she had the feeling she'd need it.

Although Angela had been sullen and silent as she dug into her costume trunk for some tights and a top for Ivy to put on, the rest of the morning was not too bad. To begin with, it was a pony Ivy was to learn to ride, not a tall, frightening horse. Paulo showed her how to mount and, once she was seated in a comfortable saddle, her feet firmly in the stirrups, he instructed her how to hold the reins. Then he led her slowly around the circle.

For all her apprehension, Ivy's first training session was not what she had anticipated at all. The well-schooled pony obediently walked and trotted at Paulo's commands. After her first nervousness, there seemed nothing to be afraid of. In fact, Ivy actually enjoyed it. At the end of an hour, Paulo seemed satisifed. "This afternoon you can watch the rehearsals. Get an idea of what we do. Tomorrow we can get down to business."

Feeling a little stiff, Ivy clambered to the ground and Paulo led the pony away, calling indifferently over his shoulder, "Go back to Sophia's, kid. She'll tell you how to get to the big tent."

Ivy had already begun to realize that here at the circus, she would be on her own, expected to find her own way. This was so different from the orphanage, where every minute of every day orphans were told what to do, how to do it, when and where to do it. This was a whole new world. A little scary maybe, but Ivy decided she liked it.

She thought she knew how to get back to Sophia's caravan, but as she neared it, she halted, confused. Somehow she must have taken a wrong turn. The caravan looked as she remembered it and was in the same location, but another woman was standing in the doorway. Someone Ivy did not recognize at all.

She was large like Sophia, but other than

her size, she looked entirely different. This woman was dressed in a floating gown of rainbow-colored stripes, a tangle of many strings of shiny beads swung around her neck. A colorful scarf was tied over her head and long, glittering earrings dangled from her ears. Her face, when she turned to look at Ivy, was heavily rouged, the eyes, shadowed in purple and outlined in black. It was only when the shiny red painted lips parted in a half-smile that Ivy felt a glimmer of doubt. Could it possibly be?

Then out rippled a deep, rolling laugh from the enormous bosom. Instantly Ivy was relieved. It was Sophia, after all! But she had been transformed into a gypsy.

"Scared you, did I? I'm sorry, love. It's me, no worry about that. Only now I'm Romany Rovina, the gypsy fortune-teller, who knows all, tells all . . . for a price!" Sophia laughed until she shook all over. Ivy had to laugh, too.

Sophia put on a mysterious air. "Cross my palm with silver, little lady, and I'll tell you your past, your present, your future . . ." Then she paused and heaved a deep sigh. "Poor little kid, I don't think I want to know *your* future with that Paulo."

"Now, don't be gettin' maudlin, Sophia," warned a voice Ivy thought she knew. "Save your predictions for the 'towners.' That's what they pay you for. Ivy don't need no more comments about Paulo."

When Ivy turned around, she saw a clown. His white, powdered face sported a marvelous painted-on grin and a bulbous nose. Straw-colored yarn hair sprouted from beneath a dented top hat, and he was wearing baggy striped pants and oversized shoes.

"Want to see the rest of the circus, meet some of the performers, Ivy?" he asked.

This time she knew immediately. It was *Gyppo!* "Oh, yes! Paulo said I could watch the rehearsals in the big top this afternoon."

"Well, come along. I'll give you a guided tour beforehand."

"Show her the midway, too, where I'll be holding out in all my glory when the circus opens."

"What is the midway?" Ivy asked.

"The midway is where the concession-aires set up their booths. They sell hot dogs, balloons, cotton candy, pinwheels on sticks, dolls, plaster dogs, stuffed animals, satin pillows, that kind of thing. Then there's dart-throwing, games of chance, ring toss," Gyppo explained. "And the special attractions like Sophia's fortune-tellin' booth and Martina, the Snake Charmer, and . . ."

"Don't forget the freaks," Sophia prompted.

"The *freaks?*" Ivy looked from one to the other.

Gyppo shook his head. "I think we could skip them this first time."

"Ah, you're too soft-hearted, Gyppo."

"Just don't like people bein' exploited, Sophia." To Ivy, he said, "They're wonderful people, really. It's just that they've been born with . . . well, they look different, that's all. There's the Alligator Man, with skin like a reptile, the Bearded Lady, and the Miniature Monahans, a family of dwarfs from Australia."

"It's a livin', ain't it?" put in Sophia. "If it weren't for the circus, what kind of job could they get? Who would hire 'em? Have you thought of that, Gyppo?"

"I suppose you're right." Gyppo conceded. "Well, Ivy, shall we go and get a good seat for the show?" He tipped his hat with exaggerated politeness to Sophia, then held out his hand to Ivy. When she took it, he squeezed hers and a loud horn blared. She jumped back in alarm, then, realizing the trick, she giggled. Sophia joined in and, pleased with himself, Gyppo roared with laughter.

Together they weaved their way in and

out of the camped caravans, Gyppo stopping here and there to introduce Ivy to some of the performers. Most of them were now attired in costumes, ready for the grand rehearsal of the opening show.

Outside one of the tents, a wire was erected, tautly suspended between a wagon and the hitching post. Walking across it was a slim, blonde lady, balancing herself delicately step by step, holding a ruffled parasol in one hand as she went. Gyppo stood very still, putting his finger to his lips to signal Ivy to be quiet. Watching her progress, Ivy held her breath and did not let it go until the performer jumped down and practiced two curtsies.

"Magnificent!" Gyppo applauded.

"Merci!" The young woman smiled. "And who is your little friend?"

"This is Ivy. She's goin' to be one of us. She's Tarantino's new act."

The rosebud mouth formed a slight pout. *"Ah, mais non!"*

"Yup, 'fraid so."

"Well, Ivy, welcome to the circus. I'm Liselle." The enchanting young woman offered her free hand.

"I don't see how you do that!" Ivy said breathlessly.

Liselle smiled. "I was born to it. I grew up

with aerialists. I started young. It takes lots of practice, that's all." She laughed lightly. "And only two rules — don't look down and don't panic."

"I'm taking Ivy over to the big top to watch the rehearsal."

"Then you'll catch *my* act. Have a good time."

They walked on, Ivy thinking Liselle the loveliest thing she had ever seen.

On the way, Gyppo introduced Ivy to a man over six feet tall called Tiny who had an act with tigers and lions. Farther on, he greeted a group of acrobats dressed in shiny white satin costumes, their short capes lined in red silk. These were the Flying Fortunatos, a family of daring trapeze artists.

As they passed a handsome, erect man attired in a Prussian officer's uniform — a crimson jacket with gold epaulets and high black leather boots — Gyppo told Ivy that he was Klaus von Bremer, one of the "stars" of the circus. He had come from Austria, bringing with him four gleaming black Arabian horses that he had trained in a number of outstanding routines.

Just outside the big top, Gyppo pointed to a group of jugglers who were tossing rings and dumbbells into the air faster than Ivy could keep track. Nearby, a woman was putting a group of small dogs, all barking and yipping, through a series of tricks. There was so much going on everywhere, so much to see.

"I'd better take you in and get you settled now so's I can go and join the rest of the clowns for our act," Gyppo told her.

As they entered, the band was tuning up, and Gyppo explained that each act was cued musically for the entrances and exits.

Sitting at ringside that afternoon, Ivy was an entranced spectator. Since she'd never before been to a circus, everything — every performer, every act — was a marvel to her.

She soon learned that at the circus, nothing was as it seemed. Just as Gyppo and Sophia had magically become a clown and a gypsy by donning costumes, so the other performers were similarly transformed. The spectacular Sheik Ahmad, in a gold lamé turban and beaded vest, putting his exotic tigers through flaming hoops, was really Tiny, the same rangy man in overalls, whom she had met earlier.

Liselle, who had seemed beautiful even in her plain leotard and tights, now appeared on the high wire as a sparkling fairy-like illusion of beauty and grace.

Ivy held her breath as the Flying

Fortunatos swung, tumbled in midair, caught each other by their hands, and hung upside down on their trapezes. She laughed until her sides ached with the antics of the clowns.

Of course, Ivy watched the performance of the Tarantinos with special interest. When the ringmaster announced them, Ivy hardly recognized the ill-tempered Angela, now a smiling, crowd-pleasing charmer, as with her sister Gina and her husband Vince in green satin costumes shimmering with varicolored sequins. They came running into the ring, followed by a magnificent white horse, mane and tail streaming out like silken banners. In the center, Paulo, in a similar costume with the addition of a crimson-lined short cape, cracked a long whip and the horse began cantering, circling the ring. One by one, the others took a running leap onto the horse's back as he went by until all three were astride, waving at the audience as the horse continued to circle. There were other tricks as more horses were brought in. Forward and backward somersaults were turned while the horse was moving. Finally, Gina was alone in the ring. At Paulo's command, she jumped on the horse in a standing position, smiling and waving both arms, while the horse never lost his gait. Ivy crossed both her index fingers and took a deep breath. Did Paulo expect *her* to do *that?*

When Gyppo came to get her, Ivy was dazed by all she had seen. Coming out of the big top, she was surprised to see Harry's elephants, now out of their red and gilt-tasseled costumes, helping the roustabouts with their work.

"Elephants not only perform in the show, they have important jobs, too," Gyppo explained.

They stood for a few minutes watching as the huge animals patiently pulled the rigging, pushed vehicles with their heads, towed some of the heavy equipment.

"We'd better get on back to Sophia or she'll be sayin' we kept her up too late from her beauty sleep." Gyppo chuckled.

At Sophia's caravan, they found her sitting at her table with her fortune-telling cards spread out on the table before her.

"Practicin' how to fool the towners with your predictions, are you?"

"Just gettin' my cards warmed up," she sniffed, tossing her head. "How'd you like the show?" Sophia asked Ivy.

"It was wonderful! I especially liked the black horses and the man who got them to dance and bow."

Sophia exchanged a look with Gyppo, then said, "Better not let Paulo hear you say that. Baron von Bremer ain't one of Paulo's favorite people. He gets green as all get out if you so much as mention his name."

"Now Sophia . . ." Gyppo admonished.

"Well, it's the truth and the kid might as well be warned. No use her gettin' off on the wrong foot with Paulo."

After Gyppo left, Sophia made tea to which she added generous spoonfuls of honey. "This will make you sleep tight, little lady. If there's *one* prediction I can really make, it's that you're goin' to have quite a day tomorrow."

Chapter Three

Even though Sophia's powers as a fortune-teller were make-believe, she had correctly foreseen Ivy's next twenty-four hours. Her training began with a physical change. When Paulo banged on Sophia's door early the next morning, he took Ivy directly over to the Tarantino tent. Both Angela and Gina were there and both looked at him nervously.

Giving Ivy a push between her shoulder blades, Paulo pointed her to a high stool and ordered his wife, "Get the scissors."

"Ah, but Paulo, it's so pretty!" Angela protested, slipping her fingers through Ivy's silky curls.

"Cut it!" he shouted. "We can't bill her as a boy with all dem curls."

A towel was pinned around Ivy's shoulders, and Angela began snipping away at her shoulder-length hair. One by one, the dark spirals fell to the floor. When she was finished, Gina presented Ivy with a mirror to see the results. She looked entirely different, just as Sophia and Gyppo had when they donned their circus costumes. Ivy felt unlike herself and Gina's "You'll get used to it" was small comfort.

However, Ivy didn't have much time to dwell on her appearance. She was too busy learning to ride. Every day for the next month, from right after breakfast until afternoon, Paulo had her out practicing on the vacant lot beyond the circus backyard.

The "backyard," Ivy had learned, was where the wagons were parked. Here, too, the circus people caught up on their laundry, and the clotheslines were always full. Performers lounged around, playing cards or checkers, or took advantage of the sunshine and stretched out on the grass to catch a few winks. The circus children were romping about while the women performers sewed or mended. There was little conversation, just the occasional sound of an elephant's trumpeting or the distant roar of the tigers and lions from their cages at the end of the lot.

Paulo, however, rarely took advantage of any leisure. Tireless himself, he was relentless in his training of Ivy. After the first day, her lessons began in earnest. He showed her how to mount a little pony named Kismet and how to hold the reins, then told her to circle the ring as he looked on. Ivy soon tired of the constant bouncing in the saddle. Her feet kept slipping out of the stirrups and her neck wrenched with each jog while the leather reins cut into her hands. She bit her lip to keep from crying. She wanted to stop, but every time they reached the spot where Paulo was standing, he would shout, "Circle!" and Ivy was forced to go around again. She lost count of how many times she and Kismet circled the ring.

When Paulo finally yelled, "Whoa!" and grabbed the reins, bringing the pony to a halt. Ivy slid off, her knees almost buckling. Paulo showed not the slightest concern, but ordered her back to Sophia's.

Ivy limped into the caravan. Taking one look at her, Sophia boiled some water and poured it into a tub. "Here, soak in this. It'll ease some of your soreness, love," she said. "It'll be different when you're actually in the act, performing," she promised Ivy. "At the sound of applause, all your troubles will disappear." Her voice took on a dreamy quality. "You just don't get over the sound of clapping, the excitement, the thrill, the music. Why, there's nothin' else like it . . . not if you go to the ends of the earth."

Practice, practice, more practice became the order of Ivy's day. There was so much to learn that she sometimes felt overwhelmed. Not only must she learn the rudiments of riding, but how to treat the horses and care for them. For even though Paulo seemed indifferent toward people, he did take excellent care of his horses.

Sometimes Ivy was almost too tired to eat, too worn out to do more than crawl into her bunk. But she didn't always fall asleep right away. Her muscles ached, twitching and knotting into spasms from the unaccustomed exercise. Her ears rang with the sound of Paulo's commands, and even though her eyes were closed, she could still see his angry face, the black eyes sparking fire, the mouth drawn back from those clenched white teeth.

At night, lying in her narrow makeshift bed, the longing to be cared for and protected — shielded from Paulo's constant barking, "Mount! Trot! Canter!" — would overtake Ivy and the tears would come.

The lack of companions her own age intensified Ivy's loneliness. At least at the orphanage she had been surrounded by other children. Sometimes on her way to the practice ring, she would stop to watch the Fortunato children playing on a trampoline. Someday they would follow their parents into the act, but now they were simply having fun. Ivy wished she could join them.

But there was no play for Ivy in Paulo's schedule. When she had satisfactorily mastered one phase of riding, he immediately started her on another. The pony, Kismet, was a mean, stubborn little animal who did his best to cause Ivy more trouble. He balked, resisted, and tried to throw her.

When Paulo finally realized that Kismet's ornery ways were delaying Ivy's progress, he replaced him with a more amenable pony. Ivy soon came to love and trust Mitzi, and together they learned rapidly.

On Sundays, Martina, the snake charmer, conducted school for the circus children. Since the children of performers missed regular school at the beginning of the circus season in May and also the entire months of September and October, when they were traveling south to winter quarters, they had a lot to make up. Ivy looked forward to these classes, for it was her only chance to be with other children.

Though Paulo grumbled about it, even Angela pleaded her case. "Paulo, the kid needs time off! You can't have her practicing all the time." And Gina would chime in, "Don't be such a slave-driver." Paulo would scowl and snarl, "Go on then. But, don't forget, we still gotta practice this afternoon!"

Ivy was a quick learner, loved reading, and was good at numbers and spelling, so Sunday became the highlight of her week. But Paulo never let her forget that her main job was to learn to ride well enough to be in the act.

With the circus season now in full swing, Ivy adjusted to life under the big top, and it soon became as natural to her as her life at the orphanage had been. Though they were constantly moving, her routine remained the same as they traveled from town to town.

After the evening performance, Ivy would often meet Sophia at her booth on the midway and walk back to her caravan with her. Sophia was moody, inclined to be silent when depressed, and at these times, Ivy kept out of her way. Somehow she understood that Sophia felt bad about her age and the infirmities that kept her from being the equestrian star she had once been.

Almost all of the circus people now knew Ivy and accepted her as one of them. Gyppo remained her best friend. Ivy adored the sweet, soft-spoken Liselle and spent as much time as possible watching her practice.

Each night after the performance, the

circus had to be broken down in what seemed a chaotic jumble of shouting men and tugging elephants. Tents tumbled to the ground and must be rolled up, packed, and ready to move. The animals must be cared for, their cages well padlocked. And the shorter the distance between towns where the circus was performing, the more quickly everything had to be done, with the long line of wagons, caravans, and animal cages ready to move on at dawn.

Except for a few stars, every circus performer had some other job besides his specialty. Only performers with top billing, like Klaus von Bremer, simply saw to his own animals and caravan and rarely put in an appearance to pitch in with the others.

It didn't take Ivy long to realize that Paulo was extremely jealous of Klaus, although his act and the Tarantinos' act were similar only in the fact that they both involved horses. He never had a good word to say about the other man and often disparaged him.

It also didn't take Ivy long to discover that Paulo was a bully. He had become increasingly anxious to get her into the act. Even if he were using her as a novelty, a small child performing always pleased the crowd. Paulo kept pressing Ivy to learn what was called the "lean-back." This involved the rider holding onto a special handle on the saddle with one hand, bending as far back as possible, and waving to the crowd with the other. It was very hard to do, but Ivy was stubbornly determined to do it.

"Lean back, lean back!" Paulo would order. "Take your hand off the reins, wave to the crowd, and *smile!*" Obediently Ivy would pull on the reins and Mitzi would rear up. It was a very difficult maneuver and had to be practiced over and over.

One day Paulo's patience and Ivy's strength ran out simultaneously. When Ivy drooped forward over the saddle, Paulo made a grab for the reins and pulled Mitzi to a stop. Then he yanked Ivy off the pony. "You stupid kid, don't you understand nuthin'?" He gave her a stinging slap across her face that snapped her head back. "Now get back on and do it again!"

It was Liselle who noticed Ivy's swollen cheek when she came into the cookhouse for breakfast the next morning. "What happened?"

Ivy put her hand up to touch her face. It was still hot and tender.

Liselle's lips tightened. "Don't tell me . . . Paulo."

After that incident Liselle would sometimes jump down from her wire and walk with Ivy over to her practice sessions. Although a "live and let live" policy was observed among circus people — quarrels kept inside each family and everyone minding their own business — Liselle's action was to serve notice to Paulo that someone was taking an interest in Ivy.

Ivy appreciated Liselle's attention and thought her the most wonderful, the bravest person she had ever known. She had watched Liselle's daring performance many times and would declare over and over, "I don't see how you do it!" Liselle offered to teach Ivy. "You might like it better than riding," she suggested with a smile.

But after trying a couple of times with Liselle holding her hand, Ivy found that heights scared her. "I just can't do it, Liselle. I keep feeling I'll lose my balance and fall."

"Everyone is scared at first. You just learn never to look down! And most of all, don't panic. If you feel frightened, stop, take a deep breath, and go on." Then Liselle would hug Ivy, laughing. "Well, darling, it's not a matter of life or death!"

Ivy gave a little shiver. She just hoped it never would be.

By the end of the summer, Paulo had her ride Mitzi into the ring at the finale of the show, circle the stands twice, then join the others for the final bows. In September, the season came to an end and Ivy had to say good-bye to Liselle and move south with the Tarantinos to the circus's winter quarters in Sarasota. Liselle's whereabouts during the off-season were a mystery, however.

"I'll see you in the fall, *chérie*," she told Ivy and laughed her lilting laugh as the circus wagons pulled out.

Chapter Four

Most circus people considered the months in Florida a vacation, a time to relax and experience a little taste of normal living. But for Ivy, those months meant more rigorous training. Every day there were hours of practice. Paulo was determined she would be an accomplished performer by the time they rejoined the circus at the start of the new season.

Even Angela was led to protest on Ivy's behalf at times. "Ah, give her a break, Paulo. She's only a kid. She needs some time off."

"Who asked you? *I'm* running this act. *I* make the decisions."

Ivy had learned that Paulo took no advice and brooked no opposition. Any attempt to question his authority only stiffened his mulishness.

Angela took the brunt of Paulo's volatile personality. Ivy knew Angela was afraid of him and had often felt the weight of his hand just as *she* had. Ivy once overheard the sisters-in-law talking. It was the day after she herself had cowered in her cot during one of Paulo and Angela's frequent arguments.

"Why do you stay?" Gina demanded.

"Where would I go?" came the despairing reply.

Angela's answer struck Ivy with dread. It was the same one Ivy asked herself when she thought she could not stand another day of Paulo's bullying. Where could she go? What would she do? Who would take care of her? She had heard enough stories from circus people about how they ran away from home to *join* the circus. But who had ever heard of anyone running *away* from the circus? Especially if there was no home to run to.

At the orphanage Ivy had learned to read. The only book she owned was the small New Testament Miss Clinock had given her the day she left Greystone, and she often drew it out from under her pillow to read at night in bed.

In the front of the book was a picture of Jesus surrounded by children. Underneath was the quotation: "Suffer the little children to come unto Me and forbid them not, for of such is the Kingdom of Heaven" (Mark 10:14).

"Suffer the little children . . ." Ivy would

whisper, puzzled. What did that mean? Were children supposed to suffer? She did not understand. Then she remembered a hymn they used to sing at Greystone: "Jesus loves me, this I know, for the Bible tells me so; Little ones to Him belong; They are weak, but He is strong."

To think that Jesus was strong and that He did indeed love children soothed some of the aching loneliness, the helplessness Ivy felt. Would Jesus *really* keep her safe, protect her . . . even from someone like Paulo?

March 1888

At the end of March, the Tarantinos packed up and headed north to join the circus for the start of the new season. Ivy was now a full-fledged member of the act. Billed as the "Boy Wonder" and dressed in a satin Spanish-style costume, she would ride out on Mitzi, circle the ring, perform the stunts she had mastered, then exit, waving and smiling to the crowd.

After the first month of performances, Ivy felt fairly secure in her routine although Paulo never complimented her and still insisted on daily practice. Now he was teaching her to do a backward somersault from a standing position on Mitzi's back. As a result Ivy had acquired many bruises and sore muscles. But she was developing a stubborn streak in her relationship with Paulo, and she refused to give in. Instead, she channeled her anger into equal determination to master the skill required for the new trick.

On the whole Ivy was glad to be back on the road with the circus, where she now had her own place. Although Ivy now stayed in the Tarantinos' tent, she spent as little time there as she could manage. Instead she visited with her old pal Gyppo and her idol Liselle.

The summer months sped by, one day following the next, one week after the other, town after town. Ivy's days were filled with practice and performance and the routine of circus life. Her bonds with Sophia, Gyppo, and Liselle grew stronger. They were almost like a family, Ivy thought with satisfaction. Harry, too, had become a close friend. He often let her help him feed the elephants. One of them, Lulu, became Ivy's favorite. Ivy would always bring Lulu a bag of peanuts and stroke the grainy-textured trunk while the elephant munched.

Paulo kept her on a short leash though, and Ivy didn't have much leisure. What little free time she was allowed, Ivy liked to spend with Gyppo. Paulo permitted her to ride in Gyppo's wagon when he rode ahead of the rest of the circus to post cardboard arrows on lampposts, trees, and fences to lead them to the next town where the circus would be performing. She also went with him when they arrived the evening before in a town to put up the posters advertising the circus.

In summertime, it was still light and Ivy would look at the neat frame houses with their white picket fences and gardens. Sometimes children would still be outside playing. Passing by, Ivy would see a mother come out on the porch and call them in to supper, or maybe she would see a father pushing a child in a swing. She would feel a quick, sharp pain in her chest. What would it be like to live in one of those houses with a real mother and father?

That second summer with the circus seemed to last forever. Actually, it was only twenty-nine weeks. They had traveled hundreds of miles, however, and played in dozens of small towns in three different states. When the weather stayed warm into September, it was decided to extend the shows for a few more weeks. Riding with Gyppo those Indian summer days, Ivy felt especially happy. The air was crisp and everything seemed alive with heightened color. Orange pumpkins gleamed in the fields, orchards were bright with red apples and golden pears, and the sky incredibly clear and blue.

Then one morning Ivy woke up, feeling distinctly chilly. From her bunk, she peeked out through the tent flap and saw that it was raining. After all the months of sunshine, the rainy day seemed strangely pleasant. But she knew it would not be good for business. People wouldn't want to come out on a wet night to sit in a drafty tent filled with damp sawdust.

She dressed quickly and slipped out of the tent. The lot was a quagmire, the deep ruts made by the wagon wheels the night before now filling up rapidly and becoming flowing rivers. Hurrying, Ivy made her way over to the cookhouse tent, jumping over puddles and sloshing through the mud, drizzles of rain dripping down her neck. All around them, the roustabouts were trying to pound in the tent stakes and unroll wet canvas as the rain poured down steadily.

As she entered the tent and got in line, Bella spotted her, winked, and asked her usual question. "How's the Boy Wonder this morning?"

Bella greeted her that way these days, ever

since Paulo had had the poster printed announcing her as "Little Tonio, the Boy Wonder." Ivy took it good-naturedly, although she still hated being billed as a boy. She would have loved to have had a costume like Angela's or Gina's with a fluted net tutu and spangles instead of the white satin toreador pants. Even the ruffled shirt and red tasseled sash didn't make up for it.

Once Ivy was seated at the performers' table, others coming in for their breakfast spoke to her in the same joking way. Some tousled her short hair and said, "If it isn't another little Tarantino . . . *Come sta?*" or "Here's the little dago prince. *Buon giorno.*" Although she knew their teasing was affectionate, a way of letting her know she was now "one of them," Ivy wished they liked her for the real person she was — a girl with her own identity. Whatever *that* was. For if she had ever had an identity, she had lost it now, she thought sadly.

Mr. and Mrs. Monahan, the midget couple, sat down opposite her, their chins barely clearing the table edge. The people in the freak show usually kept to themselves, eating at their own table. This morning, however, all the tables were apparently filled. They both said "Good morning" in their squeaky little voices and Ivy responded. She had long since overcome her first funny feelings about the people in the freak show, although she still felt somewhat uneasy around Jojo, the tattooed man. Even when he was wearing clothes like everyone else, his face was like something out of a nightmare. Still, most of them seemed like nice, ordinary people.

The Monahans commenced talking to each other, leaving Ivy to her own troubled thoughts. During the last few weeks in Florida, Paulo had begun teaching her a new stunt he wanted to introduce into the act. She wasn't learning it quickly enough to suit him. The new stunt was difficult and yesterday's practice session had been a disaster. Ivy kept making mistakes and Paulo kept yelling at her, making her repeat it over and over until blisters started to form on her hands. Paulo continued snapping out instructions, growing angrier each time she failed to manipulate the procedure correctly. Tired and shaky from hunger, Ivy had felt the urge to lash back at him. But stronger than those emotions was the determination to prove Paulo wrong when he swore at her or called her "Stupid!"

Ivy was thinking about this when she heard a gentle voice. "Good morning, *ma petite*. How are you?"

Ivy looked up into Liselle's sweet face. She started to just say "fine," but Ivy knew that her friend would be able to tell that she wasn't.

Liselle put down her tray then sat down beside Ivy. "What's the matter, Ivy?"

Wordlessly Ivy showed Liselle her palms.

The young woman's eyes widened in horror. "Beast!" she murmured, adding something in French under her breath. But it was an unwritten code of the circus that performers did not interfere with other performers. Ivy understood this, knowing, too, that most of them were afraid of Paulo.

"They're better, really," Ivy said. "Sophia put some salve on them and they're healing. It's the new stunt. As soon as I learn how to do it right, he won't get so mad at me."

Liselle made no comment. She took a sip of coffee. "So are you going to do the new trick tonight?"

"I guess. I'll try anyhow, that is . . . if Paulo says so."

"Speak of the devil . . ." whispered Liselle.

Ivy looked up to see Paulo strut into the tent. He stood at the entrance, both hands on his hips, scanning the room. Seeing Ivy, he strode over and, without acknowledging Liselle, spoke directly to Ivy. "We do the new trick tonight."

She nodded. Paulo spun on his heels and went to get his breakfast.

As they left the cookhouse tent together, Liselle and Ivy could see that the lot had become a slimy lake. Wagons were sunk up to their hubs. Above the din of rain, they could hear the shouts and curses as the men struggled to raise at least the main tent in time for the first show.

Would people really come out in this weather to see the circus?

Liselle, who had brought an umbrella, shared it with Ivy, sheltering her to the Tarantinos' tent. At the door, she cupped Ivy's chin in her hand and said softly, "See you tonight, *chérie*. And good luck with the new stunt."

Ivy was understandably nervous about the daring addition to her usual routine. She went over it in her mind, running through the steps of the act all afternoon. She would enter the ring, running along beside Mitzi, allowing the pony to circle the ring five times. On the fourth round, Ivy was to run for a few steps, then jump into a flying leap mount. At this point, she was to rise to a standing position and circle five more times, then back to the saddle position, pulling

Mitzi into a rear while Ivy leaned back and waved.

Ivy got into her costume early. She did not want to linger in the tent, where she might run into Paulo before the performance. He would just make her more nervous. Instead, she decided to walk over to see Sophia.

It had stopped raining, but the air was moist, and hovering gray clouds promised more rain, possibly before evening. On the way to Sophia's she stopped to say hello to Harry, rub Lulu's trunk, and feed her a handful of peanuts.

Gyppo was standing by the hot dog stand when she walked by, chatting with Carl. "Howdy, Ivy, treat you to a hot dog?" he offered as he spread mustard on a wiener then encased it in a bun.

Ivy's stomach was full of butterflies. "No thanks, Gyppo."

Carl, who had a part-time job as a clown, pulled a face and asked Gyppo, jerking his head toward Ivy, "Who's this? A new midget for your act?"

Gyppo laughed and patted Ivy's head gently. "No sirree, this here's a future *equestrian* star."

"Uh-huh!" Carl gave Ivy a skeptical look as he pulled his ear. "Kinda small, ain't she?"

"Big enough, I expect," Gyppo replied.

Ivy didn't want to be the subject of any more conjecture. She was already feeling uneasy about the new stunt and, with a wave, moved on toward Sophia's caravan.

Sophia was just packing up her crystal ball and various scarves on her way to set up her fortune-telling booth. Ivy thought she looked especially sad this evening.

If Ivy had had any thought of sharing her apprehension about tonight's performance with Sophia, she immediately dismissed the idea. The woman was in one of her moods, brooding over the past, missing the excitement of her entrance on her snow-white horse, his mane and tail flying just like Sophia's long golden hair in the pictures she had shown Ivy. Most of all she missed the roar of the crowd as she galloped into the big tent. Ivy had not told Sophia that Paulo was teaching her the rear-up and lean-back — the very act Sophia had always bragged that no one else could imitate. Ivy certainly wasn't going to mention it tonight.

To try and cheer Sophia, Ivy perched on one of the small blue chairs and asked, "How do you think the fortune-telling business will go tonight with all this rain, Sophia?"

"It won't stop the idiots from coming, I

reckon," she answered morosely. "A lot of giggling girls with boyfriends, most likely. No use telling *them* a handsome stranger is coming into their lives."

Since Sophia obviously didn't feel like chatting, Ivy soon left. She went around to the horse tent, to stroke Mitzi's nose and give her a few of the sugar lumps she had begged from Bella that morning after breakfast. The pony was sensitive, and Ivy was sure she communicated some of her own nervousness about the new trick to the little animal.

Then Ivy walked over to the big tent. The ground felt spongy under her feet from the morning's rain. For a fleeting moment, Ivy thought of the center ring where she would be performing. She sure hoped someone had spread enough sawdust so Mitzi's hooves wouldn't slide on the slippery ground. That could throw their timing off, especially if the pony stumbled during Ivy's running mount.

At the other side of the tent, the clowns were gathering. Ivy loved the clowns and never tired of watching their acts. Gyppo was the most versatile. He could step in for another clown who for one reason or another could not make a performance. He was usually with the group known as the "walk-around" clowns, who entered the big top all at once, performing their comical routines — tumbling and doing somersaults, climbing, hopping, jumping, piling on top of each other in a pyramid, then toppling off.

Soon Harry brought his elephants up. Ivy loved to watch them, ponderously swinging their trunks, as they lumbered in line, filed through the entryway and around the track, slowly following each other into the ring.

The back flap of the canvas door opened, and Ivy looked up to see Liselle coming in. She was wearing a warm robe over her costume because the evening was unseasonably cold. Ivy thought she looked tense, moving her feet constantly in small, mincing steps. But at the insistent brassy sound of the band's trumpet, Liselle flung off her robe. A brilliant smile replaced the tight expression around her lips, and she unfurled her parasol, ready to dance into the ring and place one foot into the looped rope to be swung up to the platform.

Ivy wondered if Liselle wasn't feeling well. Or maybe she and Ted, the circus ringmaster who was in love with her, had had some sort of tiff. Ivy hoped not, for she remembered Liselle telling her how important it was to have a calm, clear mind when you performed.

Just then Ivy felt Paulo's heavy hand on her shoulder. Behind him were Gina, Angela, and Vince with the horses. In Paulo's hand was Mitzi's lead.

He leaned over and said fiercely, "Now when you get in there, ride *ten* times around to warm up. Then ride around the track counter-clockwise so that when Mitzi rears, you'll be facing the audience on your lean-backs."

Ivy heard the band music marking her entrance into the grand parade. Her heart skittered around inside her, pumping so hard she could hardly draw a deep breath. Mitzi's ears twitched as Ivy mounted, and she could feel the pony's flanks quivering beneath her. Into the tent they galloped, starting briskly around the track. Ivy concentrated hard on following all Paulo's instructions, barely remembering to keep smiling and wave her hand in greeting.

She could hear the band playing loudly as she rode by, tensing herself for the first series of rear-ups and lean-backs. Suddenly . . . Ivy was never sure exactly what happened. But a loud popping sound went off and Mitzi, startled, lowered her head and balked. Ivy's hand loosened on the saddle handle and, before she knew it, she was catapulted off and over the pony's head. As her skull met the metal rim of the ring, she felt a stunning blow. It was her last sensation before she plunged into a whirling black oblivion.

Part 2

Abandoned

Chapter Five

St. Luke's Hospital
September 1888

When Ivy came to, she was aware of a terrible headache, a stabbing pain behind her eyes, even before she forced them open. Staring into a gray blur, she looked around dazedly. But it hurt so much that Ivy closed her eyes again.

Where was she? What had happened?

Her whole body felt stiff and bruised. One leg was held in something so hard that she couldn't move it. Had there been an accident? She couldn't think, couldn't remember. Her mind was a blank.

Ivy was conscious of being unbearably thirsty. She ran her tongue along parched lips and tried to swallow. She wished someone would come to give her a drink of water and tell her why she was here.

The throbbing pain in her left leg was awful. She must find out what had happened to her. Slowly she opened her eyes again, squinting. Gradually, one by one, objects swam into focus. Barren white walls rose on either side of her, a high window let in filtered sunlight, and a white curtain drawn around her narrow bed sealed her into a private cubicle.

Ivy tried to sit up, but it was impossible. A small moan escaped her and, almost at once, she heard a rustle of movement beside her, saw a face bending over her. The face was framed in a starched, white-winged cap. An angel? With rosy cheeks and merry blue eyes?

"So we're awake, are we?" the voice asked softly with the same kind of lilt as Gyppo's Irish brogue. "And how are we feelin', dearie?"

"I'm thirsty," Ivy croaked in a voice she hardly recognized as her own.

"Here, take a sip of water then." A glass tube was inserted gently between Ivy's dry lips. "Draw in, slowly now, so you don't choke."

Liquid flowed into Ivy's mouth and down her throat. A cool hand touched her forehead, then her cheek.

"Fever's down. That's good. Does your head still hurt?"

Ivy tried to nod, but the effort sent shafts of sharp pain splintering into the back of her head and neck. She groaned.

"There now, don't try to move. You've a

bit of a concussion. Took a very bad fall, you did. Your leg's broke." The angel made a tch-tch sound with her tongue. "Imagine now, a bit of a thing like you doin' acrobatics on horseback."

Slowly it all came back to Ivy — racing round and round the ring, managing the first standing mount, then Mitzi's hooves sliding on the slick sawdust. Ivy's reaction had come too late, for there had been a wrenching jolt, then the violent thrust over the pony's head, followed by the sharp blow on her skull just as her left leg crumpled under her, with the swift, sudden agony of cracking bone.

"I can't move . . ." Ivy murmured.

"You're all splinted up, dearie, so's your leg can knit itself back in place. You'll have to stay put for six weeks, so you might as well get used to it."

"But I can't. We're to be in Junction City next week . . ."

"Not *you!* You'll be right here at St. Luke's Hospital till you're all mended again."

"Oh, *no!*" Ivy moaned. "Paulo will be so angry!"

For the next three weeks, Ivy was cared for like a baby by crisply uniformed, smiling nurses. It was a fantasy life and Ivy, although bewildered, enjoyed the attention. From the emergency room floor she was moved into the children's ward with its pink walls, its animal and nursery rhyme pictures, and ladies from the hospital volunteers to entertain them with puppet shows and music played on a small upright piano wheeled in for the purpose.

During a rare lull from time to time, Ivy wondered why no one from the circus had come to see her. Not even Liselle. But then she supposed when they finished the season and were on their way south, they would stop to pick her up. Surely she would be all well by then.

The doctor seemed pleased with Ivy's progress when he came by on his rounds. "We'll soon have you up and on that horse again, little lady," he announced jovially. "Quick as a wink!" With a chuckle he moved on to the next patient.

Nurse Halloran took the doctor's satisfaction as credit for her own superior nursing. "See, now didn't I tell you?" she demanded when she brought Ivy her afternoon juice. "That if you were a good girl and did what you're told, you'd be out of here in no time?"

Ivy's small face clouded. "In no time" seemed as vague as "quick as a wink." She had already been in the hospital nearly a month.

"Why haven't any of the circus folks been to see me?" Ivy's voice trembled a little. It was something that had been troubling her for weeks. She was sure Paulo was too angry to come. But what about Gyppo and Liselle? And Sophia. Certainly Sophia must miss her. Of course, Sophia would need someone to bring her; she couldn't manage on her own.

At Ivy's plaintive question, Nurse Halloran got very busy, rearranging the items on the bedside tray, smoothing Ivy's bedclothes and tucking them in tighter. With her head turned away, so that all Ivy could see were the curly tendrils of red hair escaping her starched white cap, Nurse Halloran replied briskly, "Now, never you mind. It'll all work out. And tomorrow I've got a surprise for you. That is, if you mind your p's and q's."

Ivy had no idea what her p's and q's were, but the promise of a surprise was exciting. Perhaps, her friends *were* coming for a visit, after all, and Nurse Halloran was keeping it a secret!

The surprise, however, turned out to be something entirely different.

Nurse Halloran poked her head in between the curtains around Ivy's bed the following morning just after the breakfast trays had been taken away. "Are you ready?" she demanded, her rosy, freckled face beaming, her blueberry eyes shining.

"Yes!" Ivy sat up straight, expecting next to see Gyppo's grin.

The curtains parted, and Nurse Halloran stepped inside, holding up a small set of wooden crutches. "Here you are now!"

Ivy's face fell. Was *this* the surprise?

"Now, carefully bring both legs over the side of the bed, and I'll show you how to use these," Nurse Halloran instructed. She stood the crutches up in front of Ivy. "Now scoot forward." She took Ivy's hands, placed them on the cross bars, and slid the padded tops under her arms. "Just lean your weight on your hands and lift yourself . . . easy now . . . use your good leg to balance. There you go!"

For all her disappointment that the surprise was not visitors, Ivy, always a quick learner, soon became adept at using her "sticks." In fact, she learned to use them so quickly and proficiently that she was soon making trips up and down the hospital corridors, and to the nurses' station several times a day.

"A regular acrobat you are!" Nurse Halloran said, half-mockingly, half-admiringly.

Little by little, Ivy tried putting some weight on the leg that had been broken and found she could even take a few steps while letting the crutches bear most of her weight. She had so much freedom of movement now and used her crutches so skillfully that the nurses stopped telling her to go back to her bed and rest. Left pretty much on her own, Ivy visited other patients or sat in the solarium and observed the people who came during visiting hours.

She still half-hoped some of her own people would show up. Of course, now that it was already October, they were certainly getting ready to move south for the winter. She wondered who Paulo would send to get her now that she was almost completely well and ready to leave the hospital.

It was toward the end of visiting hours one afternoon that Ivy learned the truth of her situation. As the shifts were changing, she overheard Nurse Halloran chatting with Nurse Stinson, who was coming on duty. "It's a terrible shame, that's what it is," Nurse Halloran said indignantly. "What kind of people would abandon a poor little tyke in a hospital?"

"Well, who knows about them? After all, it's not like they were regular folks with real homes, real lives . . ."

"Well, I don't care what Dr. McClure says, I can't see that lively little soul going to that mausoleum."

What was a *mausoleum?*

"Come on, Tilly, you don't *know* it's all that bad."

"Don't I now?" demanded Halloran. "I pass it on my way to and from work every day, and it's a dark, gloomy-looking dungeon if ever I saw one. And those poor little things marching single file behind that high-wire fence! Looks more like a prison than a home for children, if you ask me. A more sad-faced and solemn-looking bunch I never saw in my life, I can tell you, dressed in drab, gray outfits . . ."

"But what else is there to do with her?"

"I've got an idea, but I'll have to check it out," Nurse Halloran went on. "My sister was telling me about a missionary who came to her church and told about a plan to take orphaned and abandoned children by train to rural communities in the Midwest and place them with Christian families."

"That sounds like a wonderful plan. Do you think . . ."

"That's what I mean to find out," Nurse

Halloran said determinedly.

Ivy turned quickly and hopped as fast and as noiselessly as she could back down the lineoleumed hallway. Back in the safety of her ward, Ivy reviewed what she had heard. She felt hot, then cold. They had been talking about *her!* Paulo *wasn't* coming for her or sending anyone for her. That was the awful truth. What would happen to her? The *mausoleum.* What was it? Ivy wrinkled her brow, recalling the rest of Nurse Halloran's words. The children, the gray uniforms, the high wire fence . . . it all added up to . . . to *Greystone!* They were going to send her back to the orphanage!

Later, when Nurse Stinson came around to settle her for the night, Ivy was very quiet. In spite of the fact that the nurse seemed to be trying to be extra cheerful, Ivy felt the dread creeping over her. Soon, instead of this lighted, pleasant room with its pink walls and curtains, she would be back in that cheerless dormitory. No one would come by to plump her pillow or ask her if she was warm enough or wish her "sweet dreams" like Nurse Stinson always did.

Ivy kept waking up through the night, feeling rather sick. When morning came, she did not eagerly wait for her breakfast tray or enjoy the warm porridge, the little muffins, and orange juice as she usually did.

And when Dr. McClure came by on his rounds, *he* seemed even more jovial. "Now, Ivy, I want you to try to walk across the room for me. I think that leg is strong enough to bear your weight."

Of course, Ivy had been practicing on her own for days. She had told herself she had to be all better by the time Paulo came for her. She would have all winter to get back to riding and doing her tricks. At least that's what she had thought until yesterday. Now she did not know what was going to happen to her.

"Fine, just fine, Ivy," Dr. McClure said. "I guess I can sign you out of here." He gave her shoulder a pat and left.

Ivy hadn't seen Nurse Halloran all day. When Ivy asked one of the other nurses where the nurse was, she was told it was Halloran's day off. Feeling sad, Ivy pulled the curtains around her cubicle and curled up on her bed.

"What are you doin' mopin' around like this?" The curtains were pushed aside, and Nurse Halloran herself stepped in. She was dressed in a bright green suit, her hat all aquiver with feathers and bows. She was carrying a large package wrapped in brown paper.

"Have I got news for you, Miss Ivy Austin," she said, plunking the package down on the bed and perching on the edge of the mattress. "You're going on a trip. On a *train!* Have you ever been on a train before?"

Speechless, Ivy shook her head.

"Well, day after tomorrow, you'll be riding on one!" Nurse Halloran smiled broadly. "So what do you think of that?"

"I–I don't know," Ivy stammered.

"You'll be traveling with some other children to a very nice town in Arkansas, where some very nice people are waiting to take you children into their homes and make you part of their families. Now then, isn't that the grandest thing you ever heard?"

"But–but what about the circus?" murmured Ivy shakily.

"You can forget about *that!* Good-bye and good riddance, I say!" Nurse Halloran's mouth set in a firm line. "Them that forgets *you* aren't worth worryin' about."

"You mean I'm not going back?"

"I should say *not,*" Halloran announced with a jerk of her chin. "Now, don't you want to see what I've brought you?" And without waiting for an answer, she began to untie the strings of the package.

The next morning Ivy stood shivering as

Halloran, in her starched nurse's uniform once more, helped Ivy dress.

"Now, what do you say to this?" she said, buttoning Ivy into a gray and green plaid suit. "It's practically new, even if I did get it out of the church missionary barrels. Good quality, too. All the things are donated to be sent to families of missionaries, and they don't send junk to people doin' the Lord's work in foreign lands. It's a pretty good fit, too, for all I had to guess about size. Now wouldn't you say this a fine travelin' outfit?"

Ivy nodded uncertainly. Her fashion taste, based on the circus stars she admired, ran to bright, garish colors, spangles, beads, and fluted tutus. This was much too plain and dull. Besides, it was a little small across the shoulders and felt too tight under her arms. But Ivy did not want to hurt Halloran's feelings when she'd gone to so much trouble.

"All right. Have you got everything?" She handed Ivy the small suitcase in which she had packed her nightie, a change of underwear, and two pairs of black cotton stockings. "I'll take you downstairs to the lobby where the church people will come for you and take you to the train station."

Holding tight to Halloran's hand, Ivy went down the hospital corridor for the last time. Some of the nurses at the desk waved to her before the elevator doors closed and their kind faces were lost to her forever.

In the lobby, Nurse Halloran leaned down and gave her a hug. "I have to go back on duty now, Ivy. A Mrs. Willoughby, I think her name is, will be along pretty soon. Don't worry. Everything's going to be fine. You'll make friends with the other children on the train, and at the end of the trip, you'll have a new mama and papa and a real home."

She put both her plump hands on either side of Ivy's face and gazed down at her for a long time. Ivy noticed the blueberry eyes glistening before she said, "You're a real little trooper, Ivy." Then with a rustle of her starched apron and a squeak of her high-top shoes on the linoleum floor, Nurse Halloran turned swiftly, walked to the elevator and when its doors slid open, stepped inside without looking back.

Chapter Six

Orphan Train West

Ivy pressed her nose against the window of the cab, then glanced at the woman dressed in black sitting beside her. She had arrived at the hospital and announced at the front desk, "I'm Mrs. Willoughby. I've come for the child, Ivy Austin." When Ivy was pointed out to her, she had spoken sharply, "Come along, and hurry! We're late as it is." And she led the way out to the cab parked at the curb.

Ivy had followed obediently. She had never been in a cab before and found it strangely exciting. She would like to have asked where they were going. But the woman seemed so cross, from the time she had bustled through the hospital doors into the lobby where Ivy had been waiting, that Ivy didn't dare. Ivy was used to doing what she was told and not asking questions, so she supposed she would find out soon enough.

Suppressing a sigh, she turned to look out the window again. They were going fast along the city streets, dodging carriages and horse-driven wagons, a trolley car swerving down the track in the middle, its bell clanging loudly.

Just then Mrs. Willoughby leaned forward and tapped on the divider separating the back seat from the driver with her black silk umbrella. "Driver, stop! This is where we want to go."

"Yes, ma'am. Just trying to squeeze in so's you won't have so far to walk."

"Never mind. Just let us out here." Her voice was nervously high-pitched.

The cab swerved to a jolting stop amid a jam of other cabs, carriages, and throngs of people. Mrs. Willoughby pushed open the cab door. "Come on, will you, or we'll miss our train."

The woman fumbled in her big black purse, then thrust some bills at the driver who was setting down her luggage on the sidewalk. Ivy took a long breath. She had not been outside in weeks, not since that awful day of the accident. The winter morning air felt cold and held the acrid smell of coal soot. Looking around, Ivy saw they were in front of a huge, gray building. A sign in metal letters spelled out UNION RAILROAD STATION.

"Here, you can carry this," Mrs. Willoughby told Ivy and handed her a small valise, while she hefted a huge carpetbag. With her other hand, she took Ivy's upper arm and pulled her along, hurrying through the glass doors of the terminal into the lobby. The huge depot echoed with their footsteps as they crossed the marble floor. They went through another set of doors out onto the cement platform overlooking rows of twisting railroad tracks. At the other end was a group of children huddled around two women and a man.

One of the women came up to them. "What kept you?" she asked, a worried expression on her face. "We were getting concerned."

"I'm sorry, Miss Hartley, but I had to stop at St. Luke's Hospital to pick up this girl. A last-minute addition. Can you add her to your list?"

The other woman looked annoyed, but brought out a leather-backed clipboard and opened a fountain pen. "What's the name?"

"Ivy. Ivy Austin. She is one of the children for Brookdale."

Just then the loud shriek of a train whistle pierced the air. The man who seemed to be in charge spoke. "All right. It's time to board the train. Line up, children. Move smartly now."

"You, too, Ivy. Get in line with the others," Mrs. Willoughby directed.

Ivy's heart was beating fast. Obediently, she left Mrs. Willoughby's side and moved into the row with the others on the platform. Feeling a tug on her sleeve, she turned her head. Standing right behind her was a little girl of about seven or eight. Her face was round and pale under a fringe of golden blond bangs, and her eyes were brimming with tears.

"What's the matter?" Ivy whispered.

"I'm scared," she lisped.

"There's nothing to be scared about," Ivy said with the assurance of a well-traveled veteran. "Haven't you ever been on a train before?"

The little girl shook her head.

"Don't worry. It'll be fun. You'll see."

Just then they were jostled forward as two older boys crowded into the line.

Ivy glared at them. "Stop shoving!"

"Who's shovin'?" retorted the taller of the two.

"*You*, and don't do it again."

"Who's goin' to stop me?" The boy screwed up his freckled face and stuck out his tongue.

"*I* will," Ivy promised, holding up two fists.

"Boys, over here." The woman called Miss Hartley put a hand on each of the boys' shoulders, moved them out, and marched them down to form another line boarding at the other end of the car.

Ivy felt a moist hand slip into hers, and she looked down again into the younger child's anxious face. At Greystone, Ivy had often been assigned to look after the smaller children, newcomers to the orphanage, who were frightened and needed comforting. So although this girl seemed only a bit younger than Ivy herself, it seemed natural for Ivy to protect her. "Come on, don't be afraid. Stay with me. We'll stick together and those stupid boys won't bother us. What's your name anyhow?"

"Allison," was the soft reply.

"Mine's Ivy. We'll be friends."

As she boarded the train that day, Ivy felt she was making a brand-new start. All the bad things were over, she convinced herself. She wouldn't have to think about how mean Paulo was, or how cruel they all were to go off and leave her, or anything. Nor would she waste any more time in grieving over Gyppo, Sophia, or Liselle, who had not even come to say good-bye.

One day followed the next, each one like

the one before except for the changing view outside the grimy train windows.

Everything went by so fast that it was hard to remember one passing scene from the other. Once they had crossed a wide river on a high trestle bridge. Far below, boats and barges plowed the murky waters. Then they were climbing mountains. Ivy could hear the chugging of the engine as the train wound its way around hairpin curves so that you could see the engine at one end and the red caboose at the other.

There was little for the children to do. After they woke in the morning, Miss Hartley and Mrs. Willoughby handed out biscuits and dried prunes, which served as their breakfast. About the only change in the monotony of the constant forward movement was when the train pulled into a station and there was a wait while water and coal supplies were replenished, or cars switched, with lots of jerking, slamming, and bumping. Each jolt afforded the children an opportunity to exaggerate the action by jumping up and down with shrieks of laughter. The boys particularly delighted in pretending to be knocked out of their seats, then shouting and rolling in the aisles. That is, until Mrs. Willoughby came rushing down to order them up, giving one or two a shake or an ear pull as she did.

Bunty Doogan, the boy who had shoved them when they were standing in line to board the train, was the ringleader of these antics. The girls provided an audience, giggling behind hands clasped to their mouths and rolling their eyes in appreciation of the break in the dull routine of their days.

Twice a day Mr. Mason, who was in charge of the whole venture, came through, stopping to ask the children how they were doing, then conducting a whispered conference with either of the lady chaperones at the far end of the train.

Throughout the trip, Allison had stuck to Ivy like a postage stamp. But Ivy didn't mind. Allison was a dear little girl, very sweet and shy, and did everything Ivy suggested. In a way, it was comforting at night, when the hard, plush seats were turned over to make into beds, and blankets and pillows were distributed, to curl up together and talk in whispers until one or the other of them fell asleep.

If there was a long stop along the way, the lady chaperones marched the children out on the train platform to get some fresh air, while Mr. Mason went off into the town to a market to buy fresh produce and milk. When he came back with apples or some other welcome treat, he was greeted with enthusiasm.

The days felt long and boring to Ivy who, before her accident, had been used to constant activity. Miss Hartley did have them do some simple exercises like touching their toes and stretching in the mornings. But the only other planned activity was on Sunday, when Mrs. Willoughby handed out Sunday school papers with verses to memorize and pictures to color. She passed around a box of crayons, most of them stubs from which each child could select four, which did not give the pictures much brightness or variation.

Ivy would have enjoyed having something to read. But there were no books except for the large book of Bible stories from which Miss Hartley read to them before they settled down for the night. Out of boredom Ivy got to telling Allison true stories about things that had happened to the circus people.

One morning she regaled a wide-eyed Allison with some of the daring exploits of the Fortunatos and told her about Liselle walking on the wire strung high in the tent with no net underneath, then launched into her own stunts on Mitzi.

"Did you fall off? Did you get lots of tumbles, hurt yourself?" Allison asked breathlessly.

"Sure, at first, but after I'd practiced a lot, I could do it."

"Weren't you scared?"

"No, not really. Not after the first few times."

A round, freckled face peered over the top of the seat behind them and a husky voice asked, "Wuz you *really* in the circus?"

Ivy raised her head and saw that it was Bunty. "I sure was," she retorted loftily.

His eyes got like saucers. "Cross your heart and hope to die?"

"I don't have to do all that."

"Aw, go on . . ."

"Believe it or not, I don't care which," Ivy said scornfully. "It's true."

Allison turned around. "She did, too. Ivy doesn't fib!"

Ivy shrugged. "If you don't believe me, that's your hard luck." Aware that she had other listeners, she preened a little. "I rode a horse and did all kinds of stunts — somersaults, forwards *and* backwards . . ."

"Then how come you're on this Orphan Train?" Bunty demanded.

"I got hurt. I've been in the hospital . . . so . . ." Ivy wasn't sure what else to say. She certainly wasn't going to tell them she'd been left behind when the circus went south. She thrust out her chin defiantly. "So they asked me if I wanted to come and be adopted and I said yes. So there!"

With this, Ivy turned back around and put her head close to Allison's, whispering to give the impression that she was telling wonderful secrets about circus life, not intended for the others' ears. After that, Ivy noticed Bunty and the other boys regarding her with new respect.

As a matter of fact, Bunty became Ivy and Allison's ally and protector for the rest of the trip. He turned out to be a resourceful and amusing fellow traveler. He had spent a large part of his life on city streets, having lived with a series of indifferent relatives, since his own parents had died when he was too young to remember them. Now he produced a pack of smudged, dog-eared playing cards with which he showed them a couple of magic tricks and taught them how to play a few simple card games. With his perennially cheerful personality, engaging grin, and infectious laugh, Ivy was glad they had made friends, for he managed to make the daytime hours fly. Thereafter, the journey was much more fun.

On the morning of the fifth day, Mrs. Willoughby announced that they would be arriving in Brookdale in a matter of hours. A stir of excitement rippled through the car of children. Some of them had been told that they had been spoken for already, and their new adoptive families would be waiting for them at the train station.

"Do you know who you'll be going to?" Ivy asked Bunty.

He shook his head. "Nah. I was put on this train at the last minute. I was supposed to go to an uncle, but he never showed up to get me at my old Gran's house. Well, she weren't exactly my grandmother. Sort of a stepgrandmother, I guess. Anyway, they brought me down to the train station . . . so I dunno."

There was a hint of fear in his eyes, and Ivy wished she had not seen it. She was feeling scared, too. What awaited this train-load of twenty-six children in Brookdale? Would it be the same as the two other stops the train had made? Children designated for Hopewell and Cartersville had been herded off the train and lined up on the station plat-form. There grown-ups, couples mostly, had walked among them, stopping here and there to speak to the boys and girls or peer into their faces. Sometimes they took off the boys' caps, ruffled their hair, or patted them on the head before moving on. Ivy and

Allison had watched it all from the window, had seen the children led off one at a time with the strangers who would be taking them home.

Ivy's heart pounded against her chest at the idea of being paraded like a bunch of circus animals, remembering how the elephants had been poked and prodded into line for the entrance march or the grand finale. Her stomach turned over slowly.

A keen observer, it did not escape Ivy's notice that the children who had the brightest smiles, the sturdiest builds, or the nicest manners — sticking out their hands or dropping a curtsy — were taken first by the best-looking, most nicely dressed couples.

You got what you *looked* like you deserved, it seemed to her.

Ivy turned her eyes upon her little companion. No question — Allison would be picked right away. She had the face of an angel — long, golden curls, dainty little hands and feet, a dimple at the corner of a rosebud mouth.

Ivy took a ruthless inventory of her own appearance. Her hair had grown out a little from the boyishly cropped curls dictated for her role as Boy Wonder. But her dark eyes and olive complexion gave her a foreign look some people might not like. She re-membered some of the circus people making disparaging remarks about "dagos," and she had overheard enough to realize some people were prejudiced against the Italians. Nor was she certain that she could pull off a winning smile. Now that her per-manent teeth had filled in the gap of her missing front ones, her smile had an uneven look.

The thought of being the very last child chosen sent daggers of foreboding all through Ivy's thin frame. What could she do to insure her chances of being picked among the first ones . . . and by the right people?

Something hard and hot blazed inside Ivy. Suddenly all the fury she had held back at Paulo's treatment came to the surface. She had wanted to flail out at him, kicking and pummeling him, even biting that hand that was too often raised against her, but she had been afraid he would only strike her harder.

Ivy's heart hammered and her ears rang. She breathed in shallow gasps, clenching her teeth and fighting back tears. Sadness mingled with indignation at being aban-doned by people she thought cared about her filled her with anger and anxiety. After all she'd been through, could something worse happen?

Ivy squirmed a little in her ill-fitting wool jacket. She hated this outfit. Again she looked over at Allison. No matter what *she* had on, Allison would be chosen first thing. Ivy's eyes moved over her friend. She was wearing a loose-fitting, brightly flowered challis dress with a round crocheted collar and long, puffed sleeves. Since Ivy was so small for her age, surely it would fit *her!* And the gray and green plaid suit that was snug for Ivy would be fine for Allison.

All Ivy had to do was convince her new friend to trade outfits.

Allison listened intently, her eyes scarcely leaving Ivy's face, as Ivy explained her idea.

Brookdale, Arkansas
November 1888

The train was slowing. They could hear the metallic sound of wheels braking on the steel rails. The voice of the conductor came through the cars, announcing, "Brookdale. Brookdale."

As the train pulled into the Brookdale station, Mrs. Willoughby sighed with relief. It was the last stop, and there were only seven children left — two girls and five boys. Mrs.

Willoughby was tired. The day had been long, the hour was late. She had been through this ordeal three times already this week, trying to keep the children orderly, being patient while the couples debated their choices, trying not to seem pushy or impatient when these decisions took an inordinate amount of time.

This stop, however, should be brief. The two little girls would go to families who had requested girls and signed written agreements to take them. All she would have to do was deliver the child to the family. The boys were another matter. But boys were usually no problem in farm communities where an extra hand was always needed.

Quickly she inspected the hands and faces of the children, some of whom were drooping with fatigue from the exhausting five-day trip. She went about hurriedly, straightening collars, brushing back unruly hair, tucking in shirttails.

The train jerked to a stop and Mrs. Willoughby hustled the children off and onto the platform. When they were lined up in the station house, one of the ladies from the Missionary Guild of the town's Methodist Church whispered to her, "Mayor and Mrs. Ellison have just arrived. Which is the little girl who's to go with them?"

Ellison, Ellison. Mrs. Willoughby consulted her list. She knew that one little girl was designated for the home of Brookdale's mayor, Daniel Ellison; the other child would be going to Miss Fay Stanton.

The start of a headache began to thrum at Mrs. Willoughby's temples. Momentarily, her thoughts were blurred. Hadn't she seen that name just recently? Then she remembered a few minutes before, when she had bent over to whisk the accumulation of dust from one child's high-top shoes and pull up her black ribbed stockings. Of course! *Ellison.* That was the name tape she had just sewn on the hem of the little gypsy-looking girl's flowered challis dress.

"Allison," Mrs. Willoughby said aloud, staring at Ivy, thinking of the last name of the people to whom she was promised. The name was misspelled, but no matter. She looked again at the small, thin girl with large, black eyes like a startled fawn's. At that moment a handsome, well-dressed couple entered the station's waiting room. Mrs. Willoughby noticed the deference extended by the woman who had just spoken to her; that must be the mayor and his wife. She grabbed Ivy by the hand. "Come along, child."

Ivy felt a stirring of fear. Should she tell

Mrs. Willoughby that she and Allison had traded dresses? Would she be cross? Would they be punished? She bit her lower lip nervously. One thing she had learned in the circus and at the orphanage was never to volunteer doubtful information unless you were directly questioned.

Ivy saw the lady in the violet bonnet with ribbons that almost matched her beautiful eyes, noticed the delicate nose, the softly curved mouth, the smooth face with its round, peach-bloom cheeks. She was even prettier than Liselle. This lady was the most beautiful person she had ever seen in her whole life!

Right behind her, another woman was moving toward Ivy. She was smiling, but walking with an awkward, uneven gait, as if one leg was shorter than the other. A cripple! For one horrible moment, Ivy recalled the people in the freak show in the circus. She had been frightened of them until she got to know them as the kind, interesting folks they were. But she had never really felt comfortable with them. Instinctively she drew back, holding her breath.

She felt a little push and Mrs. Willoughby's annoyed voice urging, "Go on, child. That's your new family, the Ellisons. Hurry now, they're waiting over there."

For only a fraction of a second, Ivy hesitated. Then she went forward and, miraculously, the lovely lady held out both hands to her.

LONG AWAITED
ORPHAN TRAIN
ARRIVES IN BROOKDALE

Townspeople recently greeted the arrival of orphans accompanied by representatives of two orphanages involved in bringing orphaned or abandoned children from the East to find good homes among the citizens of this county. The children range in ages from six to twelve. When the train arrived here, five boys and two girls remained of the group that left New York four days before.

Four couples who had applied for boys were eagerly awaiting their arrival. The Hassler family, the Rileys, the Torgravs, and the Binghams — all well-known farmers — welcomed the boys into their homes in the outlying districts. Two of the youngsters, brothers, were not separated.

The two sweet little girls were adopted by kind hearts in town — one by our fine mayor, Daniel T. Ellison, and the other by Miss Fay Stanton, a local seamstress. God bless them as they begin new lives with local families.

From the *Brookdale Messenger*, November 18, 1888.

Part 3

Rescued

Chapter Seven

"Never let a horse know you're afraid," Paulo had drummed into Ivy. Every time she had fallen off or the ornery little pony, Kismet, had thrown her, Paulo had made her get right back on. It had taught her not to show how she felt, no matter what. Whatever emotions she was feeling — fear, anger, loneliness — Ivy had learned to cover them.

Now, enveloped in a scented embrace, Ivy remembered Paulo's oft-repeated warning. Whatever happened — if the switch was discovered later — she would at least have had this moment.

"What a sweet little creature! But so thin . . ." Mercedes Ellison murmured. "No matter. We'll soon fatten you up, darling."

Ivy looked up into the beautiful face bent over her and felt a spreading warmth. Maybe this, after all, was the end of all the bad times. Forgetting the uneven teeth she had worried about, Ivy smiled and felt Mrs. Ellison's arms tighten around her.

"We'll be going home soon. But first your new papa has to make a speech. It won't take long, let's hope," Mrs. Ellison whispered conspiratorially.

Huddled against the rustling taffeta skirt, feeling the softness of the sealskin cape Mrs. Ellison wore, Ivy watched the mayor as he moved about the room. Dan Ellison was a stocky, powerfully built man, with blunt, handsome features, a ruddy complexion, and eyes filled with merriment. He was immaculately groomed, dressed in well-tailored clothes, thick gold watch chain dangling from his checkered vest.

He was greeting people, walking up to them with a buoyant step, acknowledging them with a ready smile and a handshake. He called most by their first names, while his gaze roamed on to the next person. Then he held up one hand, and the crowd clustered around him quieted as he began to speak.

"My friends, it is certainly inspiring to see so many generous-hearted people gathered here today to welcome these poor little waifs. Both Mercedes — Mrs. Ellison — and I were touched when we first heard of the need of these children for homes." A spattering of applause rippled through the room, but he shook his head. "No, no, we don't deserve any praise. We're only doing our civic, our *Christian* duty. Taking this little child into our home will set an example of sharing our God-given blessings and privileges with the less fortunate. Some of *you* may want to follow suit with others who may be coming on subsequent Orphan Trains." Dan nodded to a man standing nearby holding a notebook and pen. "Yes, you may quote me on that." The man scribbled busily. "And now, Mrs. Ellison and I are going home, taking our new little daughter with us."

This announcement brought a round of applause as he moved through the crowd, stopping here and there to accept congratulations, handshakes, pats on the shoulder. Finally he reached Mercedes, who stood waiting with Ivy. At the station door, he turned and waved his hat to those still remaining in the waiting room.

At this pause, Ivy peeked around Mrs. Ellison's skirt to see if she could see Allison. The fear of discovery of the mistake made her heart flutter. Then she spotted the woman she had seen limping toward her. She was seated, with Allison on her lap. The woman was stroking the long, golden curls. Allison was smiling! *She looks happy,* Ivy thought with relief. Maybe it was all right.

Maybe they were both getting the right homes in spite of Mrs. Willoughby's mistake.

"Come on, darling." Ivy felt Mrs. Ellison squeeze her hand, and she went with her new mother out the door. A splendid dark green phaeton hitched to a handsome black horse waited at the curb.

"In you go, little one," Mr. Ellison said and lifted Ivy inside, then assisted his wife, who sat down beside her and drew her close.

"What an adorable little person you are!" she cooed. "Just wait until you see the cunning room that's waiting for you."

Ivy felt a mounting excitement that bordered on nausea. What would happen if they found out they had the wrong child? What if Mrs. Willoughby realized she had sent Ivy to the wrong people? Ivy felt as if a cold hand had reached into her stomach and twisted it painfully. And what would they do to *her?* Punish her for not speaking up? Then maybe no one would want her. Out of the past came a conversation she and Sophia had had about the people in the freak show. Ivy had asked her why they had come to the circus and allowed themselves to be gawked at by the "towners." Sophia's answer struck her with new impact now. "Well, they had no place else to go, poor things. Even their own families didn't want 'em. Who would want someone like that?"

What a terrible thing not to be wanted. If they all knew the truth . . . if they knew what she had done, no one would want her either. Ivy felt a chill and shivered.

Mrs. Ellison drew her close. "Are you cold, darling? No wonder, wearing only this thin little dress . . . no jacket or even a sweater. Don't worry. We'll soon be home, and you can put on some of the pretty things I bought when we knew we were going to get you!"

Ivy managed a smile, reminding herself not to show her fear. This was all too good to be true. Better than any fortune Sophia could have predicted. Mrs. Ellison was so beautiful, with her satiny white skin and eyes set wide apart under perfectly arched brows, and she smelled of crushed violets. Ivy took a deep breath and cuddled closer, pushing away the frightening possibility that hovered over her.

"Here we are!" boomed Mr. Ellison. "Home!" Ivy sat up and looked out the carriage window as they pulled up in front of a two-story yellow frame house. Dark green shutters framed the windows. A flower-bordered walk led up to a wide porch. Could this really be happening? This was the kind of home her imagination had built on the nights she had lain awake, first in the dark dormitory at Greystone, and often on the narrow bunk in the Tarantinos' tent. Did dreams really come true?

Ivy took a long breath. No, it was real. The Ellisons were getting out, taking her by the hand, leading her up to the front door. If this was a dream, Ivy didn't want to wake up. Not now. Not ever.

That first day at the Ellisons seemed unreal. Right away, Ivy was taken on a tour of her new home. In the kitchen she was introduced to Bertha, the rosy-cheeked Danish cook, and Daisy, the housemaid, who greeted her with curious eyes but pleasant smiles.

"Now I want you to see the room we have all ready for you," Mrs. Ellison took Ivy's hand and led her upstairs.

Ivy's eyes were round with disbelief as she gazed at the white iron curlicued bed, the pink spread, and candy-striped curtains. There was even a ruffle-skirted dressing table with its own mirror and a pink dresser set.

Mrs. Ellison picked up the hairbrush and began stroking Ivy's hair, murmuring how lovely it was and how lucky she was that it was naturally curly. "But we must let it grow, don't you think? Then we can put ribbons and pretty hair slides in it." At this, Ivy beamed happily. The hated boyish look would be gone forever!

"Would you like to see what else I have for you?" Mrs. Ellison went over and opened the closet. Hanging there were several small dresses, and on the shelf below, a row of little shoes.

"For *me?*"

"Of course, for *you,* sweetheart! You're going to be our little girl now. Let's put one of these on, shall we?" She selected a scarlet dress with a wide, sailor collar trimmed with dark blue braid and held it up for Ivy's approval. "Do you like this one?" Wordlessly, Ivy nodded. "Here, raise your arms," Mrs. Ellison directed and then pulled the dress Ivy had traded with Allison over her head. Buttoning her into the new frock, Mrs. Ellison said with satisfaction, "You're such a pretty little thing. I'm going to love dressing you up."

Ivy watched as Mrs. Ellison bundled up the dress with its telltale name tape and tossed it into the wastepaper basket without a glance. Ivy felt an enormous relief at getting rid of that dress. Now no one would know she had been "placed out" to the wrong people. Or would they?

In spite of everything, for the next few days, Ivy lived in fear, breathlessly waiting — as Gyppo used to say — "for the other shoe to drop." Day after day, she half-expected the doorbell to ring and someone — possibly a frowning Mrs. Willoughby — to be standing there, demanding that Ivy leave at once. But a week passed, then another and still another, and nothing like that happened.

Maybe it was going to be all right, after all. Every night after Mrs. Ellison had tucked her in between lavender-scented sheets, had kissed her good-night and had tiptoed out the door, leaving a night-light burning, Ivy thought about her little friend. She hoped Allison was happy, too. She wished, no, she *prayed* very hard that her friend's new home was as warm and loving as the Ellison home was.

But next week she would be starting school. There she would see Allison, and she would find out herself.

It was Daniel Ellison who took Ivy to be enrolled at Brookdale Elementary the following Monday. The principal greeted them effusively, flattered to be visited by the town's mayor. "Of course, Ivy must be tested to find out in what grade she should be placed since she has no transfer school records. But she certainly looks like a bright child, Mayor. I'm sure we will be able to place her in a class of children where she will feel comfortable," Mrs. Holt assured him.

"And *I'm* sure you'll see that she fits in without any problem," Dan said with subtle emphasis. "By the way, I see that the fence down near the boy's ball court needs repairing. I'll send some of the city workers down and get that fixed for you right away."

"Oh, splendid, Mayor, thank you very much indeed," Mrs. Holt gushed.

Ivy had benefited from her lessons with Martina, the circus snake charmer. With a natural aptitude, she retained what she had learned. She easily passed the tests in arithmetic, grammar, and reading, and within an hour was escorted to the fourth grade classroom by the principal. There, after a whispered conference with Miss McGaran, the teacher, Ivy was given a desk, a notebook, and a copy of McGuffy's *Reader*.

As soon as the recess bell rang, Ivy looked for Allison. When she saw her coming from the third grade room, her worries about her new friend were put to rest. Allison, in a blue merino dress with lace-edged white collars and cuffs, looked like a doll newly dressed from a toy shop. Her golden hair hung in long curls tied with crisp blue ribbons, and she was carrying a shiny red lunch pail. Anxious to hear Allison's report about her new home, Ivy suggested that they go to a bench at the far end of the playground so they could eat and talk privately.

"So what is it like?" Ivy asked, eager yet dreading what Allison might be going to tell her about her new home.

Allison took a bite of a sandwich of sliced ham and cheese piled high between two thick slices of brown wheat bread and chewed it thoroughly before answering. "It's very nice."

"Does that lady — what's her name? — does she want you to call her Mama?"

Allison shook her head. "No, she said since she's not married, it wouldn't be proper. So I'm to call her Aunty."

Ivy thought of Mrs. Ellison's smothering hug, the smell of her exotic perfume as she had crushed Ivy to her silken breast, how she had told her over and over, "Now, you are to be my precious little girl, and I will be your mother. Can you do that, darling? Call me Mother?"

Of course! Ivy had eagerly agreed. She would do whatever this lovely lady asked. If only nothing happened. If only she could stay here forever. Whatever it took, Ivy was determined to please.

"So what is her house like?" Ivy persisted curiously, wondering if it could be anything to compare with the mayor's spacious residence.

"Well, it's small and white and it has a garden in back with flowers and two birdhouses . . . Aunty loves birds and all animals. She has a cat, too, but she doesn't let Miss Muffet — that's the kitty's name — outside. She might frighten away the birds, you see. She just sits on the kitchen windowsill in the sun and watches them." Allison took another bite.

"And do you have a room of your own?" Ivy asked, thinking of her pink and white one at the Ellisons.

"Yes, it has flowered wallpaper and little windows that look out over the garden. Aunty sleeps in the next room, and we both leave our doors open at night so we can call back and forth if we want to. She has a sewing room in the front of the house, 'cause she makes clothes for people. She made this for me. Do you like it?" Allison smoothed her skirt.

"Yes, it's very pretty. So then, you think you'll like living there with her?" Ivy rushed on, anxious to be reassured.

"Oh, yes! Aunty is ever so nice. She is the nicest person I've ever met."

"And you don't mind that she's a . . . I mean, that she walks, well, funny?"

Allison shook her head vigorously, making the golden curls bounce. "Oh, no! She told me all about how it happened. When she was a little girl, she fell out of a wagon and the wheel ran over her leg, crushing the bone, and it never grew like her other one did, and that's why she limps."

Ivy shuddered involuntarily. Her own accident came back to her vividly, filling her with horror. What if she had been crippled? What if she had had to walk with a terrible lurching gait for the rest of her life?

The bell rang. Recess was over. They gathered up the remains of their lunch and stuffed it back into their pails.

Walking back toward their classrooms, Ivy asked, "Do you think I could come over and see you one day after school, Allison?"

"Oh, yes! Aunty says she wants me to have my friends over. I told her about you and Bunty and the others on the train." Allison paused for a minute. "I wonder how Bunty is doing? He went with a big, red-faced man and he didn't look too happy about it."

"Oh, Bunty, he'll do fine. He's tough,"

Ivy said confidently. "Well, I'll see you, Allison. I'm glad that you . . ." She stopped, uncertain as to how to finish the sentence. Did she mean "glad that you got a nice home"? Or was it "glad you agreed to trade dresses" that she really meant?

After the first day, Ivy gradually made other friends. But Allison still remained her special one. Although Ivy needed the constant reassurance that the "trade" had benefited Allison, not harmed her, her fears were allayed each day when she got to school. Without doubt, Allison had the prettiest, the widest variety of clothes of any other little girl in the class. She was always dressed exquisitely — every pleat, every bow, every ruffle perfect. No one could fail to see that this child was obviously adored, her needs lovingly provided.

Little by little, Ivy lost her nagging apprehension that someone would find her out. In fact, there were days when she didn't think of it at all. Then, at other times, when she least expected it, she would remember, and a cold fear would clutch her heart.

Like the time at Sunday school about two months after she had come to Brookdale. The teacher had begun the day's lesson by writing a Scripture verse on the blackboard: "For nothing is secret, that shall not be made manifest; neither anything hid, that shall not be known" (Luke 8:17). Then turning from the board, she said severely, "Today, children, we are going to talk about lying. There are all kinds of lies. For example, it is just as much a lie to keep silent about something you know *should* be told as to tell an outright falsehood."

Ivy felt sweat gather in her palms, and her heart thumped hard against her chest.

"You may think a lie won't hurt. The first lie you tell may make you feel uncomfortable, guilty. But it's like getting an olive out of one of those long narrow bottles. After the first one, the rest come out quite easily." Mrs. Gaynor moved to the edge of the platform and gazed at each one in the suddenly subdued classroom. "Don't make the mistake of telling that first lie."

Ivy's stomach knotted. She felt a sour taste in her mouth and she swallowed hard.

Mrs. Gaynor stepped back to the blackboard, rapped her chalk sharply on the written verse, underlining it. "I want you to memorize this verse, so you'll never forget it. There is nothing so despicable as a liar. Someone you can't trust. Don't ever think, boys and girls, that you can get away with telling a lie."

Ivy felt a wave of nausea. She must have

paled visibly because Mrs. Gaynor looked worried and stopped midsentence to ask, "Ivy, don't you feel well?"

Ivy shook her head. "No, ma'am."

"Then perhaps you'd better step outside and get some fresh air." The teacher went over quickly to the classroom door and opened it for Ivy. That was where Mr. and Mrs. Ellison found her after church services. Mrs. Gaynor explained the situation to them, and Ivy was taken home and pampered ridiculously all afternoon. She was allowed to lie on Mercedes's damask-covered chaise lounge with cologne-soaked handkerchiefs on her forehead while Mrs. Ellison read to her.

It was hardly the kind of treatment to bring about either confession or repentance. But as time went on and Ivy saw the evidence of Allison's contentment, her guilt disappeared . . . or at least, it subsided for a while.

Chapter Eight

Ivy's life with the Ellisons in Brookdale began to follow a pleasant pattern that became so natural that she almost forgot there had ever been a time of terrible tension, of uncertainty. The bizarre months with the circus also grew dimmer and dimmer.

Of course, Ivy could not completely forget. Sometimes something triggered a memory, and she found herself thinking of her circus friends — Gyppo, Harry, Sophia, and especially Liselle. With a little twinge of hurt, she wondered if they ever thought of her or wondered where and how she was.

As the months passed, her life was so full and rich that she began to feel secure. The Ellisons knew nothing at all about that phase of their adopted child's former existence. They had assumed Ivy had come from an orphanage back east or a foundling home as had most of the other children. When Dan Ellison had first heard about the Orphan Train project, he had made an impulsive decision. With an election coming up next year, it might be a good political move to take an abandoned orphan into his home. Mercedes was overjoyed, for she had given up the hope of having a child of her own.

But almost the moment Dan had set eyes on Ivy, he had fallen in love with her. He had begun to take her with him on his political rounds, visiting and talking with his constituents. He took pride in introducing the pretty child as "his daughter," not unmindful that her very presence reminded people of his generosity of spirit.

He also liked to take her with him on the weekends when he tramped through the nearby woods and went fishing. She would walk along the stream beside him as he cast, keeping quiet so as not to spook the trout. Then later they would find a spot — a sunny rock or a fallen tree — to sit and eat the picnic lunch Bertha had packed for them. It was these times together that Ivy treasured most of all.

Ivy became so much a part of both the Ellisons' lives that it seemed as if she had always been there. And Ivy, always acutely aware of her good fortune, did everything to please her adoptive parents. Mercedes delighted in and spoiled her outrageously, treating her more like an adorable little sister than a daughter to be trained and disciplined.

But although Ivy had acquired nearly all of the girls in her class as friends, she still sought Allison's companionship most often. There was an unspoken bond between them. Only they could know the void left in the deepest part of their souls as a result of being orphaned, abandoned, having no one to care for them.

Ivy liked visiting the little house on Maple Lane where Allison lived with her Aunty. Here she was warmly welcomed on the days she walked home from school with her friend. They would go into the kitchen where Aunty served them cookies and cocoa and asked them about their day while she sewed. A fire would be glowing through the perforated door of the shiny, black stove, casting a bright reflection on the copper pots hanging on the walls. There were rows of blue and white china on the racks of a tall, polished oak hutch and pots of red geraniums on the windowsill, where one of the cats was always curled up. Since Mercedes could not abide cats and did not want the trouble of a dog, there were no pets at the Ellison home, so Ivy especially enjoyed playing with Miss Muffet's new litter of kittens.

Sometimes when it was time for her to leave, Ivy would stop at the gate for a minute and look back at the small frame house, so different from the mayor's elaborate residence on Front Street. It looked like some of the cottages in the villages she and Gyppo traveled through, tacking up posters to announce that the circus was coming to a nearby town. It looked just the way Ivy had always imagined a *real home* should look.

Not that she was unhappy with the Ellisons. Her life with them seemed to get better and better. Ivy felt real affection for Mother and Daddy Dan as she called them, and she knew she was a very lucky little girl to live with them.

It was a busy household; Mayor and Mrs. Ellison did a great deal of entertaining. They also went out two or three evenings a week to events and civic functions important to Dan's political career. On such evenings, Ivy loved to go into Mercedes's dressing room while she got ready.

Of all the rooms in the house, Ivy liked this room best. The furniture was of pale gray wood painted with roses, trailing pink ribbons, and upholstered in pastel needlepoint. Set in the three-windowed alcove was a dressing table with a full-length mirror. While she brushed her lustrous hair, rolling and arranging it with ornamental high-backed combs or adorning it with flowers, Mercedes let Ivy try on her hats or sample perfume from the assorted cut-crystal bottles on her dressing table. She would also ask Ivy's opinion on her selection of jewelry, often accepting Ivy's choices.

The longer Ivy was with the Ellisons, the more her adopted mother confided in her. Sometimes Mercedes would confess that she dreaded attending a certain event to which they were "forced" by political expediency to go. Wrinkling her pretty nose, she would say to Ivy, "What a bunch of bores will be there tonight, darling! I shall simply perish! Some of these people cannot put two sentences together that are interesting or even make sense! Oh, dear!" Then she would sigh dramatically and more often than not, would slide open one of the dressing table drawers and bring out a bottle and a tiny glass.

"This is my magic potion to get me through the evening," she would say, pouring some amber-colored liquid into the glass. She would then down it in one swallow, make a little grimace, recap the bottle, and replace it. Shutting the drawer, she would put her finger up to her lips. Winking at Ivy's sober face reflected in the mirror behind her, she would say in a stage whisper, "Don't tell Daddy, will you, love? It's our little secret."

Ivy had no real understanding of this incident, though it was repeated time after time. She believed there must indeed be magic in the bottle, because by the time her mother was ready to leave the house on the mayor's arm, Mercedes would be her charming, assured self with no hint of anxiety in her manner. Of course, Ivy's fierce loyalty to her new mother would never let her betray their "secret" to her father or anyone else.

Neither did she really understand a conversation between the cook and Daisy, the housemaid, the afternoon before Valentine's Day. Ivy had been allowed to make cookies to take to her class party the following day. In the kitchen, Bertha oversaw the mixing of the batter, then let Ivy roll it out on the marble counter. Ivy was using a heart-shaped cookie cutter to cut them out when Daisy came down the backstairs and into the kitchen.

"All finished?" Bertha asked her.

"Except for the missus' room. She's lying down. *Says* she's got a *headache* and don't want to be disturbed."

Something in Daisy's voice made Ivy turn her head just in time to see the cook raise her eyebrows as the two exchanged a knowing look.

Ivy went on sprinkling her cookies with sugar into which red food coloring had been dropped. She didn't quite understand Bertha's cautious warning to Daisy — "Little pitchers have big ears" — and Daisy's equally puzzling rejoinder, "And longer tongues."

September 1889

Summer came, then another fall and the school year started once again. Allison, who was bright and smart, skipped a grade and was promoted so that they were both in the fifth grade now. But the fact that she was in the same class with Ivy did not bring them closer. In fact, Allison did not seem interested in joining Ivy's small circle of girlfriends. This group was always included in outings planned by Mercedes, the parties or little gatherings at the mayor's house.

One day when they were together, Allison demanded, "Do you ever think of the Orphan Train, Ivy?"

Startled, Ivy looked at her, wondering why she had brought *that* up, wishing she hadn't. "Oh, sometimes, I guess. Why?"

"I do. I think of before that, too . . . when I

was in the orphanage."

"You shouldn't, you know. It just makes you sad. You're happy now with Aunty, aren't you?"

"Yes, I know. And I wouldn't say anything about this to Aunty . . . you're the *only* person I would ever tell. But I do wonder sometimes why my real mother gave me away."

"She probably had to, Allison. For lots of reasons. Maybe she was sick or poor or too young to take care of you herself."

"I know, but you can't help but think if your own mother would give you away . . ."

"Well, try not to think of it anymore. We're both lucky, remember? That's what matters."

"I know, you're right, Ivy, it's just that . . ." and Allison's voice trailed off.

"Let's go play with the kittens," Ivy suggested and grabbed Allison by the hand and pulled her along.

The subject was never brought up again nor discussed between them. But it disturbed Ivy. Allison's comment had stirred something deep within her, something she didn't want to feel — the realization that even though they were happy on the surface — and both of them had every reason to be — there were scars remaining that no amount of love or time would ever heal.

Winter 1891

One winter evening, when Ivy was in the seventh grade, and had been with the Ellisons for nearly three years, the past came back with a terrible reality.

It was a Friday. After school, Ivy had spent the afternoon skating on the frozen pond at the town park with a group of friends. Enjoying herself thoroughly, she was almost the last to leave, and it was rapidly getting dark as she hurried home. Humming happily under her breath, she swung through the gate. Skates slung over her shoulders, she rounded the side of the house to leave them in the toolshed. As she opened the door and stepped inside, she heard a husky voice call her name.

Startled, Ivy dropped her skates with a clatter of steel blades on the bare wood floor. She gasped and whirled to run out. The scream that formed in her throat was cut off when a rough, cold hand clapped itself over her mouth.

"Don't, Ivy, don't scream. It's me, Bunty. Bunty Doogan."

The wild pounding in her heart subsided. With mittened fingers, Ivy pried the hand away and twisted around so she could make out the figure crouching in the darkness. In the dim light slanting in from the one high window, she saw the boy's familiar but frightened face. "Bunty! What are you doing here?"

"I've run away. Couldn't take it no more, Ivy. That man, Tolgrav, was too mean — mean clear through. We never got enough to eat. Never. And no milk, even though he has four cows. Worked us from sunup till dark. He was supposed to send us to school, but he didn't . . ." The words choked off and Bunty's voice hardened. "He didn't do nothin' for us he promised."

"But where are you going? What will you do?"

"I'm gonna hop a freight train. I been listenin' and there's a train just before eleven at night. I just come here to wait. He won't miss me till mornin' when I'm 'spected to do my chores. I wondered if you . . ." He paused, then stumbled on. "I'm real hungry, Ivy. Do you think you could get me some grub? Maybe somethin' to take with me?"

All the memories Ivy had pushed away suddenly rushed back. She recalled Bunty's cheerful grin, how he had bolstered their spirits on the Orphan Train, amusing them with his card tricks, his jokes. How he had joshed with Allison so she wouldn't be afraid, and had assured Ivy that things were going to be better when they got to Arkansas.

Well, he'd been right about *her*. But evidently things hadn't been better for Bunty. She owed him. But how could she manage to pack food and sneak it out to the woodshed?

While she hesitated, Bunty said, "I hate to ask, Ivy. I don't want to get you in no trouble. Maybe, I better push on . . . I just couldn't think of nowhere else to go."

Quickly Ivy gathered her wits. "No, of course not, Bunty. I just had to take a minute to think. It'll be all right. It might be a little while before I can get back out here, but don't you worry. I'll come."

Ivy felt nervous as she hurried up the steps of the back porch and into the kitchen. Bertha was at the stove, stirring something that smelled delicious. Ivy's own stomach gave a twinge. Being outdoors all afternoon had given her an appetite. But what about poor Bunty? He must be starved. Ivy saw the pan of cornbread Bertha had just taken out of the oven. Steam rose from it in tantalizing wafts.

Bertha turned as Ivy came in the door. With one hand still holding the wooden stirring spoon, she placed the other hand on her hip and gave Ivy a stern look. "Well, missy, you're late enough. The missus was just down here, asking if you'd come in yet. They're going out this evening, so it'll just be you for supper."

That might make things difficult, Ivy realized. On nights when the Ellisons had social engagements, Ivy ate in the kitchen, right under Bertha's nose. To put together a food packet for Bunty with the cook around would be next to impossible. But she must do it. Somehow.

It turned out to be easier than she had suspected. After she had eaten, Ivy persuaded Bertha to sit in the rocker by the stove and read the evening paper while she did up the few dishes and put them away. Bertha, who had had a long day, willingly complied, glad of a chance to rest her swollen ankles.

While the cook was thus occupied, Ivy cut two large slices of cornbread and scooped a generous helping of the stew into a covered dish. A quick trip into the cold pantry yielded three Baldwin apples. She tucked these in with the rest and wrapped it all into a clean dishcloth. Looking around for something in which to carry the food out to the shed, Ivy spotted a small wicker basket. Dumping out the clothespins inside carefully so as not to make noise, she secreted the bundle inside and sprinkled some pins on top just in case. Then she hurried back into the kitchen.

"You done yet?" asked a yawning Bertha.

Ivy smiled innocently and chirped, "All done."

Still, she had to get the stuff out to Bunty. Although Ivy knew the Ellisons would not be home until late, she would have to wait until Bertha finished setting out her bread for the next day's baking and left the kitchen. Tensely Ivy listened for the cook's lumbering footsteps, making her way up to her third floor bedroom for the night. Not until then did Ivy risk slipping downstairs, creeping through the house, then darting out into the night. Outside in the freezing air, she ran to the shed where a shivering Bunty still hid. Ivy thrust the bundle into his cold hands.

"I can't stay, Bunty. And here's some money. It's not much, but my allowance isn't due and I spent most of last month's."

"Thanks, Ivy. It's more'n I 'spected."

Ivy's eyes filled with tears. "Good luck, Bunty!" she whispered, her throat choked and hurting. Then she turned and ran back through the yard into the house.

Later, when she went to bed, she could

hear rain on the roof. Ivy lay there, trying not to cry, hearing the steady downpour get louder and louder. She bit her lip, reminded of other long-ago nights when she had lain in the dark and listened to the drumbeat of the rain.

She thought of Bunty, crawling out of the toolshed and making his way down to the railroad tracks to wait until the 11:33 slowed at the crossing. She imagined him running and jumping, hoping to catch the handle on one of the boxcars and swing himself up to safety.

Ivy started to shiver and could not stop. She was terrified, thinking of Bunty out in the dark and the cold rain, running for his life. It had just been luck, "dumb luck," as Gyppo used to say, that it was Bunty not Ivy who had been "placed out" at the Tolgrav farm.

Then in the distance the mournful sound of a train whistle echoed through the night. Ivy shuddered, squeezed her eyes tight, and felt salty tears roll down her cheek as she burrowed into the pillows.

May 1892

The rest of the school year went by in a haze of happy activity. In the seventh grade, the social events among girls their age increased. Mercedes loved giving parties for Ivy and liked to celebrate every occasion. All the girls were eager to accept. What parent would turn down an invitation for her daughter from the mayor's wife? Allison was always included, even though she was younger, but more often than not, she would decline.

When Ivy asked her one day why she had turned down a particular invitation, Allison told her, "Oh, they're all such snobs, Ivy. I mean all they talk about is what their fathers do and how much money they spend on clothes and things. I don't know . . . it just makes me feel . . . well, it's just not worth it to me to spend my time with people like that."

Ivy bristled, feeling rebuked. *She* spent a great deal of time with Alice Mason and Clarabelle Jessup and Ginny Colby, the very ones Allison was referring to. "They're the most popular girls at school, Allison. Don't you want to be in that crowd?"

"No. Frankly, I'd rather stay home with Aunty. She's much more interesting than any of them."

Ivy had gone home in a huff that day. If Allison wanted to miss all the fun, it was *her* loss, she told herself.

But not too long after this conversation came a curious turn of events. On an evening in late May, Dan announced at the dinner table that he had bought a whole block of tickets to the circus scheduled to come to Brookdale that Saturday, and Ivy could invite her whole class.

Like a puppet whose strings are unexpectedly jerked, Ivy felt a sickening jolt. Blood rushed up into her head, then just as quickly drained away, leaving her dizzy; and she dropped her soup spoon with a clatter.

Mercedes glanced at her in alarm. "What in the world is the matter, darling?"

The mayor beamed. "She's excited, that's all."

"No, it's something else, Dan. What *is* it, Ivy?"

"I feel sick," Ivy said weakly, and she really did.

In the hubbub that followed, Ivy was taken upstairs and put to bed with a hot water bottle at her feet and a cold cloth on her head. After a concerned Mercedes had tiptoed out of her bedroom, Ivy lay there shivering. She didn't want to go to the circus. What if it was the Higgins Brothers' Circus, the one she had been a part of not long ago? What if she saw Paulo? Worse still, what if he saw *her* and demanded she come back to the Tarantinos' act? After all, he had papers from Greystone stating that she belonged to him. Ivy's hands pressed together tightly over her aching stomach.

To everyone's disappointment — except Ivy's — she ran a temperature for the next several days, although the doctor could not find a specific cause.

"Keep her in bed for a few days and if she doesn't break out or come down with something by then, well . . . children often get these unexplained fevers," he told the worried Mrs. Ellison.

When Ivy returned to school the following week, her friends told her what she had missed at the circus. Ivy only felt an immense relief.

In time, she thought she had put the circus and all her painful memories behind her once more. She blossomed in the affection and security of the Ellisons and the bad times seemed to be over for good.

Chapter Nine

With only two weeks left of the school term, the results of final examinations were posted along with the names of those being promoted to the eighth grade and the announcement of honors. Allison was awarded the art prize for her Arbor Day poster, and Ivy, a felt sweater patch for being on the winning girls' tennis team.

After the dismissal bell rang, a triumphant Ivy met Allison in the cloakroom. "Congratulations, Allison!" she greeted her. "Come on. All of us are going to Phelan's Soda Shop to celebrate." She flourished a dollar bill she drew from her pocket. "*My* treat!"

Allison turned away, putting her sketch pad and paint box into her book bag. "Who do you mean . . . *all of us?*"

"Well, our team, of course, and Sue Finch and Mary Anne Bryson and — I don't know who all — I guess most of the class."

"Even Ginny Colby?" Allison raised her

eyebrows. Ginny had been particularly un-
friendly to both of them. At the time they
first entered Brookdale Elementary, she had
deliberately snubbed the two orphans,
whispering behind their backs, pointedly
not inviting them to her birthday parties
while discussing her plans in their hearing.

Ivy shrugged. "I guess so. If she wants
to."

Allison buckled the straps on her book
bag carefully, then looked directly at Ivy.
"Why do you always feel you have to *buy*
friends, Ivy?"

Ivy's face flushed crimson and tears
sprang into her eyes. "That's the meanest
thing anyone has ever said to me!" she
gasped. "And I thought you were my
friend!" With that, Ivy whirled around and
ran out into the corridor.

Allison dropped her book bag and rushed
after her. "Wait, Ivy. I didn't mean that . . ."
She halted at the door of the cloakroom. Ivy
did not look back. Instead, she kept running
toward the cluster of girls waiting at the
front of the building. Tossing her head, she
linked arms with two of them, and the little
group went skipping together out of the
school yard.

The next day Ivy came to school arm-in-arm with Sue Finch. She pointedly ignored Allison on the playground and when the bell rang for classes to begin, she walked right past her without a glance. During geography, a note was passed to Ivy. She knew it was from Allison and that Allison, seated a few desks behind, was watching her, waiting to see her open and read it. Ivy put it down, still folded, until Miss Banning rolled up the wall map and told the class to take out their reading books.

With exaggerated indifference, Ivy opened Allison's note and read: "I'm sorry. Please meet me at recess."

Ivy did not look around right away. She had been deeply hurt by Allison's accusation. In fact, after she had left the other girls at the soda shop and gone home, Ivy had wept bitter tears over Allison's remark.

Was it true? Did she try to *buy* friends? Of course, she didn't like *everybody* in her class. And, yes, she did try to encourage all of them to like her. And Daddy Dan was always giving her money, telling her to take her friends to the sweet shop or the pharmacy for an ice-cream cone. So why shouldn't she?

Reluctantly Ivy admitted to herself that being liked and accepted was very important to her. Her classmates did seem to enjoy doing things with her — having treats or coming to the mayor's house on special occasions. But did they *really* like her for *herself*? The possibility that they might not was what Allison's question implied. Ivy wasn't sure of the answer.

She read the note twice, then looked around to find Allison gazing anxiously at her. Ivy gave a stiff nod and saw quick relief on her friend's face.

When the bell rang for recess, Allison was waiting outside the classroom door. Shyly she suggested, "Let's go to the far end, our old place, where we ate lunch together when we first came to Brookdale."

When they were settled on the bench, Allison opened her lunch pail and handed Ivy a small waxed-paper bag containing an apple tart. "Here, I made this last night with Aunty's recipe. And here's some homemade fudge."

Comically, Ivy struck a shocked pose. "Why, Allison, are you trying to *buy* a friend?"

At first Allison looked stricken, then catching on that Ivy was teasing her, she giggled. "Oh, Ivy, I'm so sorry about yesterday. I don't know why I said such a hateful thing. It just burst out. I think I was hoping just you and me would go somewhere after

school. I didn't want all those others along
. . . and, well, it's just that everything seems
so easy for you . . ."

"*Easy?*" Ivy was astonished. "It's you who
has it easy, Allison. You're so talented. Everybody thinks you're such a good artist and
praises you for everything you do . . ." Ivy
halted. Allison looked bewildered. Maybe
there was no use trying to explain how she
felt. Even though Allison was an orphan,
too, she didn't seem to feel worried all the
time that people were . . .

"Ivy, you *are* my very best friend and I
didn't mean to hurt you," Allison said, in-
terrupting her thoughts. "So do you forgive
me?"

"Sure, Allison, I do." Ivy took a taste of
the tart. "Ummm, this is really good.
Thanks."

That was the end of the incident between
the two friends. But its impact lingered with
Ivy, alerting her to the possibility that her
actions could be misunderstood. There
were other ways to make friends. In fact, Ivy
made a list of them and began trying to perform them: "Always be cheerful. Speak to
everybody even if they don't speak first. Do
favors for people. Help without being asked.
Compliment people sincerely — on their
dresses, their hairstyles, their hats . . ."

Eventually Ivy's list got wrinkled, smudged, and finally, lost. But some of the reminders stayed with her and soon she was considered the most popular girl in her class.

Summer 1892

To the surprise of most of the citizens of Brookdale, at the end of the summer, Allison's Aunty was to marry Matthew Lund, an unassuming bachelor. He was a talented cabinetmaker with a thriving business and a place in the country just outside the city limits, where he had taken care of his aging parents most of his life. Now both of them had died, and he was free to pursue his own happiness.

A private ceremony was planned to take place in the parlor of the modest white frame house where Fay lived and conducted her sewing business and where Allison now lived with her.

Although the Reverend Radicker was going to officiate at the wedding, Miss Fay didn't want a church affair. She felt too self-conscious about her lame leg to walk down the aisle in front of everyone, Allison confided to Ivy.

Allison would be the only attendant, and

Aunty made her a frilly, pink dress, sashed in satin. Aunty's own dress was an example of her expertise in its simple elegance.

Ivy was thrilled to be allowed to be part of the preparations. Days ahead, under Aunty's supervision, the girls iced and decorated the tiny *petit fours*, little diagonally-cut individual cakes. Aunty showed them how to make the dainty potted ham and cream cheese sandwiches on white bread, cutting off the crusts carefully and covering them with damp linen cloths to keep them fresh for the small reception to follow the wedding. While they worked at these pleasurable tasks, they talked endlessly, speculating on what kind of wedding they themselves might have one day.

A week after the wedding, the newlyweds went off for a belated three-day honeymoon to the state capitol to attend the State Fair. While they were gone, Allison stayed with the Ellisons.

Ivy, as curious as everyone else about the match, questioned Allison, and found it had come as no surprise to *her*.

Having known her since childhood, Matthew had courted Fay persistently for years. In her crippled condition and unable to have children, Fay had decided she should never marry. But Matthew had finally overcome her resistance.

But that simple explanation did not satisfy the romantic Ivy. "Are they *really* in love, do you think?"

"They got married, didn't they, silly?"

"But do they kiss and hug and all that?"

"Not in front of me, of course."

"But Miss Fay . . . I mean, she's as nice as can be, but she isn't very pretty, Allison, and, well, how can someone like her . . . I mean, being lame and all . . ."

Allison's face got beet-red. "She can do anything any other wife can do and lots better, too! She can sew and cook and garden and can . . . just everything!"

"You needn't get all huffy about it. I just wondered, that's all."

"Well, you don't need to wonder anymore," Allison said indignantly. "And Matthew is so in love with her. He brings her a rose every morning and lays it beside her plate at the breakfast table. And just the way they look at each other . . . well, I can tell, so there!"

Ivy wisely asked no more about the Lunds' love life. She had to take Allison's word that it was truly "a marriage made in heaven." But the Stanton-Lund union gave Ivy many things to think about.

Perhaps, after all, it was what people were

like on the *inside* that mattered. Maybe it wasn't necessary to be handsome or beautiful to find lasting love and happiness.

Even so, Ivy was glad *she* was nice-looking. She had never thought too much about her looks until lately. But she was filling out now, not so thin and wiry, and of course Mama was always fussing over her, telling her what lovely hair she had and how pretty she looked.

Staring at herself in the mirror one day, Ivy was startled when her bedroom door opened and Daisy, the housemaid, walked in with some freshly ironed camisoles and petticoats. She gave Ivy a strange look. "Pretty is as pretty does!" she snapped, then whisked out of the room, her chin in the air.

Somehow, Ivy had the feeling Daisy didn't especially like her. She often made such digging remarks to her. Things like, "You have it easy enough," and "You've nothin' to complain about, as I can see." Sometimes she'd catch a look in Daisy's eyes . . . envy, jealousy? "Another new dress? My, aren't *we* the fine one." Maybe it was just a feeling. Oh, most of the time Daisy was nice enough. But, deep down inside, Ivy wondered if the maid didn't like her because she was an orphan.

Chapter Ten

Spring 1893

Ivy and Allison left the school yard, dawdling as they walked down the road. It was the last week of school, at the end of their eighth year. Since a teachers' meeting was scheduled, classes had been dismissed an hour earlier than usual.

"Oh, freedom! Isn't it wonderful? I'm so tired of studying, tired of being stuck in a classroom all day!" Ivy exclaimed, swinging her books on their strap and taking a few dancing steps ahead of Allison. "I'd like to do something fun that has absolutely nothing to do with school!" She twirled around once or twice, then stopped abruptly. "I know what. Nobody expects us home this early. Let's go down to the river. It's warm enough to wade. We can take off our shoes and stockings and . . . wouldn't that be fun?"

Allison seemed to hesitate.

"Oh, come on. We can stop at Fallon's Mercantile, get some candy bars and some sarsparilla, and have a kind of picnic. I don't have to go straight home, do you?"

"No."

"So, let's go!" Ivy grabbed her friend's hand and pulled her along.

Still in a sprightly mood, they pushed into the store, setting the bell above the door jangling. The owner, Wilbur Fallon, turned around from the shelves he was stocking, but seeing it wasn't an adult customer, continued with his work. Mrs. Fallon, sitting behind the counter at the cash register, glanced at them over her spectacles, but made no move to assist them.

Fallon's was a general store, carrying all kinds of merchandise — men's heavy-duty overalls, gardening gloves, flannel nightgowns and underwear, house slippers, boots, and tools of all kinds, from rakes, spades, and shovels to pins and needles. There were assortments of candies, confections, and big round barrels of crackers and pickles.

The girls browsed around a bit until Ivy spotted, in the corner among the gardening tools, some wide-brimmed straw hats.

"Oh, look, Allison. These would be perfect to wear to the river." Ivy struck a pose, one finger under her chin, batting her eyelashes and saying in a mincing voice, "To keep the sun off our *delicate* complexions."

Always an appreciative audience for Ivy's comedy, Allison smiled, and they both walked over to the display. Ivy picked up two hats, jammed one on Allison's head, and placed one at an angle on her own. Then, putting her thumbs to her shirtwaist, she mimicked a farmer stretching his overall suspenders. "Ain't this just the ticket?" Allison responded with a giggle.

"If you try on them hats, you have to buy 'em," Mrs. Fallon's sharp voice warned.

Both girls turned to see the storekeeper's wife eyeing them accusingly.

Immediately Allison took off the hat she was wearing and looked at the price tag dangling from the brim. "The hats are thirty-nine cents, Ivy. I don't have enough money." Reaching into her pocket, she brought out only a few small coins and showed them, in her open palm, to Ivy. "This is all I've got with me."

Something in Mrs. Fallon's voice stirred a feeling of rebellion in Ivy. She glanced over at the woman, who was leaning on the counter with folded arms, a no-nonsense expression on her thin, sallow face. It was just the kind of look from grown-ups that always infuriated Ivy. Turning back to Allison and not bothering to lower her voice, Ivy replied, "Never mind. It will be all right. Come on."

"But, Ivy . . ."

Ivy caught Allison's hand, dragging her along as she sauntered toward the candy display, still wearing the straw hat perched on her head.

"Didn't you hear me?" Mrs. Fallon leaned forward, repeating in an acid tone, "I *said* you'd have to pay for the hats if you tried 'em on."

"We're taking them." Ivy gave Mrs. Fallon a saccharine sweet smile and began darting about, selecting things at random and piling them on the counter — rock candy, two palmetto fans, a box of cookies, some hair ribbons, and a package of mints.

Mrs. Fallon's mouth folded into a straight line, but she rang up each of the items Ivy placed on the counter. She paused, spearing Ivy with a glare. "That comes to two dollars and ninety-three cents."

Allison, standing beside Ivy, gave a little gasp.

Ivy lifted her chin and said loftily, "Charge it to my parents' account. That's *Mayor* and Mrs. Ellison."

At that, the Fallons exchanged a look that chilled Ivy straight to her bones. It happened so quickly she had no way of protecting herself, and she stepped back as if from a physical blow. When she recovered slightly, she swooped up the bag into which Mrs. Fallon had dumped their purchases, steadied the brim of the straw hat, and marched toward the door, Allison hurrying along after her. But before they reached the door, Mrs. Fallon said something to her husband. Although Ivy didn't catch it all, she heard the word *orphan*.

Outside, at the top of the steps, Ivy halted, feeling shaken. In the look that passed between the two storekeepers, followed by the disparaging remark, she knew she had been the target of unjustified contempt, suspicion, dislike. All her old wounds — being alone in the world, abandoned and unprotected — were reopened. She almost felt as if she were bleeding inside.

Then anger, swift and hot, swept over her. She tossed her head. "Come on, Allison, let's go," she said, and they ran down the store steps and onto the road. They didn't stop running until they got to the grassy banks of the river at the far end of town. Ivy flung herself down, panting. As she did, the paper bag containing all the purchases she had made at Fallon's split open, and the contents spilled out. Ivy started laughing. She laughed and laughed until the tears she hadn't allowed herself to show at Mrs. Fallon's insults ran down her flushed cheeks.

At length she wiped her eyes and said to Allison, "What an old witch! I'll never step foot in that store again as long as I live!"

Acacia Springs
Summer 1893

Later that summer when Ivy was fourteen, she went with Mercedes to the Acacia Springs Resort. Situated in the cool mountains on the shores of a beautiful natural lake, it was considered the Chautauqua of the Midwest. Here, as at the original site on which it was based, life was a mixture of inspirational lectures and summer pleasures. Culture was emphasized in the programs offered visitors — courses in nature study, painting, drawing, and elocution. Silver-tongued orators came to expound on various subjects — literature, philosophy, religion. Physical activities were also offered to appeal to a wide variety of interests — archery, canoeing, and swimming in the lake. In the evenings, concerts were held, featuring well-known singers and musicians. Although the arts were well represented, the emphasis at Acacia Springs was on the refinement of the mind amid the bucolic atmosphere of one of the loveliest vacation spots in the state.

For rent were small cottages, freshly painted white each year, with their peaked roofs and gables, and small porches in front on which to sit and rock while watching the parade of other summer residents strolling by. Set against the dark green of the pine woods, towering in tall splendor behind them, the houses looked like something out of a fairy tale.

The luxury hotel, rising three stories high and festooned with wooden gingerbread as delicate as eyelet, trellised pillars, and circling verandas, commanded a sweeping view of the lake. Although Ivy would have liked to stay in one of the quaint dollhouse cottages she thought so cunning, Mercedes preferred having the services of a hotel staff and took adjoining rooms for them there.

The lake in front was by turn either a glassy blue or rippling with choppy waves. Canoes and sailboats floated across the horizon while children played on the sandy beach under the watchful eyes of their chatting mamas or nursemaids.

Ivy, however, now a young lady, was allowed to do just about whatever she pleased during the day. Mercedes urged her to take advantage of the many educational opportunities, the nature walks and botany classes, while she herself spent most of her days reading novels and swinging in the rope hammocks provided for guests on the shady lawns.

Ivy never lacked for something to do or for companionship, and the days were pleasantly filled. In the evening, she joined her mother for dinner in the large dining room whose windows overlooked the lake. From their table they could watch the sunset spread its pink, mauve, and golden light across the sky and onto the lake, like a giant watercolor painting. After dinner, there was a variety of entertainment, from lantern shows and dramatic monologues to music by a string quartet.

After that first year, Ivy and Mrs. Ellison went to Acacia Springs for a month every summer. The mayor would come up for one or two weekends, then at the end of their stay, would spend a week with them before taking them home.

For Ivy, everything seemed even better after Daddy Dan came. He would arrive on one of the two-decker steamboats where Ivy would be waiting for him on the dock. They would share an ice-cream cone at one of the pagodas, then walk up to the hotel where Mercedes, dressed in one of her white frilly summer dresses, was on the porch to greet him with a welcoming kiss. As much as Ivy loved her adopted mother, Daddy Dan filled that longing spot in her heart that had been empty for so long.

When Ivy returned from Acacia Springs at the end of August, she and Allison spent what was left of the summer discussing their future. In September, they would enter Brookdale High School. With their grammar school years behind them and their childhood virtually over, much of their time was spent excitedly imagining what being in the "practically grown-up" world of high school would be like.

One afternoon they were up in Ivy's room working on their scrapbooks, an eclectic collection of copied poems, postcards, pictures, and quotations. The scrapbooks had been Allison's idea. Allison had shown artistic talent early, while Ivy, not as artistic, was equally enthusiastic. Her effort consisted mainly of cutting pictures out of Mercedes's many women's magazines and fashion catalogues while Allison drew or painted her own.

"You'll probably be an artist when you finish school," Ivy sighed, casting an envious glance at her friend's neatly arranged page. She wiped her own glue-smeared fingers with a damp rag. "You're so good! Do you think maybe one of your parents was an artist?"

Allison continued filling in a line with a carefully wielded paintbrush. "I don't know, Ivy. I don't have any idea who or what my parents were." She dipped her brush again into the water tin, then onto the color in her paint box. "I was left in a foundling home . . . that's all I know. And there's where I stayed until I was put on the Orphan Train."

"You can't remember anything?"

"There's nothing to remember, Ivy. I was only a baby." She started painting again. After a minute she added, "There is one thing, though . . ."

"What's that?"

"Well, I remember the head Sister telling one of the other nuns that they'd finally gotten permission to place me. I guess that's why nobody ever adopted me before, the reason I stayed at the foundling home so long."

"*Permission?* I don't understand."

"Your *real* parents have to sign papers, releasing you to be adopted. At least, that's the way Aunty explained it to me."

Ivy was quiet for a minute. She had never heard anything about this. Could *her* parents have signed papers? No, she didn't think so. She had been so young when she came to Greystone, and she didn't remember much before that. But Paulo must have had to have *permission* to adopt her . . . did Mama and Daddy Dan have papers? She'd never asked. Been afraid to, in case it was discovered that she wasn't supposed to have come to them at all.

Ivy glanced at Allison, who was calmly painting a flower border around a Bible verse. "Aren't you curious though? I mean about who your parents *really* were?"

"What good does it do to be curious?" Allison went on painting. "They would never tell you anything, even if you wanted to know. Aunty says the court records are sealed. That means no one can get to see them after an adoption takes place."

Ivy had a vague memory of something that floated in the back of her mind, something that had been relived in those long-ago nightmares. However, it was the circus she remembered most, and she wanted to forget that.

"Let's not talk about this anymore," Allison said quietly. "It makes me too sad."

Ivy started guiltily. "But you *are* happy,

aren't you, Allison? I mean here with Miss Fay?"

"Oh, of course! Aunty is the sweetest person in the world and I love her dearly. But I suppose it's only natural to sometimes . . . well, to long for or imagine what your life might have been like if your *real* parents hadn't given you up."

"They probably *had* to, Allison," Ivy insisted. "You have to keep telling yourself that, you know. Or maybe they just died, like both mine did."

Allison nodded. "I don't want to talk about it anymore," she said again.

"Oh, sure. We don't have to," Ivy said quickly. Someday she would have to tell Allison about the mix-up, but not now. She changed the subject. "What are you going to wear the first day of school?"

"Aunty's making me two skirts and some lovely blouses," began Allison, and for the rest of the afternoon, the topic was clothes.

That was the last time Ivy brought up the subject of their backgrounds. Although never completely free of her lurking guilt over what she had done, little by little those spasms of guilt, with fear of possible retribution, diminished. The reason it bothered her less and less was because upon entering high school, Ivy came into her element.

Part 4

Sunny, Golden Days

Chapter Eleven

September 1893

Her first morning at Brookdale High, Ivy was late. She had tried on and discarded three outfits and had fussed so long with her hair, which she was wearing up for the first time, that she didn't have time for breakfast, and dashed out of the house. When she arrived at the corner where she and Allison had planned to meet, she realized that her friend had not waited for her. Hurrying to the school, she ran up the steps of the main building and down the hall to the gym, where the entire school was to gather for the first assembly of the year.

Just as she reached the gym door, breathless and panting, she collided with a tall young man hurrying from the opposite direction. Mumbled mutual apologies followed, then he swung open the door for her, and they both slipped inside. Ivy found the nearest seat at the back, while he strode right up to the front and took a seat on the stage.

Must be somebody important, Ivy thought, blushing hotly at the memory of her clumsiness. After Mr. Stapleton, the principal, made the welcoming speech and a few announcements, he introduced the teachers on the staff, one by one. Then, gesturing toward the young people sitting on the other side of the stage, he asked them to stand as he called each name. When he said "Baxter McNeil," the fellow Ivy had bumped into stood up.

"Of course, this young man needs no introduction." Mr. Stapleton chuckled. "Everyone here knows Baxter." A round of applause rippled through the crowd. "But for the benefit of newcomers and freshmen, Baxter was not only elected student body president almost unanimously, but he is also senior class president and editor of our school newspaper, the Brookdale High *Banner.* So any of you aspiring journalists out there will have to submit to Baxter's blue pencil if you want to be published."

Ivy took another look at this Baxter McNeil as he sat down, his face a little flushed. Voted student body president by the entire school! That meant he must be outstanding, well-liked, popular — worth getting to know.

When the assembly was dismissed, Ivy

stood at the back of the room watching for Allison so that they could find their homeroom together. As other students walked out in groups of three and four, she spotted Baxter again. It would be hard to miss him. At six feet he stood out in a crowd. Not exactly handsome, he was nice-looking with clean-cut features, a shock of sandy hair, and intensely blue eyes. All at once his gaze met hers and she felt her cheeks burn with embarrassment. Humiliated to be caught staring, she quickly looked past him and gave a little nod and wave, pretending to have just seen a friend.

"Who are you waving at?" came a familiar voice at her elbow.

"Oh, just someone I thought I knew," Ivy fibbed to Allison, then changed the subject. "Sorry I was late. How do you like my hair? I had a terrible time getting it fixed."

As the two started down the corridor to the freshman classroom, Ivy, still distracted by that split-second eye contact she'd had with Baxter McNeil, put her arm through Allison's. "What did you think of that senior they introduced, the tall one?"

"I think I like it better down," Allison remarked. "Anyway it's slipping out."

Ivy looked at her, puzzled. "What *are* you talking about?"

"Your hair. You asked me if I like it."

"Didn't you hear what I said? About that senior, Baxter McNeil?"

"No, I guess I didn't. I was looking for our room number," Allison replied, absently checking the list she had received on registration day. "Here we are. Room 214 and here . . ." She handed Ivy a couple of hairpins that had dropped to her shoulder.

"Oh, fiddle!" Ivy exclaimed, taking them and sticking them randomly in her loosely knotted bun.

Ivy didn't have a chance to press further for Allison's opinion of Baxter McNeil, because the bell was clanging and they had to hurry into the classroom to find their assigned desks. But from that first encounter Ivy was determined to get to know him. At Brookdale High, however, seniors and freshmen lived in two different worlds, with freshmen on the lowliest rung of the school ladder. Seniors rarely mingled with anyone but their own peers. They had their own tables at the cafeteria, clustered together in groups at recess, had their own social activities to which lower classmen were seldom invited.

It was only at intramural sports events or activities involving the entire school that freshmen ever rubbed shoulders with the lordly upperclassmen. One such unifying element was the school paper. Twice a month, the day the *Banner* came out was eagerly awaited by the entire student body.

When Ivy learned that each class chose a reporter to turn in articles about their members, class elections, parties, sports participation, and extracurricular activities, she volunteered. Although she had no real aptitude for writing, she thought the job would be a way to meet the editor.

But as the school year moved into full swing, Ivy was caught up in the events themselves, enjoying them rather than observing and reporting them. Ivy was not disturbed when at the first freshman class meeting, after officers were elected, the new president Mike Holmes scribbled on the blackboard: "*Banner* deadline is Friday! Get your copy in to editor *pronto.*"

"That means *you*, Ivy," Allison reminded her as they were gathering up their books after the meeting. "If you've got it ready, I'll drop it by the *Banner* office when I leave my sketch." Allison had done a pen and ink sketch of the class emblem and motto they had chosen.

"Well, I haven't got it written," Ivy said with an airy wave of her hand. "There's not that much to report."

"We've had class elections. You could give the names of the officers and report that we voted to have a booth at the Fall Carnival."

"Oh, well, that won't take long. I can do that tonight and turn it in tomorrow," Ivy said breezily, picking up her books and sweater. At the door they parted — Ivy, to meet some girls at the soda shop and Allison, to take her art lesson. Miss Fay had arranged for her to take instruction two days a week after school from a local artist who taught calligraphy and did sign work for some of the town's merchants.

That evening, instead of writing her report, Ivy spent most of the evening washing her hair and deciding what to wear to the party she had been invited to on Friday. She forgot entirely about the deadline until she saw Allison the next morning.

When Ivy confessed she had not written the article yet, Allison rolled her eyes. "Ivy, sometimes you're so irresponsible. I don't understand why you volunteered for the job of class reporter if you didn't want to do it."

"I did it because . . ." Ivy lowered her voice, "I thought it would be a good way to meet Baxter McNeil. Is that so bad?"

"No, of course not, but there are other ways. Somebody else in the class would have enjoyed writing the stuff."

"Would *you?* Will you do it, Allison?"

"No, Ivy, I won't." Allison set her mouth in a firm line and walked away.

Miffed at Allison, in spite of knowing she was right, Ivy spent recess huddled over a notepad, scribbling a hasty report. Then she hurried down the hallway to the *Banner* office. She halted at the door, seeing that Baxter was in there alone.

Good, Ivy thought. *I'll have a chance to chat with him, get acquainted.* She gave her hair a pat. Knowing she looked particularly nice in her lace-trimmed, tucked shirtwaist and her dark green skirt cinched with a wide, black patent leather belt that showed off her neat waist, she advanced toward his cluttered desk. Notes were hung on a spindle at one corner, paper piled high at the other.

Ivy waited a minute but Baxter, head bent over, went on writing. She cleared her throat, but he seemed unaware of her presence. Finally, in her sweetest voice, Ivy spoke up. "Hello. I'm Ivy Ellison. I'm the freshman class reporter and I'm here to turn in my copy."

Unsmiling, he looked up, spearing her with a steady blue gaze. "You're late. You've nearly missed the deadline. Copy's supposed to be put in the box over there before lunch on Friday. I was just getting ready to leave for the printer's." He held out his hand. "Let me see it. If there are too many corrections, your piece may not make this issue."

Ivy handed it to him and stood there holding her breath while Baxter scanned the page. In a minute he flung it down and shook his head. "That's the sloppiest piece of copy anyone has ever turned in to the *Banner*. You're a freshman, aren't you? Most freshmen try to turn in their best writing, not their worst. I can't publish this because I can't read it!"

"But . . . but the names are all right, aren't they? That's what's important, isn't it? Getting the class officers' names in . . ."

"No, that isn't all that's important," came his sarcastic retort. "Look, Miss Iverson — or whatever your name is — if you can't do better than this . . ."

"But, I *can*, I mean I *will*. Please . . . give me another chance to prove it."

He started shoving papers into a worn folder and stood up. Ivy remained where she was, wondering what to do or say. The class president and the other officers would all be furious if that report didn't make the year's first issue of the *Banner*. And there was nothing Ivy dreaded more than to be the target of uncomplimentary criticism.

"I could write it over, if you want. Right now."

"Don't you have a class next period?"

"It's only Music Appreciation. I can skip it. They'd never miss me."

Baxter hesitated. He looked at Ivy steadily for a full minute. Then he remembered her. She was the same girl he'd nearly knocked over rushing into the auditorium the first day of school. Pretty little thing. Now her big eyes were wide and anxious, waiting for his answer. It *was* a pretty sloppy piece of writing and as the editor of the *Banner* he should make a point about deadlines, teach her a lesson . . . but . . .

"Well, all right. But don't let it happen again. If you can't handle the job and turn in decent copy, then you'd better let somebody else in your class do it."

Ivy took the paper he held out, sat down at a nearby desk, and started writing in her neatest handwriting an improved version of her original report. For the next ten minutes, there was no sound in the room but the scratching of her pen.

When she finished, she meekly handed it back to Baxter, who read it quickly, then nodded. "All right. This'll do."

"Thank you."

***

Spring 1894

That abrasive meeting set the tone of Ivy's relationship with Baxter McNeil for the remainder of the year. It certainly wasn't the kind of relationship she had wanted. But at least, he now knew who she was. That was better than nothing, she told herself.

Striving for Baxter's editorial approval earned some unexpected side benefits for Ivy. Her writing in general improved. Her essays, term papers, history and book reports were all vastly better for her effort.

It was only to Allison she confided her real reasons for trying so hard. Many of their confidential conversations were sprinkled with references to Baxter McNeil. But with every *Banner* deadline, Ivy's longing for some kind of change in his attitude was frustrated. Baxter never altered his indifferent, strictly businesslike manner toward her. A less stubborn girl might have given up.

As the end of the year approached, Ivy knew time was running out for her wishful thinking. Baxter would graduate in June and go away to the university where he had a full scholarship.

One afternoon when she and Allison were studying for finals together, Ivy slammed her math book shut and declared, "Someday Baxter McNeil's going to beg me to go out with him."

"Oh, Ivy, for heaven's sake." Allison gave an exasperated sigh. "I'm tired of hearing you go on so about Baxter. He's had a whole year, and he hasn't made the slightest move . . . although, I must say, you've done all but turn cartwheels."

"I don't care. I bet you five dollars I can make him ask me to his graduation dance."

"I don't believe in betting, Ivy." Allison shrugged. "And I don't know why you're so set on getting Baxter McNeil. He's a senior and you know seniors never ask freshmen to anything, much less their graduation dance. You're wasting your time, Ivy. Besides, why do you care? You have half the freshman boys hanging around you now!"

To Ivy's chagrin, no invitation to his senior graduation dance was forthcoming from Baxter McNeil. When Allison jokingly reminded her of their bet Ivy, pouting, offered her a five-dollar bill.

Smiling, Allison refused. "You know I didn't mean it. You weren't serious, were you? You didn't *really* think Baxter was going to ask you!"

"Well, it wasn't for lack of trying. I practically invited myself the last day I turned in copy to the *Banner.*" Ivy sighed. "He'll be sorry, though. Someday he'll want to court me, and I'll already be engaged to someone rich and handsome, and I'll turn him down!"

Allison laughed and finally Ivy joined in. But she wouldn't admit how crushed she really was that, for once, her charm, her attempts to make someone like her, had failed.

Chapter Twelve

Summer 1896

Ivy's and Allison's pastime of keeping scrap-books continued on into their high school years. Although they still sometimes ex-changed a poem or picture, the girls did not work on them together anymore. Their indi-vidual interests had changed and each had her own idea of what was important to record. Thus, the scrapbooks were a kind of journal reflecting the many stages of their de-velopment through the next two years.

Ivy's scrapbook was an assortment as varied as the changing nature of her enthu-siasms. At times she saved everything — in-vitations, newspaper clippings, bits of poetry, a picture or photograph, a quotation that caught her fancy, a souvenir from a trip. If she did not have time to organize and put them in any kind of order at the time, she would stuff the clippings in the back of the book until she did.

When Ivy started a new book in Sep-tember of 1894, her second year at

Brookdale High, there was some overlap from her freshman year. During that year she had cut out any item that had appeared in the school newspaper, the *Banner*, that mentioned Baxter McNeil's name — a basketball game in which he'd played or an article with his byline.

But the pages that followed were filled with memorabilia of the events and activities in which Ivy was involved her sophomore year, and any mention of Baxter disappeared. In fact, she dropped the job of class reporter in another classmate's lap. Without the stimulating encounters with Baxter, as abrasive as they often were, Ivy lost interest in journalism.

When at the end of her year-long campaign to capture Baxter McNeil, he disappointed her by escorting a studious senior girl to his graduation dance, Ivy plied her charms on more susceptible young men. For the next two years, the pages of her scrapbook were filled with dance cards, pressed flowers, Valentines, and programs from the dramatic club's productions in which she usually had a prominent role.

Ivy loved to act. It was a way of trying on another personality, experiencing someone else's emotions. Putting on a costume, she could assume another identity and immerse

180

herself in it. Ivy, off or onstage, expended a great deal of time and effort trying to lose herself. As far as she was concerned, her *real* life had begun the moment Mrs. Ellison had held out her arms to Ivy that memorable day in the train station, and there was no need to go any further back than that. What Ivy most wanted to forget was the smell of sawdust, the sound of the circus calliope, the echo of Paulo's voice, the snapping crack of his whip.

Mercedes insisted on having Ivy's picture taken every year. These, along with the group class picture, were ritually pasted in at the beginning of each new section of her scrapbook.

Sometimes, on a rainy afternoon, when she had nothing better to do, Ivy would take out her old scrapbooks, lingering over pages that were particularly meaningful. Like the first ones in her freshman-year scrapbook.

" 'To Thine Own Self Be True' was the theme of the Class of 1894's Valedictory address, given by Baxter McNeil to the assembled guests, parents, and students at the graduation ceremony on June 10th . . ." began the article Ivy had pasted in her book.

She remembered that day clearly. Sitting with her classmates, she had felt mingled regret and pride as Baxter rose from his seat on the stage and took his place at the podium. How handsome he had looked in his navy blue blazer, stiff-collared white shirt, a frilly white carnation tied with green and gold satin ribbons in his buttonhole. He had delivered his speech in a clear, confident voice and had received a well-deserved round of applause.

Oh, Baxter, why didn't you pay any attention to me? We could have had some really wonderful times together. I'm not dumb, you know. I can carry on as good a conversation as Susan Bailey any day! You just never gave me a chance, Ivy thought as Baxter took a bow, shook hands with Mr. Stapleton, the principal, then resumed his seat, looking satisfactorily flushed.

Ivy sighed. Maybe it just wasn't to be. And there certainly were other boys who were happy to bring flowers and candy and sit with Ivy on the swing on the Ellisons' porch on summer evenings or take her to church socials, square dances, and taffy pulls in the winter.

Turning the pages, she came to the ones commemorating her sixteenth birthday. Well, not her real birthday. Since no one was quite sure what day that was, Mercedes had decided that they would celebrate the day on which she had been adopted. There was always a party, presents, a lovely dinner, and an elaborately decorated cake.

She flipped another page, coming to a quotation that had been exquisitely lettered on a delicately painted card. "A faithful friend is a strong shelter; and he that hath found one, hath found a treasure." Allison had made it for her. Even though Ivy and Allison no longer enjoyed the same social activities, Ivy still considered Allison her closest friend. After all, they would always share the indelible bond of being on the Orphan Train together.

One of the gifts Ivy had received that birthday was a Kodak camera from Daddy Dan. So the next pages were a gallery of her snapshots. The earlier ones were often out of focus, heads of subjects lopped off, and there were whimsical shots of friends posed in trees, arranged in pyramids, or posed in some other illogical setting that Ivy, amateur photographer, had directed.

There were lots of pictures taken at Acacia Springs, where Ivy still accompanied her mother every summer. She was glad she had printed the names of those friends she made during the summer vacations because otherwise she might have forgotten some of their names.

Stuck in the back of the book was a brochure. On the cover was a photograph of a young woman in a traditional riding habit, seated on horseback. In the background stood a rambling, gray stone structure with a name in Gothic lettering underneath: "ELMHURST, A Finishing School for Young Ladies." Ivy scanned the description once more. "Discriminating parents who desire their daughters to reside in a cultured atmosphere that emphasizes manners and study of the arts as a requisite in their education would do well to choose Elmhurst. Our staff of unsurpassed background provides a balanced program of instruction in social skills, healthful physical sports — archery, horseback riding, ballroom dancing — as well as exposure to music and art appreciation — all the influences which give young ladies poise, polish, and that intangible mark of refinement. After a year at Elmhurst, your daughter will graduate, epitomizing the ultimate definition of a lady."

It was Mercedes's ardent hope that after Ivy graduated from Brookdale she would agree to attend Elmhurst, but Ivy was stubbornly opposed to the idea. Her adopted mother had no clue that it was the picture on the cover of the brochure that had triggered Ivy's adamant resistance.

Two images had brought back Ivy's worst memories. Elmhurst reminded her of Greystone, the orphanage to which she had been taken as a bewildered, frightened five-year-old. And, of course, Ivy never wanted to get on a horse again. When Mercedes coaxed, "Do think about it, won't you, darling?" Ivy took the brochure, but had never read any more than the first paragraph, for she had no intention of going.

On the whole, however, the next two years of Ivy's life followed a smooth, happy path. It seemed as if the dark shadows from her past would not shut out the sunshine of these carefree high school days.

At breakfast one morning, a week after school closed, Mercedes surprised Ivy by asking, "How would you like to have Allison go with us to Acacia Springs this year?"

"Really, Mother? Oh, yes, that would be great fun. Do you think Miss Fay would agree?"

"Well, why don't you see how Allison feels about it, and then I'll speak to her." Mercedes smiled, pleased that her simple suggestion had made Ivy so happy.

That very afternoon Ivy hurried over to Allison's, confident that her friend would be as thrilled and excited about the prospect as she. First, Ivy decided, she would suggest they go down to the river, always their favorite place for sharing confidences and plans. There Ivy would tell her about Acacia Springs, then pop the surprise invitation.

However, when Allison came to the door and heard Ivy's suggestion about spending the afternoon down at the river, she shook her head regretfully. "I can't, Ivy. I promised Aunty I'd finish this dress for her. Mrs. Barlow is coming for a fitting in the morning."

"Could I help so you'd get through sooner? It's such a nice day, it would be a shame to spend it inside."

"Can you take out basting stitches?"

"Sure!" was Ivy's immediate reply then she dimpled, "Show me."

Allison laughed and opened the door wider. "Come in."

Leading the way into Miss Fay's sewing room, Allison turned the dress over and pointed out the larger stitching beside the tiny ones on the beautifully done French seams. "Just snip and pull," she explained, "but very carefully so you don't tear the cloth."

The girls settled down and worked steadily for a few minutes. But the task wasn't as easy for Ivy as she had expected.

She put down the sewing impatiently and, unable to contain her surprise longer, burst out, "Allison, do you think you could go with us to Acacia Springs? It was Mother's idea. She thinks you're a good influence on me. But, of course, I can't imagine anything more fun!" Ivy laughed gaily.

To her dismay, Allison shook her head. "That's very kind of Mrs. Ellison, Ivy, but . . . I don't think so. Not that I wouldn't enjoy it. But I'm going to have to work this summer. Even if I get a scholarship to the Art Institute after we graduate next year, I'm going to need money for clothes and other expenses. Aunty says I can have all the egg money and the proceeds from the vegetables. So I plan to make the garden larger so we'll have more to sell. That will take a lot of time and work."

Ivy was silent. The old shadow of guilt descended, twisting her in a stomach-wrenching grip, reminding her again of what she had done. If she had spoken up, it would have been *Allison* not *Ivy* who went to the Ellisons. If *they* had adopted Allison, there would be no need for her to work all summer, no need for a scholarship, for that matter. No doubt Dan would have sent Allison to the best art school in the country.

Ivy felt suddenly sick. Carefully laying

down the dress she was working on, she stood up. "I'm sorry, Allison, I've got to go. I just remembered. I have some errands I have to do for Mother."

Allison looked astonished. "I thought you wanted to go to the river after this."

"I know but I forgot . . ." Ivy's heart pumped. Lies, more lies! Just like the olive bottle Mrs. Gaynor, their Sunday school teacher, had used as an illustration so long ago. The first lie was hard to get out, but each succeeding one was easier, until the lies just popped out, one after the other, like so many olives.

Ivy hurried out of the house, down the porch steps and out the gate in the picket fence. She felt the weight of all her past lies, the burden of all her sins. She saw herself as the scapegoat of ancient times to whom the village people tied their offenses, faults, and crimes before chasing it out into the desert as a symbol of atonement.

Mindlessly, she began to run down the road, not knowing in which direction she was headed, wanting only to escape. Would she never be rid of it? Sometimes she forgot for a short time. After all, Allison seemed happy. She was certainly secure, well-cared for, loved. But when something like this came up about money, involving the future,

Ivy realized the enormity of the act she had committed.

Ivy ran faster, feeling as if she were choking. Her hair began to tumble out of its ribbons and her breath came in short gasps. On and on she ran until she found herself on the path that led down to the river. Finally, out of breath, her hair streaming down her back, she flung herself down in the tall grass, panting.

She buried her face in her hands. Just look what she had done! Even if she confessed at this late date, how could this mess ever be straightened out? How could she ever explain? How could she ever be forgiven?

Everyone would hate her. She would be forever branded as a liar. She would have to leave town. But where would she go? What would she do? Tears burst from her in deep, wrenching sobs.

"Ivy! What on earth's the matter? Are you hurt? What happened?"

Pushing her hair back from her hot face, Ivy looked up and into Baxter McNeil's troubled gaze. Of all people, *Baxter McNeil!* Ivy felt her face flame. What was he doing out here? She had not seen him for what . . . nearly two years? Not since he'd graduated Brookdale High and gone off to the state university. Ivy hastily wiped her eyes with the back of her hands, unaware that the childish gesture stirred his protective masculine heart.

"Why, my goodness, Baxter McNeil! You're the very last person I expected to see," Ivy said, struggling to sit up and smoothing her wrinkled skirt. "What in the world are you doing down here?"

"Fishing," he said dryly, which of course was obvious. He was carrying a fishing rod, and a wicker creel was slung by a leather strap over one shoulder. Ivy felt even more embarrassed.

He crouched down beside her, sitting on his heels. "Can I do something to help? What's wrong, Ivy?" he probed gently.

It was too late to try to pretend there was *nothing* wrong. Her tears told him something definitely *was*. But of course she couldn't tell him the real reason, so she tried to make light of it. "Oh, it's not much." She shrugged. "My wickedness catching up with me, I suspect. I *should* be home doing chores or errands for my mother. But I played hooky and came running down here and twisted my ankle. It hurts like the very dickens."

Baxter didn't seem convinced, but he did not pursue it further. Instead, he lowered his lean body to sit down on the grass beside her. This gave Ivy a chance to collect herself.

In a minute she asked brightly, "So, Baxter, how's college? Are you home for summer vacation?"

"No, just for a few days. I've got a summer job on a newspaper near the university that starts on the twentieth. So I have to go back." He turned his head to look down at the river glistening in the sun. "I didn't realize how much I'd miss this place. Good old Brookdale. Couldn't wait till I got away. Now I can't wait to get back. I talked to Mr. Barnes, the editor of the Brookdale paper, to see if there might be an opening as a reporter when I finish school. He was non-committal." Baxter sighed then glanced at her speculatively. "What about you? When you finish school, what are *your* plans?"

"I don't have any, really."

"You ought to think about college, Ivy. You're smart."

"Oh, I don't know. Daddy has suggested going to the Normal School for Teachers in Pemberton. But I don't much want to be a teacher."

"There are other things besides teaching, Ivy. There are more and more opportunities for educated women these days."

He was beginning to sound too much like

Daddy Dan to suit Ivy, and she picked up her hat. "Well, there's time enough to make up my mind. It's just the first week in June. I've got the whole summer. Besides next year seems a long time away."

"It'll go faster than you think." Baxter shook his head. "It doesn't seem like nearly two years since I graduated Brookdale High, and here I'm halfway through college. Yep, I really do miss this place."

"You *miss* it?" Ivy was incredulous. *"High school? Brookdale?"*

"I miss the small town, where everyone knows you. I guess it's true what they say, 'You can take a boy out of the country, but you can't take the country out of the boy.' " He grinned.

"Baxter, you're not a country boy! Your father's a lawyer and you've always lived in town, not in the country!"

"It was meant as an aphorism, Ivy, that's all."

"Oh, you and your big words! You always did try to intimidate me, Baxter McNeil!"

"But I never managed to, did I?"

Ivy tossed her head. "Well, not for lack of trying. Of course, you were *everything* at high school — student body president, editor of the school paper. It was pretty ter-rifying to a lowly freshman."

"I don't think I terrified *you*, Ivy. You don't scare easily." He looked at her curiously. "I don't imagine there's anything you're afraid of."

"You might be surprised," she retorted, then thinking the conversation was getting too serious, she started to get up.

Baxter frowned. "Do you think you can manage to walk back to town on your ankle?"

Ivy had almost forgotten her fib about twisting her foot. "Oh, yes, I'm sure."

Baxter unwound his long frame and got to his feet, reached down for her hand to pull her up. "Easy now," he cautioned. "Better test it first, see if you can bear your weight on it."

Ivy made a good show of it. "It's all right now."

They started walking slowly to the road and then toward town, Ivy purposely favoring one foot to perpetuate the myth of the sprained ankle. Baxter slowed his longer stride to hers and walked her all the way home. They talked about mutual acquaintances from high school and church.

When Ivy told him about Allison's working for a scholarship to art school, Baxter said, "She's a talented young lady. But you are, too, Ivy. You ought to think about what your father suggested. At least go to college, then you can decide what else you might want to do."

"Well, Mama and I are leaving for Acacia Springs next week," she said flippantly, "I'll think about it up there."

At the Ellisons' gate, she paused. "Well, good-bye, Baxter. It was nice seeing you again."

His eyes regarded her steadily for a moment as though he might say something more. Then he gave a little nod. "You, too, Ivy. Have a nice summer." With a wave, he turned and walked down the street.

Watching him go, Ivy felt a small pang of disappointment. Why, she didn't know. The chance meeting with Baxter McNeil had been a strange coincidence. He was better-looking than ever, but he was still as bossy and critical as when they had had those clashes about deadlines and copy at the Brookdale High *Banner*. Hmph! Who did he think he was anyway, saying all those things about college and how she ought to be thinking about the future? Why did he think he knew what *she* should do?

She remembered the mad crush she had had on Baxter McNeil her first year at high school. It seemed a long time ago now, and she had gotten over it. Hadn't she?

★ ★ ★

During the next few days, Ivy was still in a turmoil of mind and spirit thinking about Allison. Was there nothing she could do? Maybe there was. She could possibly make sure somehow that Allison got to go to art school, whether she received the scholarship or not. Maybe Ivy could squirrel away part of the generous allowance the Ellisons gave her, money she often squandered on foolish, impulsive purchases she didn't need. Daddy Dan was always slipping her an extra five or ten dollars, telling her with a wink to go buy something pretty for herself. Yes, that was the least she could do.

In spite of her disappointment that Allison had not accepted their invitation, that summer was one of the happiest Ivy ever spent at Acacia Springs. At seventeen, she was old enough now to be part of the young crowd at the hub of social activities. Her unusual looks and charm attracted many, and she never lacked for invitations to the events. During those weeks much of the old guilt subsided. When they returned to Brookdale, Ivy found that Allison had also had a happy summer and had earned a tidy sum of money. Their reunion was unshadowed, and both friends looked forward to their last year at Brookdale High, which passed with remarkable speed as memories were made that would forge their friendship even more solidly.

Chapter Thirteen

Spring 1897

Overnight, the gymnasium of Brookdale High School was transformed into an exotic palace ballroom. Allison, as head of the decorating committee, had performed a feat of magic, making all the gym equipment — the scoreboards, the basketball hoops, the balance beam, the hurdles — disappear. In their places were minarets, a mock fountain in the middle, with glistening strips of silver paper cleverly arranged to cascade like water. All around the room, arcaded porticoes were bordered with mosaic, painstakingly constructed of dozens of colored-paper cutouts. Billowing gossamer draperies formed tented alcoves in which low, round tables were surrounded by plump pillows for sitting. Flickering candles in papier-mâché Aladdin lamps cast rainbow-colored lights on the floor, which was now waxed and polished for dancing. Above the entrance, flanked by posts wrapped with marbleized paper to give the effect of varicolored marble pillars, a banner printed in Arabic-style lettering spelled out "Class of 1897." Before the doors were opened to the arriving seniors, no one else except the hard-working members of the committee and some junior volunteers had seen it. When the seniors entered, they walked into a virtual enchanted fairyland.

Ivy clutched Allison's arm in excitement. "How did you ever manage it?"

"I copied it from a picture in *Arabian Nights*. Does it really work?"

"Does it ever! It's simply gorgeous. You're an artistic genius, Allison!"

"Oh, Ivy, you always exaggerate." But Allison looked pleased.

Others joined in the enthusiastic praise until Allison was almost giddy.

Then she was whisked off by the class president to dance, leaving Ivy alone . . . but only for a moment. A voice behind her asked, "May I have this dance?"

Ivy thought she recognized the voice, but wasn't sure until she spun around. "*Baxter!* What are you doing here?"

"The alumni were issued invitations, you know. We're having our class reunion later this week, too. Shall we?" He held out his arm to escort her onto the dance floor.

Surprised, Ivy picked up her skirt and

floated into his arms as the orchestra began playing.

"You're looking especially lovely tonight, Ivy."

"You look quite splendid yourself, Baxter. I don't think I've ever seen you all decked out in a shirt, tie, and dark suit." She laughed. "Not even in church!"

Baxter grinned. "I don't think I've had this one on since my own graduation night dance, to tell you the truth."

"You mean you don't go out dancing in the city? There must be lots of attractive young ladies in St. Louis who would be thrilled to go out with an up-and-coming journalist."

"You don't do much gallivantin' any-where on a reporter's salary . . . particularly not in St. Louis, Ivy."

"What a shame. The poor things don't know what they're missing. And here you are at a high school dance, stuck with a hometown girl."

"That isn't exactly how I look at it, Ivy. I was afraid your dance card would be all filled, and I wouldn't have a chance."

"Want the truth, Baxter? Four years ago, I would have killed for the chance to dance with you." She tilted her head to one side and looked up at him coquettishly.

He seemed shocked. "You should have told me. I would have invited you to *my* graduation dance."

"No, you wouldn't have, Baxter. Remember, I was — in your words — the worst excuse for a class reporter you'd ever seen!"

"Good grief, Ivy, are you quoting me directly, or are you making it up? I couldn't have actually been *that* obnoxious, even as an editor, *could* I?"

She nodded solemnly, although her eyes sparkled mischievously.

Baxter tried to look appropriately contrite. "Would you accept a retroactive apology?"

"Yes . . . provided you'll take back all those awful things you said."

"I do. I probably didn't mean them. You weren't *that* bad."

"I tried hard to prove you wrong. You can't imagine how much in awe I was of you then. You were . . . well, older . . . three years ahead of me and such an important person at school. I was trying terribly to make you notice me."

"By writing bad copy?"

"You said you were going to apologize!" Ivy pretended indignation. "I worked hard. I wanted your approval more than anything." She lowered her eyes for a minute.

"There! I probably shouldn't have told you, but now you know my secret."

He narrowed his gaze reflectively. "I guess there are a lot of things I don't know about you, Ivy."

"What would you like to know?"

"Everything."

"*Everything?* No, that's not a good idea. One shouldn't want to know everything about another person. There should be some mystery about someone . . . even someone you care about."

"You're probably right. Maybe, *especially* someone you care about." His hand holding hers tightened.

Ivy's heart turned over and she found it suddenly hard to breathe. But daring to discover the truth, she looked up at him and asked impulsively, "Do you care about *me*, Baxter?"

His eyes met hers steadily. "Yes, I do, Ivy. A whole lot."

"But you don't really know me."

"I'd like to. Very much."

They circled the room again, then Ivy drew a little apart and asked, "How much longer are you going to be in Brookdale?"

"Nearly two weeks."

Her eyes sparkled. "Well, that should give us enough time to find out about each other, shouldn't it?" she asked softly.

To Ivy, the next two weeks were unbeliev-able. It was like having a good fairy grant your most cherished wish. It seemed impos-sible to her that Baxter McNeil, of all people, now found her irresistible. She re-membered the hours she had literally *pined* for him. How hard she had worked to get him to notice her. How she had fantasized his asking her out, imagining what she'd wear, what he'd say. And now, it was hap-pening!

It was a heady sensation. Ivy had stars in her eyes, while her feet seemed to dance on clouds. Baxter McNeil, her secret love throughout that first year at Brookdale High School, was now hanging on her every word and wanted to spend time exclusively with her.

Even in the midst of her new happiness, however, Ivy felt insecure. When Baxter told her how he had been attracted to her even back in high school, Ivy found it hard to believe him.

Only Ivy knew that beneath her gaiety, her vivaciousness, her popularity, always lurked the fear of being abandoned, of losing yet another person she had come to love. Life for her was like walking the high wire with a yawning drop underneath, where one misstep would send her plunging to disaster. Sometimes with a chilling flash of remembrance, Ivy would recall seeing that moment of terror in Liselle's eyes that last night at the circus, the same night *she* had been injured. Trembling herself, Ivy had watched Liselle mount the rope that took her high up to the dizzying platform from which she would take that first step out on the wire, the crowd holding its collective breath. Time and time again that scene played itself out in her mind. Subconsciously Ivy applied Liselle's oft-repeated rules to her own life: "Don't look down and don't panic!" Ivy would shudder, wondering what would happen if somehow she were found out, the deception revealed, her lie discovered. Would anyone love her *then?*

When Ivy was with Baxter, she covered her uncertainties well with a ready smile, a happy-go-lucky manner, hoping he'd never guess what lay just under the surface. Before he had to return to the city, she and Baxter spent part of every day together. They took long walks, often out to the river, walking along its banks, talking endlessly — at least Baxter did. He told Ivy his plans, his goals, his ambitions for becoming a published journalist. But the more they were together, the more difficult it was for Ivy to hide her deep-seated insecurities.

The Ellisons liked Baxter and were cordial and friendly when he came by to see Ivy. But neither of them had any idea it was anything more than an affectionate friendship. They might have been alarmed had they known the intensity of Baxter's feelings for Ivy.

Two days before he was to leave, he came for dinner at the Ellisons. Afterwards, he and Ivy went for a walk in the summer dusk. When it began to get dark, they strolled slowly back to the house and sat down together on the swing on the side porch. A pale oval moon hung in the mauve evening sky.

"You will write to me after I'm gone, won't you, Ivy?" Baxter asked rather anxiously.

"Well, I'm not much good at letter-writing, Bax, never had much practice at it. But of course, if you write, I'll write back." She tipped her head and looked up at him. "That is, *if* you won't blue-pencil my letters!"

He laughed and slipped his arm around her shoulder. For a few minutes the only sound was the swing's gentle squeak.

Then Ivy sighed. "I hate to have you go.

The city seems a long way off."

"Not too far, actually. And it's not as if it's forever. You know I plan to come back here and go to work at the *Brookdale Messenger*."

"You can't be sure you'll get a job at the *Messenger*, can you?"

"Well, maybe not, but I know I'll be back, Ivy. Brookdale is my home. This is where I want to live, spend the rest of my life and one day be editor of the paper." There was a teasing note in Baxter's voice as if he were trying to offset the melancholy they both felt at their parting.

They swung for a few minutes in silence, the swing creaking on its chains. Ivy looked toward the house where the lights shone out from the parlor onto the porch. She knew Mercedes was waiting for her to come inside and that saying good-bye could not be put off much longer. Tomorrow night Baxter was obligated to spend with his own parents and family before he left on the train the following morning.

Baxter, sensing her thoughts as he often did, whispered, "I'd like to kiss you, Ivy. May I?"

"I thought you'd never ask," she said, nestling back against his shoulder to receive his gentle kiss. When she opened her eyes, his face was very near. Even in the shadowy light, she could see that he was still looking at her.

She sighed and put one hand along his cheek. "Oh, Baxter, it's going to be such a long time . . ."

"I'll try to get home . . . maybe at Christmas, Ivy."

"But you said you had to save your money. What about your board, room, the expenses?"

"Yes, but I'll work it out. I'll be back."

Some deep inner memory clutched Ivy like a cold hand squeezing her heart. How many times had she been told "I'll be back," only to have that person disappear from her life forever?

Baxter drew her toward him gently. "I love you, Ivy." He kissed her again, and she tried to believe that in that sweet, tender kiss was a promise that would be kept.

In the middle of the next night, Ivy woke up from a sound sleep. She sat straight up in bed, not knowing what had awakened her. She waited, listening, then it came — the long, lonely sound of a train whistle echoing through the clear summer night. The same sound that always brought the prickling along her flesh, the indefinable aching, the yearning in her heart.

The day after Baxter left, Ivy went out to see Allison. She had been so preoccupied with the romance that she had hardly seen her friend since graduation. Of course, Allison was aware of what was happening between Ivy and Baxter, but the two had not really had a chance to talk. Ivy could not wait to confide her new feelings to the friend who had always shared her secrets . . . except, of course, one. But that one was far from Ivy's mind when she pushed through the gate and went past Fay's flower beds and herb garden onto the porch.

She knocked briefly, then opened the front door, calling as she did so, "Anybody home? It's me!"

Allison came rushing into the hall, waving an envelope and a letter in one hand. "Oh, Ivy, I'm so glad you've come! I've just received the most wonderful news!"

Miss Fay was right behind Allison. "Hello, Ivy, you're just in time to celebrate with us."

"What is it? What's happened? Don't keep me in suspense."

"Here, read it for yourself." Allison thrust the paper toward her.

Ivy noted the letterhead first — "The Art Institute." Quickly she scanned the page, then let out a happy cry. "Oh, Allison, how wonderful! I'm so proud of you!" Ivy hugged her.

"I was just going to pour us all a glass of fresh grape juice," said Fay. "So come along to the kitchen. Or better still, I'll bring it out onto the porch. It's such a pretty day." She disappeared into the kitchen at her hobbling gait.

The two girls looked at each other for a full minute, then Ivy said, "It's all your dreams come true, isn't it, Allison?"

"Oh, yes. More than I ever really hoped for. Just think, Ivy, I'm going to St. Louis. I've never been to a big city like that before and . . ."

"St. Louis is only the first step, Allison! You'll be a famous artist. Next, you'll be going to Paris!"

Allison shook her head, her face suddenly serious. "No, not Paris, Ivy."

"Why ever *not?*" demanded Ivy, surprised. "*All* artists study in Paris for a year or two. They go to museums, to the Louvre and . . ."

"I don't have a birth certificate, Ivy. You can't get a passport to go abroad without one. You see, at the foundling home in New York there was just my first name pinned to my clothes." She gave a rueful little smile.

"No other identification. I don't know who my parents were, although I feel sure my mother loved me. The nuns told me I was well-cared for and beautifully dressed." She threw out both hands in a helpless gesture. "I don't have a clue as to what my father's name was. I can't even prove I was ever born."

"What do you mean? You're *here*, aren't you? Doesn't that mean you were born?"

"Not legally. You have to have a birth certificate. I can't go to Paris without a passport, and I can't get a passport without a birth certificate."

Ivy was stunned. She had never thought of such a thing. As she stood there staring at Allison, a conversation she'd had with her adopted mother only a short time ago came to mind. Mercedes had mentioned that perhaps after the election next spring, they could take a trip to Europe.

"Wouldn't that be lovely, dear? Traveling is so educational, and we could have such fun together, sightseeing and shopping."

Did Ivy herself have a birth certificate? And if she did, had the orphanage given it to Paulo Tarantino when he adopted her? Feeling chilled, Ivy shivered involuntarily.

There was no chance to say any more because they heard footsteps coming back down the hall. Allison put her forefinger to her lips, slowly shaking her head. Ivy realized Allison didn't want to discuss it further. But Ivy suddenly felt stricken. She had been so happy lately she hadn't thought much about her background. Now, this new information was like another door banging shut, another barrier placed on her life.

In spite of her genuine happiness over Allison's scholarship, Ivy felt strangely depressed when she got home. She was aware of Mercedes's anxious glances cast her way throughout dinner and tried her best to appear cheerful.

"I ran into Mr. Stapleton this afternoon in town, Ivy, and he asked me what your plans were. He said how bright you were and that he hoped you would go on with your education. I told him I had suggested Elmhurst to you, but that you weren't very interested, that is, unless . . . you've changed your mind?"

"No, I'm not and I haven't." Ivy's tone was firmer than she intended and she felt immediately contrite. "I'm sorry, Mama, but I really don't want to go."

"Have you *really* looked at those brochures, Ivy?" Mercedes persisted gently. "You know we could take a trip up there — it isn't that far — and look it over for ourselves. Are you sure you wouldn't like to consider going, dear?"

"No! I told you, Mother, I don't want to go away."

"But why not, Ivy, dear? I really don't understand." Mercedes seemed genuinely puzzled. "Elmhurst is one of the finest finishing schools in the state. They offer many cultural advantages — piano and voice lessons and all sorts of other activities you would enjoy. Like archery and horseback riding, for example. Wouldn't you like to learn to ride, Ivy? I've always thought it was such a ladylike sport, and you would look elegant in a riding habit."

Ivy shook her head. "No, Mama, honestly. I'd much rather stay here with you and Daddy than go away. I'll find plenty to do. I can learn to sew or take drawing classes right here in Brookdale. Besides," she added positively, "I don't like horses. Not at all!"

Ivy excused herself on the pretext of having to shampoo her hair. She hardly made it to her bedroom before she was overcome with near hysterical laughter. Learn to ride horseback? She pressed her hand against her mouth to silence the uncontrollable laughter. If her mother only knew . . . All the old rage and rebellion welled up

211

inside Ivy against Paulo, his relentless training, his unbridled anger, his oaths, the crack of his whip. In seconds the laughter had turned to tears. Ivy flung herself on her bed, buried her head in one pillow, and pulled another over her head so no one could hear her anguished sobs.

She remembered in vivid detail the day she had flung herself onto the couch in Sophia's tent after one of Paulo's ruthless sessions. "I hate the circus! I hate horses, and when I grow up I never want to see or ride one again!" she had sobbed.

But Sophia had sighed, shaking her head. "Once you get sawdust in your hair, you never get it out."

"Well, *I* will!" Ivy had told her defiantly.

Recalling that scene, Ivy sat up and pounded the pillow furiously. "And I *will!* I *have!*" she said through clenched teeth.

A little later there was a gentle tap at her bedroom door and Mercedes opened it and peeked in. She was carrying a teacup. "Aren't you feeling well, dear? Did I say something to upset you?"

Ivy sat up and shook her head vigorously. "No, Mother, of course not. I'm just feeling a little down . . . with Allison going away and all . . ."

"Exactly," said Mercedes, sitting down

on the edge of the bed and handing her the cup of fragrant jasmine tea she had brought her. "And that's understandable. But you must remember, Ivy, you and Allison have different lives, and you each have your own path to take. Allison's talent is going to dictate her future. And I want *you* to have something to look forward to now that your high school days are over. You haven't found yourself yet and I think . . . well, that's why I suggested Elmhurst would be such a good idea. It would give you time to think about your own future, expose you to some possibilities. It's only twenty-five miles from Brookdale, only a short train ride, actually. And you could come home whenever you wanted to. Besides, it's right near Wainwright College and there would certainly be many delightful social occasions. Won't you at least think about it, darling?"

"Yes, Mama, I will." Impulsively Ivy hugged her, feeling wretched for her lack of gratitude.

Acacia Springs
August 1897

Because of the mayoral election in June, the annual vacation at Acacia Springs was delayed until August that year. With Dan successfully returned to office, Ivy and Mercedes went off on their trip as usual.

Ivy had reveled in the popularity she had enjoyed the year before. But this summer, with thoughts of Baxter, she wasn't as eager to enter into the social life of the resort. In fact, she had determined to take advantage of some of the educational programs offered that she had bypassed in favor of the more frivolous pursuits the previous summer.

On the first day of their stay, Ivy and her mother were enjoying the buffet breakfast served on the screened-in veranda of the hotel. Sipping coffee, Ivy looked over the printed schedule of events, trying to decide which one to try.

"What a beautiful spot!" Mercedes said rapturously, gazing out at the quiet lake. "How marvelous it is that we can enjoy all the glories of God's creation here."

Ivy suppressed a smile. Mercedes did not appear eager to explore "all the glories" of nature, even though she urged Ivy to go to the beach or swim in the lake. "Are you sure you wouldn't like to come along with me this morning, Mother?" Ivy asked, knowing almost certainly that she wouldn't. Her mother preferred the more sedentary plea-sures — reading in a hammock slung under a tree or sitting in one of the rockers, chatting with some of the other lady guests on the porch.

Ivy walked over to the main building to sign up for one of the programs scheduled for that morning. A group was just forming for a nature walk and Ivy decided to go along. The lecture, given by a rather pompous individual, centered on the varieties of butterflies to be observed in this particular part of the country. At the close of his talk, there would be a field trip. He suggested that they go in pairs. One participant would be issued a net, the other a notepad, and together they were to make notes of the specimens they saw and collect them if possible. He would then demonstrate how to pin the specimens to a board, and they would discuss the species each represented.

The thought of performing such a procedure horrified Ivy. Instinctively she wrinkled her nose, and as she did, caught the amused glance of a rusty-haired young man nearby. He was having difficulty suppressing his laughter. Ivy returned his boyish grin with a smile, then turned away to go in search of some other pastime for the morning, when he moved toward her. "I beg pardon, miss, may I introduce myself? I'm Bradley Porter, a fellow guest at the hotel. I believe we are both of the same mind about the end point of this venture. But dare I suggest we might enjoy the walk anyway?"

Ivy consulted her fob watch pinned to her tucked shirtwaist. It was already late, and alternate programs had begun. She might as well accept the suggestion.

Within a few minutes she discovered Bradley Porter to be an engaging fellow with an irrepressible personality and an outrageous sense of humor. They hit it off at once. Agreeing to reject the object of the walk, they picked up their butterfly net and notepad as partners and went out with the others on the field trip.

Under his breath, accurately imitating the pontifical voice of the leader, Brad initiated a game that sent Ivy into fits of mild hilarity. They began to carry on a ridiculous conversation, referring often to the listed butterflies they were supposed to be hunting.

"Have you perchance come upon my *Hesperia vesicolor?*" Brad asked seriously.

"I think not. But it may have been that I saw the *Erycina phareus* flying by with her companion *Polyommatus endymion*," Ivy replied with the same intensity.

"Oh!" Brad struck his forehead in mock dismay. "Then I must have missed them

216

both, interested as I was in the flight of *Papilio ulysses*."

After a few such exchanges they dissolved into helpless laughter and were reduced to leaning weakly against trees to regain their equilibrium. When they at last resumed some semblance of control, they found they had fallen way behind the others, and Brad suggested they sit down in the shade for a while.

"So you're from Brookdale?" he asked Ivy.

"Yes," she replied. "Why?"

"It seems a coincidence, but I'd never heard of the place until a week ago, and now I've heard of it twice in less than ten days," he said, frowning as though this was a most interesting and unusual occurrence.

"Oh?"

"I have a cousin who's moving there. Has a job at the bank. His name's Russell Trent." He grinned mischievously. "He's not a bit like me, so don't worry. He's straight as an arrow, very smart, intelligent." Brad winked. "I'm the black sheep of the family, but I'm more fun than Russ." He threw back his head and laughed heartily. "You know there has to be one in every clan. I have two older brothers and they're all doing great. My folks have given up on me if

217

I don't make it through the next two years of college. But Russ . . . now he's another story altogether. He's an only child and his mother's darling. And why not? He's a splendid chap. I'm not jealous or anything like that . . ." Brad broke off and furrowed his brow comically. "But why am I spending all this time telling you about my cousin, pointing out all his upstanding, fine qualities? Instead, I should be trying to make an impression on you myself."

"Oh, but you *are!* You *are!*" Ivy laughed merrily, unaware that months later she would recall this very conversation.

Chapter Fourteen

Elmhurst
Fall 1897

When Mercedes and Ivy returned home, Allison had already left for St. Louis and the Art Institute. Brookdale seemed impossibly empty and dull to Ivy with both her best friend and Baxter gone. Impulsively she decided she would go to Elmhurst, after all. Overjoyed at her decision, Mercedes was for once moved to swift action. Arrangements were made, trunks packed, and within three weeks Ivy was at the station, ready to board the train to Woodley Falls.

Waiting to leave, Ivy was struck with the familiar uncertainty and fear of the unknown. But once on her way, she felt a tremendous surge of freedom. At Elmhurst she would be starting a whole new phase of her life. No one there knew anything about her except that she was the daughter of Daniel Ellison, the mayor of Brookdale. Just as Brookdale knew nothing about her circus background, her classmates at Elmhurst would know nothing about her Orphan

Train experience. She could start here with a clean slate.

As it turned out, Elmhurst was an excellent decision. Ivy was immediately accepted by the other girls and soon became the popular center of a fun-loving group. Elmhurst itself, with its spacious grounds bordered with boxwood and its winding paths under ancient elms, became her world and Ivy reveled in belonging. Its mellow brick buildings, red-tinged Virginia creeper clinging to the walls, and the small chapel where daily services were held soon grew dear.

Her letters home were happy ones, filled with news of all her activities. She did not, however, sign up for horseback riding.

At first, Ivy looked forward to Baxter's hastily written letters, and she tried to answer them regularly. But she often failed, for Ivy found it difficult to put her feelings into words, and last summer's magic gradually faded with the onset of winter and the press of her exciting new world. When Baxter wrote regretfully that poor health had forced his father to give up his law practice and that a shortage of money would prevent him from coming home for Christmas, Ivy was deeply disappointed. With this unexpected development, she wasn't looking forward to the Christmas holidays.

Christmas 1897

She could not have been more wrong. When she walked in the door, the Ellisons' house was already gaily decorated, and a beautifully shaped evergreen stood in the parlor, waiting to be trimmed.

"Welcome home, darling!" Mercedes greeted her and showed her a handful of invitations to Christmas parties. At one of these Ivy had an unexpected encounter that would alter the direction of her life.

The very next evening, she attended a party at the home of one of the town's most prominent citizens, Henry Oliver, president of the Brookdale Savings and Loan. It was an annual affair, a buffet supper, given the week before Christmas. This event was always considered the opening of the holiday season in Brookdale. Of course, the mayor and his family were honored guests.

When Ivy arrived with her parents, their hostess took Ivy by the arm and led her a little apart. "There's someone I want you to meet, dear. He's just come to town . . . the new assistant cashier at the bank." Mrs. Oliver lowered her voice to a stage whisper. "A bachelor and very eligible, I might add. Come along. I'll introduce you." She then propelled Ivy toward a young man standing on the other side of the room. From his rather aloof expression, Ivy thought he looked bored and she was not all that eager to meet him. But she could not be rude, so smiled graciously as Mrs. Oliver introduced them. "Mr. Trent, I'd like to present the mayor's daughter, Ivy Ellison."

Instantly the bored look vanished. All at once the evening that had seemed decidedly dull took on new possibilities. The young woman with Mrs. Oliver was extraordinarily attractive. Not beautiful, but definitely interesting. Dark hair swirled above a small, oval face, flashing brown eyes that were slightly almond-shaped, shadowed by long lashes, flawless olive skin with a tinge of apricot blush — an enchanting combination. Her crimson velvet dress accentuated her distinctive coloring and showed off to great advantage the slender, tiny-waisted figure.

"Delighted, Miss Ellison," he said, bowing over Ivy's extended hand.

"I'm sure you two will find lots in common to talk about," gushed Mrs. Oliver. Shaking her fan at them playfully, she drifted away to her other guests.

Left with this stranger, Ivy wondered what they could possibly have in common, but there was a niggling memory in the back of her mind. Where had she heard the name Russell Trent before?

"I must say this is a most pleasant coincidence, Miss Ellison. Although I didn't expect to meet you so soon, I've heard all about you."

"Oh, no!" Ivy pretended dismay. "Not from Mrs. Oliver, I hope? I'm really not one of her favorite people. I used to pick some of her prize flowers from her garden on my way home from school."

"That must have been at least ten years ago!" Russ raised his eyebrows. "No, it wasn't Mrs. Oliver. As a matter of fact, it was my cousin, Bradley Porter."

Immediately the puzzle was solved. "*Brad?* Brad Porter. Of course! We had some good times together last summer at Acacia Springs."

Well, Russell Trent didn't look a thing like his red-haired, freckle-faced cousin. In fact, he was very good-looking. Ivy made another swift appraisal. With the aloof expression replaced with one of smiling interest, one might even consider him handsome. His sharply molded features and neatly combed hair reminded her of one of the male models made popular by the artist, Charles Dana Gibson. For some reason, an image of Baxter flashed into Ivy's head.

Baxter, who never knew or cared what he was wearing, was most at home in a baggy coat sweater or an old corduroy jacket, his tie askew. Momentarily distracted by the contrast of the impeccably groomed Russell Trent in his dark suit, a high, stiff collar, and gray silk cravat, Ivy brought her attention back to what he was saying.

"I got a long, enthusiastic letter from Brad recently, and I can assure you that my cousin is not in the habit of using hyperbole." Russell paused, eyeing her appreciatively. "In the letter, he told me that if I had any second thoughts about the wisdom of accepting a position in Brookdale, I should wait until I had met *you*."

"That was an extravagant statement," Ivy said, wrinkling her nose playfully. "I certainly hope you don't base your career decisions on that kind of recommendation."

"Not usually. But this time I think my cousin's advice was right on target." Russ's eyes, which were very blue, twinkled. Then offering her his arm, he asked, "Would you care for some punch, Miss Ellison?"

The evening, which Ivy had considered a social obligation to be endured, turned out to be quite entertaining and enjoyable. Mrs. Oliver had been right. Ivy and Russell found a wide assortment of things to talk about.

For one, Russell's closest female cousin had attended Elmhurst and he had often been invited to social occasions there while he was attending the nearby men's college, Wainwright.

"I always enjoyed those occasions very much," he told Ivy adding, "though I haven't been back since her graduation."

"Well, we'll certainly have to do something about that, won't we?" She smiled.

"I hope you mean that."

Russell had all the social attributes, an assured confidence that comes with a certain kind of background, an ease at repartee and conversation, besides being a superb dancer. He was a direct contrast to Brad, his fun-loving, irreverent cousin. Still, Ivy was thoroughly enjoying herself when Mercedes signaled it was time to leave. He seemed just as reluctant to see her go. As he helped her on with her hooded velvet evening wrap, he asked, "I hope I may be allowed to call on you, Miss Ellison, while you are home for the holidays?"

"By all means, Mr. Trent, I would be very pleased if you would," she said demurely. Secretly, Ivy was flattered that she had so quickly sparked the interest of Brookdale's newest "most eligible bachelor," as Mrs. Oliver had described him.

The very next day Russell sent Ivy a note, asking if he might call the following evening. He arrived with a bouquet of red roses and a box of chocolates and was invited to help trim the Christmas tree. By the week's end, Russ appeared to be seriously courting Ivy. At first, Ivy thought him rather too precise in his manners and speech. However, she found she enjoyed being treated as all the etiquette books specified a gentleman should treat a lady.

Ivy also enjoyed being escorted by someone who had been so readily accepted into Brookdale society. The Ellisons were delighted with Russ. He was such a personable young man, correct in every way, and his prospects were excellent.

One person who did not share the general approval of the newcomer was Allison. For Ivy, this was the proverbial fly in the ointment. Of all the people Ivy hoped would approve of her new escort, it was her best friend. But from the moment Ivy had introduced them, she could tell that Allison did not like Russell. Ivy couldn't understand why. If it had been anyone but Allison, she might have suspected it was jealousy. But their friendship went far beyond anything so petty.

At the holiday parties both young women

attended, Allison kept her distance, and when she and Ivy were alone together, she showed an annoying indifference when Ivy rhapsodized about Russ. Gradually, Ivy stopped confiding the details of their developing relationship to her.

Russ noticed Allison's coolness toward him and mentioned it to Ivy one evening when he brought her home from a party. "Your friend doesn't like me," he remarked matter of factly.

When Ivy tried quickly to explain that Allison did not make friends easily, Russ made no further comment.

The following afternoon, while the two friends were wrapping Christmas presents together, Ivy told Allison that Russ had mentioned her attitude toward him. When Allison only shrugged, Ivy persisted in trying to find out her reasons.

"Well, if you must know, I think he's stuffy, a bore, and full of himself! I can't, for the life of me, understand what you see in him."

"Then you must be blind!" Ivy retorted. "He's just about the best-looking fellow in this town, besides being charming, mannerly, and a splendid dancer!"

"Is that all?" Allison said sarcastically. "Sorry, I must have missed all that."

"Isn't that enough?" Ivy demanded.

"Looks and superficial manners don't mean *anything*. You certainly can't gaze at him admiringly or dance all the time you're with him. What do you talk about, Ivy?"

"Talk? Well, we talk about . . . everything . . . I don't know. Just whatever comes into our minds, I guess."

"Well, think about it. I remember you telling me how much you and Baxter found to talk about last summer. You were so thrilled, or have you forgotten?"

"Oh, well, *Baxter*. Baxter is different," Ivy said lamely. "I mean, he's so intelligent and all . . ."

"That's exactly what I mean. I've tried carrying on a conversation with your Mr. Russell Trent, and he has practically nothing of importance to say."

"Come on, Allison. You don't discuss art or politics or religion at a *party,* for heaven's sake!" Ivy sputtered. "Russ and I *do* fun things together. Like the taffy pull at the Edmonds's, and we're going ice skating tomorrow, and then there's the Dickens play that the Dramatic Society's putting on . . ."

Allison shook her head. "I'm sorry, Ivy. I shouldn't have said anything. It's really none of my business."

That ended the discussion. Ivy was still

uncomfortable with Allison's criticism, but she had decided she was not going to let it spoil the rest of her holidays.

Russell would be spending a few days with his family in Cartersville over Christmas. But he would be back in Brookdale to celebrate New Year's Eve and to escort Ivy to a gala supper dance. After that, she would be going back to Elmhurst. Until then, no matter what Allison thought, Ivy was going to enjoy herself.

The day before he was to leave, Russell Trent sat at his desk at the Brookdale Savings and Loan, staring out the window. All morning long there had been snow flurries. The sky was an odd shade of gray blue, slung with low-hanging clouds. He had been unable to apply himself to his work with his usual concentration. Why? Because he couldn't get Ivy Ellison out of his mind. He realized he thought about her constantly when he wasn't with her. It was most unusual for someone of Russ's analytical nature, and he couldn't figure out why she had taken possession of his waking thoughts as well as his dreams at night. She wasn't beautiful, although her looks were rather unique. But it was more than looks, there was something intangible, something he couldn't quite get his finger on that made her so attractive. He enjoyed being around her, knew that her vivaciousness counteracted his own inclination to moodiness. She made him laugh and he found her naturalness and spontaneity charming. Yes, he had been quite captivated by Ivy in a way he had never thought possible.

Startled out of his reverie at the sound of her voice, he swiveled his chair around just in time to see Ivy enter the bank and greet someone. She looked smart and stylish in a persimmon-colored coat with beaver collar and cuffs, and she was wearing a saucy hat with a feather that curled fetchingly alongside her cheek. She smiled and waved to him, but did not stop to chat. Instead, she went directly up to one of the teller's cages.

Russell left his desk and crossed over to speak to her. "And what brings you out on this cold morning?" he asked, looking down into sparkling eyes, feeling his heart speed up at an amazing rate.

"Money! Why else would anyone come to a bank?" she teased. "I have some Christmas shopping to do."

"You're pretty late, aren't you? It's nearly Christmas."

"I know but . . ." A dimple appeared at one corner of her intriguing mouth, "I've added a few names to my list."

After she departed, Milt Barens, the teller who had handled her transaction, remarked to Russell, "That's a pretty young lady and a *mighty lucky* one, too."

"Lucky?"

"You know, of course, that she was one of those waifs brought here on the Orphan Train."

"Orphan Train?" Russ was puzzled.

"Never heard about that? It used to bring little kids from orphanages back East. People adopted them. I'd say Ivy was lucky because the mayor and his wife took her in. They'd no children of their own, and they've spoiled her to a fare-thee-well . . ."

Russ made no comments. He went back to his desk in a rather somber mood. Ivy . . . an *orphan?* Perhaps a *foundling?* Given up at birth? By an unwed mother? He shuffled the sheaf of loan applications on his desk, but somehow could not recover his concentration.

On the train to Cartersville the next day, Russell had time to think about the last ten days. Events had moved with remarkable swiftness. Maybe too rapidly. He needed to consider all aspects of this new and rather amazing thing that had happened to him.

Ivy Ellison. He smiled at the thought of her, but sobered almost at once. What he had found out the day before would undoubtedly have a profound effect on their relationship.

As he neared his hometown station, Russell could not help wondering what his mother would say if she knew about Ivy's rather embarrassing background. Rebecca Trent was very strong on background and breeding. One of her favorite expressions used, whether praising someone or dismissing them as "not our kind," was "Blood will tell."

He knew his mother would ask him how he liked Brookdale and would question him tactfully but closely about his social life there. Russell was her pride and joy, and her interest in his life and career was keen. She was particularly anxious that he make the right choice in a bride, knowing how important the *proper* wife was to a young man on the ladder to business success.

As predicted, upon his arrival, his mother was eager to hear all about his new life in Brookdale. Russ found himself being guarded in his responses. Knowing how much she enjoyed hearing about his activities, he felt guilty about not being as forthcoming as usual. One reason, he realized, was because he was unsure of his own feelings about Ivy Ellison, and he didn't want to open himself up to a lot of questioning.

But Russell was surprised to discover that he missed Ivy dreadfully, even after only one day. He had not expected that, and it caused him some anxiety.

Without her, his days at home seemed long and tedious. He was completely uninterested in attending any of his hometown social events and especially indifferent to his mother's suggestion that he escort one of the local young ladies to the various parties to which he was invited. Instead of enjoying his short vacation, he felt restless and eager to get back to Brookdale . . . and Ivy.

As it turned out, on his return trip he did not spend much time wondering why he missed Ivy so much. He realized, with mingled uneasiness and excitement, that he had fallen in love with the one girl in Brookdale of whom his mother might not approve. That is, if she learned Ivy's strange background.

It was this information that Russ hadn't felt disposed to confide in his mother. However, the more he thought about it, the less he worried. Ivy couldn't have grown up in a more gracious household than the Ellisons, for she had been given every advantage. Her grace and social skills were above reproach. She would be an asset in every sense of the word to a man on his way up, Russ finally decided. Besides, he did not mean to spend the rest of his life in a small town like Brookdale. He had higher goals, greater ambitions, and with Ivy at his side when he moved to another town, a bigger bank, a more prominent position, who would ever question his wife's heritage?

When Ivy opened the door for him the night of his return to Brookdale, looking so absolutely lovely in a dress of midnight blue taffeta, Russ put aside all his misgivings. This was the girl he loved, and when the time was right, he would propose to her.

When it was time for Ivy to return to Elmhurst, he insisted on taking her to the train station and seeing her off himself. Since the mayor's day was filled with appointments after the holidays and Mercedes had a bad head cold, Russ's offer was gratefully accepted. They stood waiting on the train platform, their breath pluming in frosty puffs as they said all those last-minute things newly-in-love people say to each other.

Then the train thundered into the station and clanged to a stop. People started boarding the train. Porters trundled luggage carts to be loaded onto the baggage car.

"All aboard!" came the warning shout.

Russell walked with her to where the conductor stood ready to assist her up the steps into the train.

Russell stood watching as the train slowly pulled out, waving to Ivy whose face was pressed against the window. When it finally disappeared down the track, Russell breathed a sigh, regret mingled with relief. Now he could get back to his work at the bank. Ivy was a disturbing presence in his usually regimented life.

Back in her room at Elmhurst, Ivy was placing a silver-framed photograph of Russell on her bureau just as her roommate walked in the door.

"Oh, my goodness! Who is *he?*" Marcella oohed.

Beaming, Ivy turned around. "My new beau," she said proudly.

More and more Baxter's letters to Ivy went unanswered. It wasn't that she purposely neglected her correspondence with him. It was just that she didn't know what to say, how to tell him that she was caught up in a new romance. Russell Trent was experienced in the ways of courtship and used them to advantage. He sent bouquets, messages in the language of flowers that Ivy, to her delight, had to learn to interpret. He wrote little notes, mailed her small surprise gifts, coded postcards to decipher. He was enough older than Ivy to appear sophisticated and worldly. His position at the bank and in Brookdale society appealed to her own yearning for acceptance and social status. His dashing good looks and suavity intrigued her. And best of all, he was attracted to *her*. It added up to a very tempting combination.

Baxter was a much more complicated person and demanded a great deal more of Ivy than Russell. Russell seemed content that she was pretty, vivacious, and a charming companion at parties. Ivy did not realize that the fact that she was the Ellisons' daughter had influenced Russell's initial courtship. But by the time he had discovered that she was adopted, Ivy herself had won his cautious heart.

February 1898

When the Valentine Dance became the main topic of conversation at Elmhurst — whom to invite, what to wear, who would be voted Queen of Hearts, and which girls would make up the court — Ivy was forced to consider which young man to invite as her escort.

She knew Baxter was pinching pennies in order to be able to stay at the university to complete his final year and was sending out letters of application to newspapers, hoping to land a job as soon as he graduated. He certainly couldn't afford all the expenses entailed in the biggest social event of the year.

It would just make him feel bad to mention it, Ivy decided. So, instead, she sent the invitation to Russell Trent. And when Russell came to Elmhurst for the Valentine Dance, he brought Ivy a dozen red roses and a silver heart-shaped locket.

For weeks after the dance Russ had attended as her escort, Ivy floated in a lingering romantic mist. Her status at Elmhurst had been immeasurably enhanced by her handsome beau, and the other girls flocked around her, vicariously enjoying her romance as it unfolded. When florist boxes were delivered for her, they fluttered about while she read the enclosed card with a mysterious smile. Her friends recognized Russell's handwriting and teased her by prominently displaying his letters to her on the hall table downstairs. Ivy, of course, gloried in being the center of attention.

To her own surprise, she realized that at Elmhurst she was happier than she had ever been. Here she was not haunted by the feeling that sometime, some way, the truth would come out, and she would be branded a liar.

But it was always there, just under the surface, waiting to spring forth like that heartstopping moment in Sheik Ahmad's wild animal act, when he purposely turned his back to put the main lion through his tricks and Shauna the tiger had pounced on him.

It was exactly that horrifying sensation Ivy experienced one afternoon after walking across campus with Marcella to the little sweet shop they patronized for an ice-cream soda between classes. On passing the news-stand, Ivy saw the big black headlines of the newspaper: CIRCUS STAR PLUNGES TO DEATH. She halted, clutching her companion's arm.

"What's the matter, Ivy?" Marcella asked in alarm. "You're white as a sheet!"

All Ivy could do was point to the paper.

"Oh, well, do you want to buy a paper and read about it?" Marcella got out her change purse.

Ivy was shaking, and she thought she might faint. Marcella glanced at her anxiously, then led Ivy over to a bench at the edge of the campus path. "Here, sit down. I'll go get the paper." She was back in a minute while Ivy gained control of her trembling. "I still don't understand why you're so upset. Is it about this?" She tapped the newspaper she held. "It's only a circus performer."

Ivy's first impulse was to blurt out the truth. "She was my friend!" But she caught herself just in time. She couldn't explain. But now all that she had kept hidden in that secret room came tumbling into her mind. Nobody knew about it, certainly not the Ellisons. Even Allison knew very little and had probably forgotten what she did know.

Marcella was regarding her curiously. Ivy had to say something, so she managed a half truth. "I . . . it's just that when I was a little girl, I saw her perform. She was beautiful and so very, very good. What could have happened?"

"Here, I'll read what it says," Marcella said and began: "The Higgins Brothers' star aerialist, Liselle, was killed instantly yesterday when . . ."

The words spun out into the autumn air and took Ivy back to the smell of summer and sawdust and the sound of the calliope. She saw herself standing in the doorway of

Liselle's tent, watching her put on her special slippers that had soles with tiny narrow ridges, wrapping the ribbons around her slender ankles. Her golden hair glinted under the band of rhinestones. Liselle's satin bodice, scattered with beads, glittered above a short skirt of gauzy layers of gilt-trimmed ruffles. She looked up and saw Ivy and smiled a smile that made Ivy's heart sing. It was so genuinely sweet, not artificial or painted on like one of the clowns. Liselle looked like a fairy to the little girl Ivy had been, with all the luminous qualities of goodness, lightness, kindness . . .

"So, then, how do I look, *ma petite?*" Liselle had asked, standing up and pirouetting, her arms held out. When she stopped, she had put one dainty finger under her chin and bowed to Ivy, just as she did in the center ring after each performance.

"Beautiful!"

Liselle had laughed, a lilting sound. "Thank you *ma petite!*" She moved about the tent lightly, then with a final glance in her mirror, picked up her parasol. On her way out of the tent, she lay a cool hand alongside Ivy's face, cupping her cheek for a moment. "*Adieu!* Wish me luck!"

"The performer was pronounced dead at the hospital," Marcella read. "There were no survivors. The aerialist had no family."

Not true, Ivy thought brokenly. The circus was her family. Liselle might have been an orphan, just as Ivy was — it was one of the things that had drawn them to each other — but what were Gyppo and Sophia and Gina Fortunato and Ted Douglas, the ringmaster who loved her . . . if not Liselle's family?

"Come on. Let's go get our sodas," Marcella said, folding the paper and tucking it under her arm as she stood up.

Ivy felt dazed. She looked at her friend, puzzled that she could remain so unmoved. Liselle was dead! Then she realized that her roommate couldn't know, couldn't possibly know. Ivy had to remind herself that the circus was something she wanted to forget, a life she despised. Hadn't they all deserted her, abandoned her? She did not want to be reminded of any of it . . .

"Yes, all right, let's go," Ivy said briskly. She stood up, linked arms with Marcella, and they started off to the soda shop.

But it was not that easy for Ivy to forget. That night she lay sleepless in her bed, seeing Liselle in her imagination, balancing delicately above the awestruck crowd, the ruffles of her parasol fluttering as she navigated the dangerous wire, stretched taut above the crowd. Time after time she had succeeded, had swung down amid thundering applause, and had taken her bows before gracefully exiting the ring. What had happened *this* time? The question begged an answer. After her own disastrous attempts at wire-walking, Ivy remembered Liselle's explanation.

"Practice, patience, performance. That's all there really is to it. But you must stay perfectly calm. Inside. You must never go up on the wire if you are upset, you know? Your mind must be clear, your attention, your concentration absolute! Never, *never* look down! And don't panic." She snapped her fingers. "Then it is very, very simple."

But it hadn't worked that way. Had she forgotten her own good advice and gone up after a quarrel? Had her attention been distracted, her concentration diverted? Had she looked down? Panicked?

"Oh, Liselle, I'm so sorry," Ivy moaned into her pillow, wishing there had been some way she could have stayed in touch with the kind young woman who had befriended her so long ago.

Whatever the papers said, Ivy knew Liselle would not go unmourned.

"*Adieu! Adieu,* dear Liselle," Ivy whispered, knowing that one part of her heart would always keep the lovely performer alive.

Maybe it was after this shock that Ivy began to value Russ Trent's attention in a different way, not just as flattering and fun. She began to consider him seriously as insurance against future tragedy. Russell Trent was, as Mrs. Oliver had pointed out, a *very* eligible young man.

Chapter Fifteen

Acacia Springs
Summer 1898

That summer at Acacia Springs was magical. In the month of Ivy and Mercedes's stay, Russell came up two weekends in a row and, on the third, he proposed to Ivy. The evening of his proposal could have been choreographed for a romantic operetta.

After dinner they went to the dance at the pavilion. After one set, Russell waltzed her smoothly and gracefully out onto the porch.

"Let's take a walk," he suggested, and arm in arm, they strolled down to the lake beneath Japanese lanterns strung between the leafy trees that lined the walk. As if on cue, a lovely pale round moon rose over the water, paving a shimmering path to the other shore. Strains of music echoed on the soft summer air, a background to the rhythmic slap of the water against the wooden pilings of the dock.

Humming a little under her breath, Ivy held her skirt, moving it back and forth as she swayed to the melody. Russell caught her around the waist and they danced slowly around and around.

"Ivy, I have something to ask you. I came up this weekend especially for that. Before I came, I went to see your father and . . ."

"Went to see Daddy? Whatever for?"

Russell hesitated, but kept one hand on her waist. With the other, he reached into the inside pocket of his blue flannel blazer and brought out a ring box. "For this. It's . . . well, you'll see." He pressed the small spring and the lid flew open. A perfect diamond glittered in the moonlight. "I want you to wear this. It's an engagement ring, Ivy."

Allison was the first person Ivy told the very next day after she returned to Brookdale. She invited Allison over and, with an air of great secrecy, whisked her upstairs to her bedroom, then flung out her left hand, wiggling the finger on which the diamond sparkled.

Her friend's reaction to the news of her engagement was disappointing. There was no ecstatic exclamation of surprise, no hug or wishes for her happiness. Instead, Allison stared at Ivy in shocked dismay. "I just don't believe it! What about Bax?"

"What *about* him?" Ivy pretended a nonchalance she did not feel. She drew herself up, bracing for what she was afraid her friend was about to say. Hadn't Allison always been her confidante? The one person she always felt she could trust with her secrets? Except, of course, for the one Ivy still kept buried in her heart. All through high school Ivy had poured out her longings about Baxter, and her friend had rejoiced when their romance had bloomed last summer.

Allison looked at her, aghast. "How can you ask that? How can you *think* of marrying Russ when you love Bax?"

"But I love Russ. He's everything I've ever wanted . . ." Ivy began, but Allison cut her protest short.

"Ivy, I know you. You can't tell me you don't love Baxter anymore."

"Of course, I love him, but I'm *in love* with Russ."

"Have you told Baxter?"

"No, how could I? We just got home yesterday. *You're* the first one I've told. I thought you'd be happy for me."

"I would be, Ivy, if I thought —" She stopped abruptly. "You know Baxter's coming home, don't you? I saw his mother in town the other day and she's so thrilled. He's got a job with the *Brookdale Messenger*.

Didn't he write to tell you?"

Guiltily Ivy thought of the two unopened letters from Baxter that were lying on her dressing table when she came home from Acacia Springs. She shook her head but didn't explain.

"Maybe he planned to surprise you," Allison said, then shrugged. "He's going to be heartbroken when he finds out. Please think about what you're doing, Ivy. You can't really be giving up a man like Bax for someone like Russ . . . surely not!"

Ivy bristled. "What do you mean 'someone like Russ'?"

"Anyone can see Russ is shallow. Why, he isn't half the man Bax is. Bax has character and integrity, a sense of humor . . ."

Ivy got up and flounced over to the window, twisting the curtain pull. "Then why don't *you* marry him? You sound like you're in love with him."

"Oh, Ivy, don't be a fool and marry someone you don't really love just because he's good-looking and personable and . . ."

Ivy spun around and speared her friend with an icy gaze. "I think you've said enough, Allison. I thought you'd understand."

Allison stood, picked up her straw hat and painting case. "That's just it, Ivy, I *do* understand."

Slowly, almost sadly, Allison walked to the door. Her hand on the knob, she hesitated and glanced back, but Ivy was staring out the window and didn't turn around.

After Allison was gone, Ivy felt bereft. Her best friend was the one person she had wanted to share her happiness, to rejoice with her that dreams — even *abandoned orphans'* dreams — can come true. *No matter what, I'm going to be happy!* Ivy determined, wishing her feelings matched her determination.

The Ellisons were pleased that Ivy was happy and had made such a satisfactory match. They welcomed Russell warmly, and wedding plans were discussed. But first there had to be an engagement party and Mercedes must have time to assemble an elaborate trousseau for her daughter.

The announcement of the engagement in the society section of the *Brookdale Messenger* of Miss Ivy Ellison's betrothal to Mr. Russell Trent stated that a December wedding was planned.

Wanting to make up before she left again for the Art Institute in September, Allison came over to see Ivy. "I'm sorry if I hurt you, Ivy. I hope we'll always be friends."

Relieved, Ivy hugged her. "Of course, we

will! And you will be my maid of honor, won't you? That's why I wanted a Christmas wedding, so you'd be sure to be here."

Allison assured her she would.

"I want Miss Fay to make my gown and you can choose your own colors and design them both!" Ivy declared.

Greatly relieved, she suggested they go downtown and look at patterns and materials. This spur-of-the-moment decision resulted in a chance encounter that revived some unpleasant memories. Coming out of the one fabric store in town, they came face to face with Mrs. Fallon, the owner of Fallon's Mercantile. She looked startled, then quickly rearranged her expression to force a tight smile.

Ignoring Allison, the woman spoke directly to Ivy. "I read in the paper that you're engaged to be married, Miss Ellison. I'm sure there are many purchases you'll be making in preparation for the event. So, I just would like to remind you that we have expanded our merchandise greatly in the past three years, enlarging our stock and upgrading the quality. I can assure you it compares favorably with any you might buy elsewhere." She gave Allison a severe look as she went on, "Even ordering from the city is not always reliable nor is it always satisfactory. I just hope you will pass this information on to your mother . . . the mayor's wife."

The last few words were spoken with saccharine emphasis. Then glancing at Allison again, she said acidly, "I wonder why Mrs. Lund does not avail herself more of our ample stock of fabrics. It would be so much more convenient for her, as well."

Neither Ivy nor Allison dared look at each other lest they betray not only their astonishment at Mrs. Fallon's pushiness but their shared dislike of the woman. Neither had forgotten how she had treated them when they were youngsters.

Ivy recovered sufficiently to respond with equally exaggerated politeness, "Thank you, Mrs. Fallon, I will certainly remind my mother."

Mrs. Fallon's beady eyes blinked once, and Ivy felt she had not missed the edge of sarcasm in her reply.

After Mrs. Fallon passed by and the girls went down the street in the other direction, Ivy exclaimed, "The nerve of that woman! I wouldn't buy a spool of thread in her store."

"Be glad you don't have to. Although Aunty *does* order some of her finer materials from the city, she still has to deal with Mrs.

Fallon occasionally. But she usually finds it a disagreeable experience."

In spite of the relaxed camaraderie of the afternoon, when they parted at the Ellisons' gate, Ivy discovered that their differences were still very near the surface when Allison asked, "Have you written Baxter yet?"

Ivy stiffened. "Not yet. But I will."

"Well, don't wait too long. His mother told me he'll be home at the end of the month."

Ivy felt an uneasy flutter that she tried to ignore.

Allison still hesitated. "It would be too bad for him to find out from someone else."

"Oh, Allison, for pity's sake. Stop worrying. I *will*."

As she had done so often in the past, hoping to avoid unpleasantness, Ivy did procrastinate in writing to Baxter. Something she would later bitterly regret.

September 1898

On an early September afternoon, a week after the engagement party, Ivy was in her bedroom sitting in her windowseat in the sunshine, brushing dry her freshly washed hair when Daisy tapped at the door.

"You have a caller, Miss Ivy," she said

with a kind of sly pertness.

"Who is it?"

"It's Mr. McNeil, miss."

Baxter! *Here?* Ivy's stomach plummeted.

Allison was right. She *should* have written Baxter promptly, breaking the news of her engagement. She clenched her teeth. *Well, as the saying goes, my chickens are coming home to roost. Serves me right for putting it off.* Brush in hand, Ivy sat motionless, trying to think what she should do next.

Daisy stood at the door, obviously impatient. "Should I say you'll be right down, miss?"

"What? Oh, yes, I guess so." Ivy put her hands up to her still damp hair and shook it a little. "That is, I'll be down in a few minutes."

As she got up and moved over to the dressing table, Ivy tried to remember what Baxter had said in his last letter to her. She had not read it very closely, in fact, she had scanned it quickly. But she felt sure he hadn't said anything about a trip home any time soon. She should have paid attention when Allison told her about seeing Mrs. McNeil. Well it was too late now. She'd just have to face the music.

While she frantically caught up her hair and secured it with a ribbon, letting it hang loosely down her back, Ivy wondered what to say. What if Baxter had come, thinking things were just the way they had been between them last summer? With a passing glance at herself in the bureau mirror, Ivy went resolutely downstairs.

From the bottom of the steps Ivy could see into the parlor where Baxter waited, hands plunged in his jacket pockets, standing at the bow window. There was something about the set of his shoulders that told her he was very angry.

At the sound of her footsteps Baxter spun around. Ivy drew in her breath. She was right. He *was* angry. He stared at her, then pulled a scrap of newsprint out of his pocket and held it up, shaking it. "So! You're engaged? Funny, I should have to find out by reading it in my hometown newspaper because you didn't have the decency to tell me yourself. Who is this fellow? How come I never heard about him from you?"

"Baxter," Ivy began in a conciliatory tone, "I just — well, after all, we haven't been corresponding regularly . . . at least not for a long time . . ."

"As I recall, *I* wrote. *You* didn't. Even when I asked you in *my* letters why you weren't writing. The last time I heard from you was a postcard from Acacia Springs in

June. Even then, I don't think you mentioned Russell Trent or that you were about to announce your engagement!"

"I don't think I owe you any explanation," Ivy said. "You know we've kind of drifted apart in the last year." She paused, then continued in a softer tone, "I meant to write you, Baxter, honestly I did. But I knew you were busy with your work, your friends in the city. After all, it wasn't as if . . ."

"If what, Ivy? Have you forgotten all that we talked about last summer? The promises we made?"

"That was . . . well . . ."

"Oh, are you going to tell me, that was *then* and this is *now?*" Baxter demanded. "Ivy, you knew I was going to come back here and try to get a job at the *Messenger* even though I could make more money in St. Louis. As a matter of fact, I was offered a job, but I turned it down to come back here. Why? Because of you . . . don't you know that?"

"No, Baxter, of course I didn't know that."

"I told you I loved you, Ivy. Doesn't that mean anything? I never told anyone else that." He flung out his hands in a pleading gesture.

"I'm sorry, Baxter, but —"

254

"*Sorry?* Is that *all,* Ivy?"

"I didn't mean to hurt you. But while you were gone, I fell in love with Russ and that's all I can say."

Ivy started to move away, but he grabbed her wrists, forcing her around to look at him. "I said I wouldn't believe it, not until I heard it from your lips. Tell me it isn't true, Ivy."

"It *is* true, Bax. I'm engaged." Ivy tried to keep her tone cool, tried to free her hands from Baxter's strong grip. "Russ and I are going to be married in December."

Baxter's eyes burned, his voice was harsh. "Yeah, my mother told me all about this Mr. Trent, the up-and-coming banker. Are you so needy for status and security that you'll do something you know isn't right for you and not care who else you hurt in the bargain? Does this fellow *know* you, Ivy? I'm sure he doesn't. Not the way I do. I know you and love you, in spite of understanding that you've got this need — this silly, stupid need — to prove yourself. And you're going to use this unsuspecting . . . well, he must be out of his mind!"

"That's a terrible thing to say! You don't even know him! You're just jealous!" Ivy said furiously.

"Of course I'm jealous. But it's more than

that." Baxter dropped her hands and shook his head, slowly and sadly. "You know you're marrying a fantasy, don't you? I ought to shake some sense into you, Ivy, before you wreck your life and wreck that poor fellow's, too. He can't live up to your poor, little-girl dreams. No man could. I wouldn't try. But I do love you and I could show you the kind of love you really need — two people caring about each other, working hard, building a life together . . . not floating on clouds." He'd let go of her wrists, but now his arms went around her, drawing her into the curve of his embrace. Then he kissed her.

At first, Ivy pushed against him, planting her palms on his chest, but he held her tight, kissing her so demandingly she automatically responded.

When Ivy finally broke away, she was breathless and swayed unsteadily on her feet. "You shouldn't have done that, Baxter," she said when she managed to find her voice.

"Maybe not, but I wanted you to remember what it was like to be kissed by someone who knows you and loves the real *you,* not some kind of make-believe person."

He let her go and stalked out of the room.

Ivy felt shaken. She started to call him back, but resisted the impulse. What nerve! She felt the adrenaline flow through her body. Baxter McNeil! Who did he think he was? Her indignation rose as from the window she saw his departing figure push through the gate. But her hand went to her mouth, her fingers touching the lips still warm from his kiss.

Ivy filled the next few days with frantic activity, doing anything to avoid dwelling on the scene with Baxter and mostly trying to avoid Allison.

Her behavior appeared very strange to Mercedes, who followed her upstairs one morning after breakfast to ask, "Shouldn't you go over to Miss Fay's and talk to her about the wedding dress, dear? You said Allison was designing it, didn't you? Won't she be leaving to go back to the Art Institute in a few days?"

"Yes, I suppose so," Ivy replied crossly, busying herself folding handkerchiefs and putting them in the wrong bureau drawer.

Tactfully Mercedes withdrew, thinking Ivy and Allison must have had some kind of falling out. Still, that was unusual. Although they were as different as could be in personality, the two girls had been close friends ever since coming to Brookdale on the same Orphan Train.

A half hour later Ivy stuck her head in her mother's sitting room door, announcing that she was off to the Lunds to consult with Miss Fay and Allison about her wedding dress.

As Ivy approached the familiar house, she felt decidedly awkward. Still, if she hoped to mend the rift between them, she would have to take the first step. Rehearsing what she would say when Allison came to the door, Ivy was surprised when instead it was Miss Fay who welcomed her. She told Ivy that Allison had taken her drawing pad and paint box and gone out sketching. Disappointed, Ivy followed Miss Fay into the sewing room. She tried to concentrate while Miss Fay showed her the sketches Allison had made and spread out swatches of fabric from which to choose.

"With a December wedding, we can use rich materials such as velvet and satin," Miss Fay said thoughtfully. "The way Allison has designed the gown, the bodice will be tucked with lace insertion, the sleeves puffed at the top, tapering to the wrist ruffles."

As they were talking, Ivy heard the back door close and footsteps come down the hall, and she knew Allison had returned from her outing. She could almost see her friend hesitating in the kitchen, wondering whether or not to join them.

Then, in a minute or two, Allison looked in. "Wedding plans?"

Miss Fay turned around. "Yes, come on in. We need your artistic help."

"Your sketch is beautiful, Allison," Ivy said sincerely. "I love it."

"Thank you." Allison flushed with pleasure at the compliment. "I wanted it to be the loveliest gown imaginable," she said shyly.

The awkwardness between the friends was bridged in the discussion that followed. But when Ivy left, she only wished that Allison approved her choice of a bridegroom as heartily as she did her choice of a wedding dress.

Part 5

Scandal

Chapter Sixteen

The elaborate trousseau Mercedes had insisted on assembling for Ivy required much time for shopping, ordering from out-of-town stores, and fittings on the wedding gown.

"It is a dream dress, Miss Fay!" Ivy declared as she stepped down from the little platform where she had been standing in the sunny sewing room. Miss Fay, on her knees, her mouth full of pins, could only nod vigorously.

"Allison is simply an artist," Ivy went on as she eased herself gingerly out of the bodice so as not to get stuck with the many pins holding it together.

Replacing pins into the plump, red apple-shaped pin cushion, Miss Fay said, "I hope I can do it justice."

"Oh, you will!" Ivy gave Miss Fay an impulsive hug. "It's going to be the loveliest wedding gown any girl ever had. Thank you!"

On her way home, Ivy dawdled. It was such a beautiful, golden Indian summer afternoon that she was tempted to stop by the bank and try to entice Russ away from his desk to walk with her down by the river. Of course, she knew he wouldn't. She smiled fondly. He took his job much too seriously to follow a whim. His conscientiousness was one of the things she admired about him.

Ivy was humming as she came in the front door of the house. She stopped at the hall mirror to untie her bonnet ribbons when something made her pause. A steady buzz of voices was coming from Dan's study. Strange, she thought. What was her father doing home this time of day? He usually lunched with his cronies at the Downtown Club. Then Ivy recognized her mother's voice, too. There was something different about its pitch. Although she could not make out the words, Ivy felt a prickle of anxiety. Something was wrong. The Ellisons rarely argued and yet — a thin thread of foreboding zigzagged through Ivy — there was something disturbing about that closed door, the intense rise and fall of their voices.

For a heartbeat she remained absolutely still, listening. Then slowly Ivy turned around and stood uncertainly before moving across the hall to the study door.

She raised her hand and tapped lightly. There was a sudden cessation of the conversation.

"Yes, who is it?"

"It's Ivy, Daddy."

She thought she heard her mother murmur something that sounded like a protest.

Then her father spoke, "Come in."

Cautiously she opened the door and entered. She looked from one to the other. Obviously Mercedes had been crying. Her father was behind his desk, standing as if he had been pacing and had stopped at her knock.

"Is something the matter?" Ivy asked, her heart pounding.

Mercedes sniffled, wiped her eyes with her dainty handkerchief and shook her head. "Nothing that need concern you, darling."

"Nonsense, Mercy. Of course it concerns Ivy. You can't keep this from her. Besides, it will be all over the papers tomorrow if young Baxter McNeil has anything to say about it."

"Baxter? What does Baxter have to do with it?"

But they didn't seem to hear her question, for her mother burst out, "Surely Jack

265

Handley won't print any unfounded allegations!"

Jack Handley? Editor of the *Brookdale Messenger*? What were they talking about?

"That's what I've been trying to tell you, Mercy. He has all the proof. That's why he came to me. He wanted me to deny it. To give him reason not to print any of this. Jack's hands are tied. They have to go with the story."

"Daddy, please, what's happened?"

Nervously rearranging the items on his desk — moving the inkwell, adjusting the blotter — he began speaking in a shaky voice. He told her what would soon be public knowledge. That he had been accused of malfeasance in office, in other words "misconduct or wrongdoing by a public official." Favoring certain contractors in granting contracts, regardless of fair bids, seemed to be the main allegation.

Ivy felt the blood drain from her head as her world came crashing down once more.

That it should have happened in September had a certain irony. Fall had always been Ivy's favorite time of year. When she was with the circus, it was the time when they moved to Florida for the winter. The pressure of performing was over, and Paulo

266

had allowed her to make the trip in Gyppo's wagon for the month-long trek. They left — animal cages, house caravans and all — after the last show and did not roll into Sarasota until early October. Ivy had enjoyed passing through the towns, especially the farmlands where hay was stacked in the meadows and pumpkins turned fields into seas of orange-gold, and trees in the orchards hung heavy with crimson and russet fruit. She loved the morning mist in the valleys, the bright sunshine gilding the trees by midday, and the smell of burning leaves in the purple dusk as the train of wagons halted to camp overnight.

Yet underneath there had been a certain melancholy that as a child Ivy could never quite understand. Did it have something to do with the time of year or simply that there was always a sense of being alone — despite her new "family" — that threatened to snatch even brief interludes of peace? Just as now, when at the peak of happiness with her coming marriage and surrounded by people who loved and cared about her, Ivy had lowered her defenses, and then like a sudden bolt of lightning, disaster had struck, shattering her carefully constructed world.

As Dan predicted, the very next day the

scandal broke, headlining the morning edition of the *Brookdale Messenger*: GRAND JURY TO INVESTIGATE MAYOR ELLISON FOR ALLEGED MALFEASANCE IN OFFICE. Late that afternoon he came home from his office ashen-faced, and shut himself in his study.

Mercedes remained in bed all day with a headache. Ivy had spent most of the day bringing her mint tea and changing the soothing cologne-soaked cloths for the aching brow. From her mother's darkened bedroom window Ivy saw her father come home, and she slipped downstairs. Listening outside his closed study door, she heard the desk drawers opening and shutting, then smelled the odor of burning paper. What was he doing? Destroying incriminating evidence?

It seemed like hours that she paced the hall outside, fearing the worst, wondering if she should knock and ask if she could help in any way. As she was hesitating, the study door opened and Dan stepped out.

Seeing Ivy, he asked, "Where is your mother?"

When she told him, he frowned, then said sadly, "No wonder, poor soul. I'll go up and see her in awhile. But first, Ivy, come in. I need to talk to you."

Ivy followed him back into the study. She glanced surreptitiously at the fireplace where gray, curling ashes still smoldered. So he *had* been burning papers. With a sinking heart, she allowed herself no further speculation.

"Now, listen to me, Ivy, we don't have much time and there are some things you have to know, things you'll have to do." Dan lowered his voice to a hoarse whisper. "This news has hit your mother hard. She's not able to . . . well, I have to depend on you. I don't know how this . . . this mess is going to work out. But, in any case, hard times are ahead. The grand jury's been called to hear testimony against me. They'll move fast and dismiss the charges or . . . they may indict."

Ivy dared not ask what that meant. Her knees felt like water, and she sat down on a chair opposite the desk, her hands clenched in her lap.

"They'll probably take steps to freeze my bank account so I won't be able to draw out any money, so we'll need cash," he went on. "I'm sure I'm being watched or will be by tomorrow. So I need you to do something important for me." He opened a desk drawer and brought out a slim leather case and handed it across to Ivy. "In this case is a

269

key to a safe-deposit box at the Pemberton Bank. There are several hundred dollars in bills in it. I want you to go to the bank and take them out."

Ivy tried to suppress a gasp. At her reaction, Dan shook his head vigorously. "No, it's not any of the money they claim I stole. This is money my mother left for me. You never knew her. She died before you came to us. I'd almost forgotten about the money until I was cleaning out my desk today and came across her passbook. Now you go over there and get the money. It's not much, but it will tide you and your mother over in case . . . well, in case something happens. Understand?"

Ivy nodded.

"It's ironic. I never touched that box. At the time I knew Mama couldn't have much, and I certainly didn't need any money. But now . . . well, it's almost like she was an angel watching over us, isn't it? Coming to help us now that . . ." He halted, shaking his head. "She'd be so ashamed if . . ." Dan clenched his hands until the knuckles whitened. Then struggling for composure, he continued, "Well, anyway, it's there for you to use. You're sure you know what to do, Ivy?"

She nodded. "Yes, sir."

"Good girl."

★ ★ ★

That evening Russ arrived at the Ellison house. He was pale, tight-lipped, the newspaper rolled under his arm. Watching him approach, glancing almost furtively over his shoulder as he came up the walk, Ivy briefly entertained an unwanted thought. Had he waited until after dark to come so as not to be seen at the home of an accused felon? Quickly she rejected that idea as unworthy and hurried to let him in.

"Is anyone here?" was Russ's first question.

"No, Daddy is with Mr. Prescott, his lawyer, and Mama is asleep upstairs. Oh, Russ, I'm so glad you're here." Ivy picked up the newspaper he had laid on the hall table and twisted it viciously. "How can they print such awful lies about Daddy?"

"They've used the word *alleged*," Russ reminded her grimly. "Newspapers can get away with a great deal, Ivy. They can print unsubstantiated charges in the headlines, but *retractions* often merit only small print on the back page."

Ivy shuddered. "Let's go into the parlor. There's a fire in there." She rubbed her hands together. "I've been cold all day."

"Nerves, probably," he commented distractedly.

Ivy moved over to the fireplace, then turned around and looked pleadingly at him. "It's all so horrible. I feel so sorry for Daddy. For all of us. And this is such a bad time with your folks coming this weekend."

Russ looked uncomfortable and cleared his throat. "Ivy, I don't think this is a good time for my parents to come to Brookdale."

"But, Russ, when will I meet them? I know this isn't the best possible time, but we'll all soon be family. Shouldn't families support each other in times of trouble?"

Russ's face reddened. "It would be too embarrassing, Ivy. For them *and* for your father, especially under the circumstances."

Ivy started to protest, but something in Russ's expression stopped her. She felt as if a sudden draft of icy wind had blown upon her. She turned away, her heart racing, experiencing a moment of panic. It was familiar. It was that same kind of breathless fear she'd felt just before she did the stand-up and lean-back as Mitzi cantered around the circus ring. It was familiar and scary. It had happened the night she had been hurt . . .

"Well, I know you must be tired, Ivy, after all you've been through today," Russ said. "You need some rest. I'd better go."

Ivy wanted to cry out, "Don't! Please

272

don't leave me alone. I'm frightened and I'm afraid of what's going to happen." She wanted Russ to take her in his arms, hold her, tell her everything was going to be all right. Instead, she managed a wan smile and walked with him to the front door and out onto the porch.

"Try not to worry, Ivy. Maybe this can all be explained. Let me know if I can do anything."

It seemed to Ivy that the offer was made reluctantly. "Thank you, Russ. I'll be fine," she assured him.

"Well, then good night." He leaned toward her, brushing her cheek lightly with his lips.

Ivy stood at the edge of the porch steps, watching him walk briskly into the shadows. Shivering, she went back inside and quickly shut the door.

Again Dan's predictions were right on the mark.

The day after the grand jury announced its recommendation to indict Daniel Ellison, two red-faced, embarrassed sheriff's deputies appeared at the house with a warrant for his arrest.

He asked for a few minutes of privacy while he bade his family farewell. None of them could find words, even Daniel who had been such a master with the apt phrase, the glib remark. As the three of them clung together, the only sound was Mercedes's sobs. Finally, Dan pulled away and went downstairs to surrender himself to the deputies to be taken away.

From the upstairs window, Ivy watched this man she loved, the only father she had ever known, being escorted to the police wagon. Even as her heart was breaking, she could not help feeling a kind of pride in his erect bearing.

Gallant to the last, he turned at the curb and, glancing up at the second floor window, Dan lifted his hat and bowed. Ivy felt Mercedes slump helplessly against her, and she put her arms around her mother.

As the police vehicle drove away, Ivy felt a premonition that she was now stepping into a new role, exchanging places with the woman who had been a mother to her. Dan's last whispered words to her had been, "Take care of your mother, Ivy." This she was determined to do, to fulfill his trust in her.

Ivy felt as if she were living in some kind of hideous nightmare, one from which she could not awaken. She slept badly, lying awake for hours, her mind filled with random thoughts. When she did fall asleep, she started up suddenly, thinking she heard voices somewhere in the house, echoes of the old days when Mercedes and Dan had hosted parties to which people had vied for invitations. Remembering how happy they had once been, Ivy would feel the weight of the terrible thing that had happened to them. But there were no tears. Ivy felt she had no more tears to shed.

Ivy moved through the next few weeks in a trance-like state, her emotions seesawing between rage and despair. Much of her anger was directed against Baxter McNeil. To think that the man who had once declared his love for her had been a part of this terrible disgrace that now engulfed her life. The worst torture of all was Ivy's thought that she herself, by rejecting him, had caused his vendetta against her father. Had he in some subconscious way set out to ruin *him* as some kind of punishment for what *she* had done? Why else would Baxter have dug into records, relentlessly sought evidence? It was an almost unbearable burden. Yet Ivy felt it might be justified. Guilt haunted her days and made her nights miserable.

Ivy knew her fluctuating moods made her

unfit company for anyone. Even Russ made excuses not to come every evening, and Ivy could hardly blame him. How could she be anything but moody with her father in jail, awaiting trial?

Sleepless nights were not all Ivy had to endure. More and more her mother retreated from the reality of what was happening. Closeted in her bedroom, Mercedes slept most of the day, and often when tiptoeing in to check on her, Ivy found an empty wine glass on the table beside her chaise lounge.

The story of the mayor's arrest, splashed daily in the papers in the weeks leading up to his trial, had shocked the entire community. Every time Ivy left the house, she could feel hostile eyes boring into her, as former friends watched from behind their starched lace curtains. She could only imagine the gossip, the cruel, harsh things people were saying.

On the few occasions when Ivy had ventured downtown, it had been very evident how people now viewed the ex-mayor's family. Those who once would have made a point of crossing the street to speak to her now made it a point to *avoid* her. Ivy could read the unspoken condemnation that her father had taken other people's money —

theirs — and used it for his own purposes. The very clothes she wore must now be a topic of conjecture — surely his wife and daughter must have known what he was doing, were aware that the money with which they bought their fancy outfits, the shiny carriage, was *stolen!*

Then one morning Ivy came downstairs to find the kitchen empty, the stove cold, and a note from the cook demanding her wages be sent to her daughter's address in Woodley Falls, saying she would not work in the home of a "criminal."

Indignant, Ivy marched upstairs and, shaking the note the cook had left, declared, "Well, we'll just have to hire someone else. Where did you get Bertha, Mama? Shall we contact the employment agency?"

"There's no use, Ivy," Mercedes replied dully. "I doubt if anyone would come to work for us now." She paused, twisting her handkerchief agitatedly, her whole body rigid. "There's no money to pay them even if we could get servants."

Mercedes put both hands up to her temples, closed her eyes as if in pain. "I don't know *what* we're going to do, Ivy, I really don't. Sell everything, I suppose. Although there's a lien against all our belongings — the phaeton, the furniture. I don't know what to do. Mr. Prescott, Dan's lawyer, has loaned us just enough to see us through the trial. Of course, after that, we must pay him back." She gave a harsh, bitter little laugh. "With what, I haven't a clue."

Ivy thought of discussing their dilemma with Russ. After all, he was a banker, and bankers were supposed to know about such things. But Russ had more and more distanced himself. Perhaps he felt that being too close to the Ellisons meant guilt by association. No, this was something *she* would have to figure out, muddle through on her own, Ivy decided. Again all the old feelings of loneliness and despair swept over her. Even with her adopted mother living in the same house, Ivy was alone . . . again.

Chapter Seventeen

The courthouse steps looked very long and steep to Ivy the morning of her father's trial. She and Mercedes had not spoken all the way from the house into town. Once or twice Ivy had glanced over at her mother anxiously. But the heavy veil she wore hid any expression. She had moved like one in a trance all morning. *Please, God, help us!* Ivy prayed desperately.

When they drew up in front of the red brick building, Mercedes seemed about to falter. Then, as if drawing on that inner reserve used in the past for public appearances, she collected herself. With only a second's hesitation, she lifted her chin defiantly and got out of the carriage without assistance.

Then, linking arms, the two mounted the steps together. Holding their heads high and looking straight ahead, they passed between a line of curious spectators.

Inside, the bailiff recognized Ivy and

nodded to her as he opened the courtroom door. Ivy followed her mother's rigid figure down the aisle to the row of seats behind the defense table. Her father was nowhere in sight. His lawyer, Mr. Prescott, talking in confidential tones with his assistant, glanced briefly over his shoulder as she and her mother seated themselves.

Hoping to get some reassurance from the man who was to defend her father, Ivy started to speak. But with a curt nod he turned back to continue his conversation.

Chilled by his glacier-cold gaze, Ivy's stomach lurched. She had not been able to eat any breakfast. Now she felt queasy. She hoped she wasn't going to be sick. She clamped her teeth together and clenched her hands until her nails bit painfully into the palms.

A door at the side of the courtroom opened and her father entered, accompanied by a sheriff's deputy. Ivy felt Mercedes's hand clutch her wrist, digging into it, and heard her quick indrawn breath.

Ivy forced herself to look at her father. In the month he had been incarcerated awaiting trial, Dan Ellison had lost all his healthy ruddy color. His dark hair was more thickly threaded with gray than she remembered. But it no longer gave him an air of distinction. Instead, it made him look old, gaunt. For a minute he seemed to search the packed courtroom. Then he saw them. A muscle in his cheek twitched and an expression of anguish passed like a shadow over his face, and Ivy realized he was both comforted by their presence and grieved by it. She knew he dreaded what they would hear.

Lies, all lies! she told herself fiercely. She didn't care what the newspapers said, what Baxter McNeil alleged in his scurrilous article!

At the hammering of the gavel and the barked words, "This court is now in session, the honorable Judge Wilson presiding," the hum of voices and the shifting and movement throughout the crowded courtroom gradually lessened. The trial began.

Afterwards, Ivy couldn't recall exactly the testimony of each witness, nor could she keep them all straight. Friend or foe? She couldn't be sure. They had all seemed to know her father. Well, of course, everyone in Brookdale knew Mayor Dan! Some of them must have been the recipients of his kindness, some act of generosity or favor on his part. Could they all have turned against him now? Even as she listened, she simply couldn't absorb all that was being said. Without realizing it, she had wrapped a protective shield around herself. Only the judge's resonant voice jolted her out of her self-imposed trance back into reality.

"Testimony having been completed, the jury will now retire to deliberate. Court in recess until they have reached a verdict."

Without a glance at either of them, Dan Ellison was led out of the courtroom by the bailiff. *Back to his prison cell,* Ivy thought with throat-choking emotion.

There was a stir of activity behind them, the sound of shuffling feet as people filed out, the buzz of conversation. Ivy blinked.

Her mother tugged at her sleeve. "I'm feeling rather faint, dear. Would you please get me some water?"

Alarmed by the ghastly pallor of Mercedes's face behind the veil, Ivy immediately got to her feet. "Of course, Mother. Right away. I'll be back in a minute."

Aware that she was the target of curious glances, Ivy hurried out of the courtroom into the hallway. There she spotted the water cooler at the other end, and not looking to the right or left, she walked down to it. She filled two small conical paper cups with water and was just turning to take them back into the courtroom when she ran straight into Baxter.

For a minute they stared at each other.

Baxter found his voice first. "Ivy, I'd like to . . ." That was as far as he got.

"Well, if it isn't the prize reporter!" Eyes flashing, voice edged with sarcasm, Ivy confronted him. "So how does it feel to be a sneak, to prowl around, looking under rocks or anywhere else to find some kind of dirt to fling at someone? Smear a good man with trumped-up charges, innuendoes?"

Baxter paled, but his tone was low and calm as he replied evenly, "I didn't have to look very far. The evidence was all there. Your father didn't try very hard to hide his deals. Seemed almost as if he wanted it to be discovered, to be found out, stopped . . ."

"Oh, *really?* You think people like to be accused of being dishonest? Then try it. I don't believe a word of what you printed about Daddy."

Baxter's voice was strained yet steady as he spoke. "Ivy, you know better than that. You know I take pride in my integrity. Have you forgotten? I almost lost my scholarship because I wouldn't bend the truth."

"Spare me your oratory on truth and justice, Baxter McNeil. I believe I heard you give that speech at your high school graduation." Her voice was bitter. "It's a pity that's all it was — empty rhetoric. Your rules of conduct must have changed. Now it's anything for a headline." She could hear herself becoming incoherent. Her hands began to shake and she felt drops of water spill from the paper cup. "If I didn't despise you so much, I'd feel sorry for you."

Ivy brushed past him and reentered the courtroom. Her hands were still trembling so from the encounter that there wasn't much water left in the cup she handed her mother. Mercedes gave her a curious look but didn't ask any questions. Sipping their water, both locked in their own thoughts, they sat silently.

Minutes later, the bailiff announced, "Court in session," and the jury came filing back into the courtroom. The judge pounded his gavel and asked, "Have you reached a verdict?"

Ivy's hand closed convulsively, crumpling the paper cup.

The days after her father's sentencing passed for Ivy as if she were moving slowly through a dark tunnel that had no end. She and Mercedes had been allowed a short time with Dan before he was transferred from the local jail to the state prison. A policeman was just outside the door, and Ivy recalled that little had been said. Their grief had been too deep for words.

Afterwards, when they went home, Mercedes collapsed. Dr. Miller was called and he prescribed laudanum to make her sleep.

"It's shock. Understandable," he told a worried Ivy. "A good, long rest is what she needs now. It will give her time to recover."

Ivy wasn't sure. It seemed to her that all Mercedes had done since Dan Ellison's troubles began was escape into sleep.

Left on her own, Ivy wandered about the silent house, mentally wringing her hands. What would they do now? To whom could she turn for guidance in all the decisions that had to be made? Mercedes was of no help. Creditors were closing in, the house was to be sold, everything else was to go at sheriff's auction.

At the end of her rope, Ivy decided she would go to her father's lawyer. Surely he could give her some advice. But at the law office, the atmosphere was decidedly hostile, and when Ivy asked to see Mr. Prescott, she was told he was busy. The excuses varied — one was that he would be in court all day, another that he was with a client and could not be interrupted — but all were transparent.

Finally it struck Ivy that her father's lawyer no longer wanted to be of service.

After all, his client had been found guilty, a situation which did not enhance Mr. Prescott's own reputation. After all he had defended a man who had defrauded a whole county.

Trying not to let Miss Price, his secretary, see her embarrassment, Ivy attempted to compose herself. She stood up and walked to the door with as much dignity as she could muster. The secretary's chill voice followed her, reminding her acidly that her father's legal fees had not yet been paid. Without replying, Ivy marched out of the office and walked all the way home, burning with humiliation and rage.

The For Sale sign on the lawn was another reminder of their predicament. Tired and discouraged, Ivy went into the house. The vans had come the day before and had taken most of the household goods to be sold at auction. The empty house was depressing. Seeing the pile of bills on the hall table accentuated it. Where was she to get the money to pay them?

She stood in the hallway, staring at them in the echoing silence. Upstairs, Mercedes was sleeping away her life, not knowing, not even caring what Ivy was going through. All the old feelings of abandonment and loneliness rose up, and a sob tore from the depths of her soul.

Then, among the envelopes scattered on the table, she saw familiar handwriting. Eagerly she picked it up, ripped it open.

"Dear Ivy, Aunty has written me about the awful thing that has happened and I am so sorry. I wish I could be there to stand by you, give you whatever comfort and support I possibly could. It is hard to be so far away when your best friend is in trouble. May I suggest you go see Aunty? She is such a wonderful person, Ivy, and I know she could comfort you in a way I never could. I am praying for all of your family, your parents and you. Always your friend, Allison."

Tears blurred the page and Ivy pocketed the letter. She would take Allison's suggestion and go to see Miss Fay. It would have to be tomorrow though. It was already late afternoon, and Russ was coming over this evening.

Ivy dressed with special care that evening for Russ's visit. She fastened her lace fichu with the silver bar pin, Russ's first gift to her, and buttoned the matching lace cuffs on the cranberry taffeta dress. She pinched her cheeks to give them some color. Everything had been so hectic lately that she had not given much thought to her appearance.

There had been too many important things to attend to, decisions to make, too many worries. Maybe, tonight, she could share some of them with Russ. They hadn't had a chance to talk about anything personal in weeks. She had longed for a strong shoulder to lean on. As luck would have it, these had been particularly busy weeks for Russ, too. The bank examiners had been in town and there had been several out-of-town trips that had taken him away from Brookdale just when Ivy needed him most.

But now that the trial was over, maybe they could talk about resetting their wedding date and go on with their plans for the future.

Before going downstairs to wait for Russ, Ivy stopped by her mother's bedroom.

Mercedes was sound asleep. Examining the laudanum bottle on the bedside table, Ivy noticed that it was almost empty. Frowning, she decided she must speak to Dr. Miller and ask him if it was wise for Mercedes to continue taking it every single night. She turned down the lamp on the dresser, then went out, closing the door quietly behind her.

In the parlor, Ivy tidied up, plumping a sofa cushion, rearranging some picture frames on a table. The plant on its stand in the bow window needed watering. She must start attending to such things, she thought, then reminded herself that they would soon have to look for another place to live, a small, inexpensive place, once the house sold.

Pulling back the stiff lace curtain, she peered out into the darkness. Winter was almost upon them. *Where has the lovely fall gone?* she wondered wistfully. Seeing Russ turn into the gate, Ivy hurried to open the front door.

"Oh, Russ, I'm so glad to see you!" she exclaimed. "It's all been so dreadful, I'm afraid it's beginning to get to me. Thank goodness you're here, I've so much to talk to you about."

She raised her face expectantly for his kiss. But Russ was looking past her. "Let's go into the parlor, Ivy, I have something important to tell you."

Puzzled, Ivy murmured, "Of course," and led the way, a vague uneasiness stirring within.

Only one gesture betrayed his outward composure. Fingering his silk cravat nervously, Russ began to speak in a tone Ivy had never heard before — cold, matter-of-fact, as if he had rehearsed it all. The words hardly mattered; it was what he was saying that struck like a blow. Russ was going away, taking another position at a branch of the Brookdale Bank near St. Louis. "You can see what an opportunity it is for me. I couldn't possibly turn it down."

Ivy winced. "I see," she said slowly, understanding clearly more than she wanted to. What she really wanted to do was grab hold of his coat lapels, cling to him, and plead, "Don't leave me! Oh, Russ, please, please, take me with you! We could get married right away . . . just as we planned. Oh, not a fancy wedding . . . but at least we'd be together and . . ." But the expression on Russ's face stopped her impassioned plea before it reached her lips. She saw what was behind all those reasonable words. Russ had no intention of ever marrying her. Not now that she was tainted by scandal. It would ruin him to be married to the daughter of a convict! She saw it all in one blinding moment of truth.

Humiliation filled her. Ready as she had been to fling discretion and pride to the winds, she now saw his eyes . . . and she knew. The cold, unvarnished fact was Russ wanted out — out of their engagement, out of the marriage, out of anything that tied him to her and the disgrace that surrounded her.

She turned away so he wouldn't see the tears rushing into her eyes. There was really nothing more to say. He'd meant everything to her. She was angry with herself for giving him that power over her.

Behind her, she could hear Russ shifting from one foot to the other. "I never meant to hurt you, Ivy . . . for things to end this way." For the first time his voice revealed some uncertainty.

"It's all right, Russ. I understand." Ivy's voice was remarkably steady. "Now, will you please . . . just go?"

The ensuing silence seemed to stretch endlessly. Then without another word, Russ left. She heard his footsteps moving across the now carpetless floor of the parlor and along the hall. A minute later came the sound of the front door closing.

Ivy remained standing very straight, every nerve strained. Had this really happened? Had Russell Trent simply walked out of her life? Was love so easily ended, support and caring so casually laid aside? Had his feelings for her changed so quickly? Had he never meant all those things he said? Had she been wrong about him all along? Could he have ever really loved her?

Ivy looked down at her left hand, at his ring still on her finger, and she began to laugh. Should she run after him in the darkness, calling out to him, "Wait, Russell! You forgot to take back your ring!" The irony of it stung. Her laughter was edged with hysteria. Soon it turned into tears, then to deep, heart-wrenching sobs.

In spite of what Allison had said or Baxter McNeil had warned, she had truly believed Russ loved her. She was ready to give herself to him, sure that he was someone who would protect and care for her. Instead, he had abandoned her. Ivy sank slowly onto the bare floor and buried her face in her hands, sobbing. The dark cloud that was always hovering descended, and the perilous abyss that was under the tightrope she always walked yawned again. Was this retribution for her long-ago lie?

Chapter Eighteen

After Dan Ellison was transferred to the state penitentiary, there was a six-week probationary period before he was allowed to have visitors. Ivy learned they would be notified the first visitors day he would be eligible to see them.

Ever since the verdict had been handed down, Mercedes had been in a state of collapse. Sometimes Ivy could hardly get through to her. Trying to get her to make a decision about some of the pressing matters facing them, Ivy was frustrated with her vague answers, and her slurred speech. The help Ivy needed was not going to be forthcoming from her mother. At least, not any time soon. Perhaps not ever. As the days passed in the half-empty house on Front Street, Ivy fought off her fear of the future.

More and more she was forced to accept the frightening reality that *she* would have to make some of the decisions. One, for example, was the need to find another place to live, a small, inexpensive place. Perhaps a flat in one of the large old houses on the other side of town, a section that had been left to deteriorate when the new road had been built through the center of town. Although Mr. McCready, the realtor, told Ivy they could stay until they found something "more suitable" or until the house sold, Ivy knew that she would have to look for a rental soon.

Finally the letter came from the State Bureau of Prisons, stating that Prisoner 234800, Ellison, would be allowed visitors the following week. It had been among the other mail, mostly bills, pushed through the slot in the door. Ivy was reading it when the doorbell rang.

Still holding the letter in her hand, she opened the door. There was Miss Fay, exquisitely dressed in a pearl gray outfit of her own making, a bonnet tastefully trimmed with satin ribbons and silk violets.

"I hope I'm not coming at an inconvenient time, Ivy," she said hesitantly. "I haven't come before because I didn't want to intrude. But Allison has been so anxious about you, I promised her I would stop by, then write and give her a report of how you are."

"Come in, Miss Fay. You'll have to forgive me. I'm a little upset at the moment. I just received the official notice that my father can have visitors . . . at the penitentiary." Ivy's voice broke.

"Oh my dear, I'm so sorry," Miss Fay said, distressed.

"Well, it's probably providential you came today," Ivy said, leading the way into the parlor. "I need to talk to someone. Mama is resting, but she did appreciate the note you sent. It was so good of you to write. Not many did." There was a trace of bitterness in her tone.

Moved by the sympathetic caring in Miss Fay's eyes, the wall she had built to dam her emotions cracked and tears came. "I still can't believe someone like Daddy is in *prison* along with real *criminals* — robbers, rapists, murderers . . ." Ivy shuddered. "It's just too much to bear."

"But we are often called on to bear things we cannot," Miss Fay said gently. "And you *must* bear it, Ivy. Not only for your own sake, but for your mother's sake as well."

"Oh, yes, I know that." Ivy fumbled for a handkerchief to wipe her eyes. "But it's so hard. So much has happened all at once. On top of everything else, my engagement is broken, Miss Fay," she said sadly. "You might tell Allison. Not that I think she will be too sorry to hear it. She never liked Russ anyway."

Miss Fay put out her hand and covered Ivy's. "She'll be sad that you've been hurt, Ivy. She just didn't think he was right for you."

Ivy shrugged. "I guess *he* didn't think he was either."

"I wish there were something I could do to help you through this difficult time, dear."

"I don't seem to have the strength to face it all."

"You must ask for it, Ivy. Just enough for each day. That's all any of us has. I know this from my own experience." Miss Fay lowered her voice confidentially. "When I was a young girl, I loved to dance more than anything in the world. And then I had the accident. My leg was so badly crushed the doctors told my parents I'd never walk again, let alone dance. I was in bed, flat on my back, for months. I was in despair. It was as if the whole world darkened. I couldn't see any future for myself. Even when eventually, my bones did mend, I was crippled. I didn't think I would ever be happy, didn't think anyone would ever love me, for I could never bear children. I couldn't see anything ahead for me."

Miss Fay smiled, and Ivy was amazed how her smile transformed her rather plain features. Why, she was radiant, almost beautiful!

"But I was so wrong. I have a wonderful life. And if I hadn't had my accident, I might never have learned to sew, would not have been able to support myself as I have all these years. Then I was given the gift of a child who has filled my life with love and happiness. And now, I am married. I have everything I thought was lost to me forever."

"But how did you manage to go through it?" Ivy was hanging on every word.

"I had a praying mother for one thing, Ivy. And a loving aunt who taught me to sew while I was recovering in bed. She taught me something else, too, something even more valuable — Bible promises. She would write one on a square of cloth and show me how to embroider it. Of course, while I was stitching, I was also learning the verses. Little by little, God's Word was imprinted on my mind, my heart, my soul."

Ivy was silent. She normally wasn't much of a prayer. Her prayers had been of the desperate kind recently as she cried out in anger and despair.

"Even after all these years, those same

verses come back to me at times when I most need them."

"We used to have to memorize Scripture verses in Sunday school," Ivy confessed. "But that's been so long ago that I . . ."

"Ask the Lord to bring them to mind — the ones that would be most helpful to you now," Miss Fay suggested softly. "There's nothing mysterious about it, Ivy. God is eager to help His children. You have only to ask." She smiled. "Now, I really must go, dear."

Ivy went with her out onto the veranda. "Was there one particular verse that helped you most?"

"There were so many that it's hard to pinpoint one." Miss Fay was thoughtful. "However, Second Corinthians, chapter twelve, verse nine: 'My grace is sufficient for thee: for my strength is made perfect in weakness' seemed particularly appropriate when I felt so helpless." Miss Fay patted Ivy's cheek. "Good-bye, dear. God bless."

Ivy stood watching Miss Fay limp down the street, remembering another verse she had heard Miss Fay quote many times. That one had certainly proven true for her. What was it? Oh yes — Joel 2:25. "I will restore to you the years that the locust hath eaten . . ."

★ ★ ★

After Miss Fay's departure, Ivy looked at the instructions that accompanied the notice of Dan's eligibility to receive visitors. "Number of visitors: Limit two. All packages brought to prisoner must be inspected and approved. Only the Bible and titles on the approved list of books may be given to prisoner." On and on the restrictions went.

Ivy winced at the thought of her father having to submit to this kind of supervision. What must it be like for him now? Free-spirited, generous, jovial Daniel Ellison — reduced to a number and a regimen of discipline meant for the lowest type of common criminal. Ivy felt a mix of emotions — a kind of sick fear of going and yet the terrible longing to see him.

Knowing she couldn't put it off, that preparations for the journey to the state prison must be made, Ivy fixed a cup of chamomile tea and went upstairs to tell Mercedes about the letter. Her mother burst into tears, declaring she could not go, could not stand the long train ride or the ordeal of visiting Dan in prison.

"But, Mother, you *have* to go! Just imagine how lonely Daddy's been, how he's longing to see us. We can't disappoint him. You *must* pull yourself together," Ivy begged. "For his sake, *please!*"

Amid near hysterical protestations that she wasn't up to it, Ivy finally convinced her that it would be too cruel for them not to go. At last, weakened and tearful, she agreed.

The night before their visit, Ivy found it almost impossible to sleep. She kept waking up, feeling chilled and nervous. Before her alarm clock went off, she woke up with a jolt. A gray dawn filtering into her bedroom cast an eerie light. Struggling up through the fogginess of sleep, Ivy suddenly became fully awake when she realized what day it was and where they were going. She threw on her robe, went in to wake her mother. "Thy grace is sufficient for me," she whispered under her breath, repeating the words all the time she helped her mother dress and got ready herself, praying it would brace her for the ordeal they faced.

The day before, Ivy had arranged for a cab to take them to the train depot. On the way, through the predawn mist that rose in swirls, wrapping around the lampposts, their mutual silence was heavy with the weight of their combined dread. When they arrived, there was a lone figure inside the station house where a single light was burning. Ivy knew it must be Mr. Goff, the stationmaster, the only one on duty this early. At the ticket window she greeted him, "Good morning, Mr. Goff. I'd like two round-trip tickets to Radford."

He glanced up briefly and Ivy was sure he recognized her. Without speaking, he ducked his head, his face shielded by a green eyeshade, punched out the tickets, and slid them back to her. Silently he took the money she slipped through the opening. Ivy felt her face burn. She was positive he knew who she was.

Ivy picked up the tickets and turned away. She recalled the many times Dan had brought her here to see her off to Elmhurst or to Acacia Springs in the summer. She remembered the cordial greetings then exchanged between the two men. Today there had been none of the cheerful jesting, asking where were they off to, no wishes for a pleasant journey or a safe and speedy return. She might have been a total stranger.

Certainly Mr. Goff had to know why these two women would be out this early on a dark, damp morning. Why would they purchase tickets to Radford if not to visit the state penitentiary? Not to acknowledge her had been a deliberate insult meant to humiliate her.

Ivy went back to the spot where Mercedes

stood like a stone statue. They did not have long to wait. Hearing the train whistle as the engine rounded the bend, Ivy felt that old shuddering sensation. She gritted her teeth and gripped her mother's arm tight until the train pulled to a stop.

They boarded the train and made their way down the narrow aisle to their seats. Again Ivy was assaulted by the past. The cindery smell of coal dust, the mustiness of the coach, the odor of sleazy upholstery, the lingering scents of food from dozens of lunches carried aboard and eaten during travel, pinched her nostrils and caused a sudden queasiness. She had been so occupied with seeing that her mother drank her coffee and nibbled on some toast that she had let her own get cold and bitter. Not that she could swallow anything anyway.

As the train lurched down the tracks, building speed, Mercedes leaned her head back against the seat and closed her eyes, her way of showing Ivy she did not want to talk. It was just as well. She herself had no words to offer either in sympathy or reassurance. They might be in this together, but they were suffering separately.

Ivy's pain was different. Being on the train brought back all sorts of feelings and fears she thought she had forgotten. All the old apprehension she had felt as a child on the Orphan Train about what would happen to her upon arrival at her destination, came back now. As the train wheels clacked, Ivy relived her memories. She thought of Allison, of how they had traded dresses just before reaching Brookdale, and of how that simple act had changed both their lives forever.

The rhythmic swaying motion of the train was almost hypnotic, moving Ivy into a strange state where past and present merged. She stared out the window into the still, dark morning. The glass became a mirror reflecting her face. Gradually the reflection became that of a little girl, eyes too big for the tiny face, dark with fear. Ivy's mind wandered back over the years. What if she had not given into the impulse of coveting the pretty flowered challis dress Allison had been wearing? Then it would be *Allison* riding this train on this terrible journey instead of her. *She* would be safe at home with Miss Fay and Matthew . . .

Mercedes's plaintive voice jolted Ivy back to the present. "Oh, dear, I feel a little nauseous. The motion of this train is quite upsetting." At once, Ivy was all attentive concern.

She dug into her handbag and brought

out a small package of mints and offered them to her. "Here, Mother, this will help."

"Thank you, darling." Mercedes sighed, placing one on her tongue. "How much longer do you think it will be?"

"Not too long. Another hour, maybe."

Mercedes, looking distressed, leaned back and closed her eyes again.

Ivy wished there were some way she could make the train move faster. She wished she could do something to make this trip easier for her mother, no matter how much she dreaded reaching their destination.

Ivy pressed her hands tightly together in her lap, praying. *Dear Lord,* please help *Mother,* help her get through this, please . . . please! Then she remembered Miss Fay's method. "Thy grace is sufficient . . ." she murmured from between clenched teeth.

A light drizzle was falling when they got off the train. Dazed and uncertain, they stood for a few minutes looking around for some clue as to which way to go from here. Ivy walked to the end of the platform. In the distance, looming like some crouching monster, she saw the outline of a great gray stone structure on the hill overlooking the town. Her throat felt tight as she swallowed. That was it . . . the prison where Daddy was incarcerated. She blinked back stinging tears. She couldn't give way. Not now. Squaring her shoulders, she walked back to her mother, who already looked fatigued.

"Wait here, Mama," she told Mercedes, knowing her mother would never be able to walk the distance to the prison. "I'll see if I can find a cab."

Inside the dingy depot, at the booth marked INFORMATION, Ivy steeled herself to ask how she might get to the state prison.

The man looked up and answered her query indifferently. "There's a horse car that meets the train on Fridays, visitors day. It's outside on the other side of the street from the station."

"Thank you." Ivy went back outside. Taking her mother's arm, she led her across the street. She didn't see any type of conveyance like the man had described. But she did see a group of people huddled on the strip of pavement opposite. Apparently they were waiting for something. An older couple, standing off to themselves, kept their heads down, lest a stranger be allowed to see their naked pain. Were they going to see a son in prison? Among the group were two or three women holding themselves apart as if not wanting to be associated with the rest. Instinctively, Ivy felt an immediate bonding. She knew these were women, who like her mother and herself, were going to visit their men in prison, perhaps for the first time. How did she sense that? Maybe there was some kind of invisible yet identifiable mark that they all wore, like the numbers stamped on prisoners' uniforms.

Within minutes an omnibus pulled by two plodding horses rounded the corner and came to a stop.

"All that's goin' up the hill, tickets are fifty cents apiece," the driver growled from the depths of his coat collar pulled up around his ears.

Ivy got the money out of her pocketbook and handed it up to him. He grunted, and she assisted Mercedes up and into the closed wagon. The three other women followed silently, each taking a seat by herself. Ivy felt as if her heart were being smashed, ground into bits, yet softened by compassion for these fellow sufferers. Each was both alone and linked by the same human tragedy. Was this the Gethsemane of the soul?

As the wagon bumped and rocked its way up the winding hill toward the prison, Ivy looked out the window at the barren hills. This cheerless landscape must be the view from Daddy's tiny cell window, a man who had loved the outdoors — loved flowers, trees, rivers, lakes, and birds. Ivy felt sick. She clamped her teeth together and swallowed hard.

When they reached the top, the driver got down and wrenched open the creaky bus door. "Be back here at three sharp, for them that's gotta catch the four o'clock train," he barked. "Ain't none other till nine tonight if you miss it."

Ivy held her mother's arm firmly and followed the little group through the front door. They were asked to identify themselves — give the prisoner's number, show their notification letters, their visitors' permits — and surrender the packages each one had bundled all the way. Ivy had packed their basket carefully, putting in all the things she knew Dan enjoyed — oranges, a box of chocolate-covered cherries, some peppermint drops. She had also put in a pen and pencil set and some stationery.

The guard, inspecting it, rummaged through the things, then took out the pen, saying in a surly tone, "Prisoners ain't allowed sharp objects."

"But," Ivy began, wondering how one could write without a pen. But the guard jammed everything else back into the basket, wound a tag with a number on it, and snapped, "This will be given to the prisoner. Pass on. Next!"

They were ushered through a door marked VISITORS' WAITING ROOM into a cavernous area with gunmetal gray walls and high windows through which pale winter light seeped. Mercedes sank down onto one of the wooden benches along the walls.

Ivy's hand tightened on her arm. *Oh, Mother, please don't faint!* she begged silently. *Dear Lord, help us!*

At the grating sound of a bolt sliding back and the twist of keys in a lock, a door at the other end opened. "This way," called a loud voice, and the guard jerked his head toward the passageway. This led into another room, divided into two sections by a floor-to-ceiling mesh fence. A shelf-like table ran down the visitors' side, with chairs placed at intervals in front of cubbyholes. The guard motioned for them to take a seat. "One at a time."

"You go first, Mother. Daddy will want to see you first." Ivy walked with Mercedes over to a chair and eased her into it. Just then there was another loud explosion of slamming doors and the gritty sound of bolts being slid across metal locks. Ivy strained to peer through the links of the fence and saw a line of gray-uniformed prisoners file in. When she saw Dan, she pressed one hand to her mouth, suppressing a cry.

He walked with a kind of shuffle that twisted Ivy's heart. Where was the jaunty, confident stride so much a part of the man? When he saw them — Mercedes seated, Ivy standing behind her, he flushed a deep red, his mouth tightening into a straight line. He seemed visibly shaken. A kind of shudder went through him. Then he straightened his shoulders and came forward, taking the seat on his side of the fence.

"Hello, my darlings!" he greeted them huskily, attempting a smile.

"Oh, Dan, oh, Dan . . ." was all Mercedes could manage.

A look of pain crossed his face. "There, there, darling, you mustn't cry. It's not too bad, not really . . ." he said soothingly.

Ivy realized he had forgotten her in his effort to comfort his wife, who now sobbed brokenly. She took this opportunity to observe him more closely. She saw that as his first flush of gladness or embarrassment had faded, his skin had a grayness, a pallor that almost matched the rough gray denim prison garb he wore.

What would prison life do to a man like

Dan Ellison? What had it already done? When it came her turn to talk with him, what could she possibly say or do to help him?

Ivy helped Mercedes up from the chair and led her over to the bench against the wall. There she slumped, still sobbing. Knowing there was nothing she could do for her at the moment, Ivy went back and took her place in front of her father's cubbyhole. "Oh, Daddy, I'm so sorry." She put her hands flat against the wire mesh separating them, and he placed his palms against hers.

"Dear girl, *I'm* the one who should be sorry. To have brought this upon you and your mother. Believe me, Ivy, if I could change things . . . if I had it to do over . . . if . . ."

"I know, Daddy." Ivy bit her lower lip, feeling her teeth cut into the soft flesh. "What can I do? Do you want anything, need anything I can send or bring next time? We brought you some oranges and some other things. But they took the basket and said they'd give them to you later."

He made a gesture of dismissal with one hand and leaned closer to the wire mesh. "That's not important, honey. Now, listen, Ivy, you've got to take care of your mother, keep her from . . . well, from giving in to depression. You know how she is. I have to count on you now. I know I can. You're strong. I noticed that right away about you, even when you were just a child. I know you were afraid, wondered how it was going to be living with a pair of strangers. But you never let on. You were such a spunky little thing. My heart . . ." He choked and couldn't go on.

"Oh, Daddy!" Ivy felt as if she, too, would strangle.

Just then a shrill bell clanged, echoing through the hollow room. Startled, Ivy jumped.

"Time's up!" the guard shouted. There was a scraping of chairs on the bare cement floor as the visitors reluctantly stood, preparatory to leaving. There were anguished good-byes as the prisoners also got to their feet.

Dan leaned close to the screen. "Good-bye, Ivy. Remember everything I said."

"I will, Daddy." Ivy watched him get back into line. She waited until he moved through the door, hoping he might look back one more time. But he didn't. Slowly Ivy lowered the arm she had raised to wave.

With a shuddering sigh, she went to Mercedes. Helping her mother to her feet, Ivy led her through the outer rooms until they

311

were outside the prison in the fresh, free air.

Soon after that first prison visit, Ivy went over to Pemberton and took the money out of Minnie Ellison's safety deposit box at the bank. There was a little more than six hundred dollars, but it enabled her to pay the first and last months' rent on a small but partially furnished apartment in an older residential section of Brookdale.

Since most of the furniture, the mirrors, paintings, china, silver, even some of Mercedes's jewelry, had been sold to pay creditors, there were only a few things to move. But Ivy did her best to arrange them in such a way as to make the strange rooms more homelike.

There was still two hundred dollars left, but Ivy knew that with food and other incidental living expenses, it wouldn't last long. She would soon have to find work. She regretted that she had turned down Dan's repeated offers to send her to the Normal School for Teachers in Pemberton. There she might have learned something useful to secure her future. Instead, she had frittered away her time at Elmhurst and then pursued Russell Trent. Now she wished she had been as determined in her pursuit of a teaching certificate.

The ordeal of moving had so exhausted Mercedes that when the next prison visitors' day approached, she absolutely refused to go, saying she was not up to the long trip. So Ivy went alone.

Dan did not seem too surprised nor too disappointed that Mercedes had not accompanied her. "It's probably better. Seeing me like this must have been devastating for her. And I don't want you to come again either, Ivy."

"Oh, Daddy, of course I'll come. I *want* to come," she protested.

He shook his head. "No. Definitely not. I'm serving my sentence. I'm getting the punishment I deserve. But it has nothing to do with you. It's easier for me not to have you come, Ivy. Please oblige me in this. It may be hard for you to believe, but the time *will* pass. When you're young, a year seems a long time, five years forever. But . . ." He gave her an ironic smile, "I'm becoming a model prisoner. I may even get time off for good behavior. And one day this will all be over, and we will look back on this and have learned from it."

"But, Daddy . . ."

He held up a hand. "Hear me out, Ivy. I've had a lot of time to do a great deal of thinking about this. I see the mistakes I've made. But when I get out of here, things are going to be different. I'm becoming a different man and with God's help, I'm going to change even more. But until then . . . now, listen to me, Ivy, I can't do much to protect your mother. That has to be your job now. As things have turned out, it's up to you. But I know you've got what it takes." Dan smiled. "I remember that first day I saw you in the train station. You had a cocky little way, head up, shoulders set, ready to meet the world on your terms. It amused me then. Now I'm counting on it."

Ivy was almost too choked up to whisper good-bye as she put both her hands on the mesh screen separating them, felt Dan's palms against hers one more time.

It was with a saddened heart Ivy left him that day, for she had no idea when she would see him again. He was right. Five years did seem a lifetime.

All the dreary way back to Brookdale on the train, Ivy was plagued with fearful thoughts. What was she to do? Where could she go to get a job? What would they do if she could not find one? There was no one to turn to, no one to advise her, no one to help. She was an orphan all over again. Just as lost, lonely, and vulnerable as she had been three times before in her life. Maybe she'd never get over being an orphan.

Part 6

Shadows

Chapter Nineteen

Ivy saw the sign — HELP WANTED: Sales Clerk — prominently displayed in the front window as she passed Fallon's Mercantile. She paused, then walked quickly on, trying to pretend she had not seen it, avoiding the signal her mind was giving her.

During weeks of fruitless job-hunting, Ivy had searched the newspaper, circled want ads, and answered them with letters in her best handwriting to the box numbers listed. From some she received no reply; others requested a personal interview. Over and over her hopes had soared, only to plummet as possibility after possibility failed to materialize. Aside from not having any previous work experience, Ivy suspected there might be another reason she was turned down so often . . . her name — Ellison. The minute the prospective employer saw that name on her application, one of two things happened: Either the interview was abruptly concluded with a curt "The position is no longer available," or some transparent excuse was given.

Fallon's Mercantile was the last place in the world Ivy wanted to work. But she needed a job desperately. And it *was* a job, Ivy's conscience reminded her. There was only a little money left from the small inheritance from Grandma Ellison, and it was nearly the end of the month. Their rent would be due soon, as well as their account at Miler's Grocery. Those two bills would take the last of it. It would be irresponsible not to try.

Ivy circled the block. It seemed ironic that she was reduced to this option. Her dislike of the Fallons battled with the urgency of her need. Everything within her resisted the idea of approaching either of them.

It was so humiliating.

She glanced at her tiny jeweled lapel watch, a gift from her parents when she had finished at Elmhurst. It was almost six. Soon the store would be closing. It was too late today, wasn't it? Customers lingering over last-minute purchases. Mrs. Fallon impatient, probably tired from being on her feet all day. Hardly a good time to apply for the job. Finally Ivy won her argument with herself. Relieved, she hurried home. She knew she had behaved in a cowardly manner, simply putting off what she should have done. Tonight she would pray hard for enough courage. Be firm with herself. Nothing else had worked out. Tomorrow she would have to apply for the job at Fallon's. It seemed the only course open to her.

That evening, Ivy fixed a simple supper of baked potatoes and salad and served it attractively, keeping up an air of determined cheerfulness in the hope of gently prodding Mercedes out of her lethargy. It was a disheartening effort and hardly ever successful.

Ivy decided not to mention her plan to apply for the job at Fallon's. Although Mercedes had accepted the fact that Ivy had to find some kind of work, bringing it up always brought about a storm of weeping and recriminations over the past. If Ivy got the job, that would be time enough to tell her mother. Instead, she wheedled Mercedes into a game of Authors until her mother was ready to retire.

When the bedroom door closed, Ivy surveyed what she now called her job-hunting outfit and decided it needed pressing. Moving as quietly as possible so as not to disturb her mother, Ivy got out the ironing board and heated the iron on the stove. Ivy did not have too much experience ironing.

Daisy had always done it for Ivy as part of her duties.

All that seemed so long ago — the servants, having things done for her . . . another lifetime. There was no use looking back, spending time in regrets, wishing things were different. Ivy had determined not to become bitter, nor to withdraw from life. She saw how destructive it had been for Mercedes.

I will face whatever comes as a challenge to overcome and not be defeated by it, she told herself. But like most such wise admonitions, Ivy found it easier said than done. Applying for a job with the Fallons seemed almost too big a challenge, she sighed as she hung up her suit, ready to wear tomorrow.

Ever since moving into the new apartment, Ivy had slept on the cot in their small parlor. She had covered it with a paisley shawl and assorted throw pillows to resemble — by quite a stretch of the imagination — a sofa. But since they never had any company, what did it matter that Ivy slept on it at night? That night, however, anticipating the interview she dreaded, the narrow couch seemed lumpier than ever and Ivy found it difficult to relax enough to sleep soundly. Her alarm clock shrilled her awake much too early the next morning. As she sleepily reached out to shut it off, she remembered what she had to face that day.

She decided to get to the store before it opened and wait outside for the Fallons to arrive. It would be less embarrassing to make her application before customers arrived to overhear. *I must get over this foolishness. Millions of people all over the world go to work every morning and no one thinks anything about it.* Even circus people went to "work." Suddenly she remembered Sophia's remark about the freaks. "It's a job, ain't it? Who else would hire someone like that?" That unexpected memory startled Ivy. *That could be said about me!* she thought ironically.

After she dressed, she viewed herself critically in the mirror and frowned. She was too pale. Her eyes looked puffy, with faint lavender shadows under them from her miserable night. Buttoning her jacket, she noticed that it felt somewhat loose. She'd lost weight lately. She hoped she didn't look too thin, too fragile, not strong enough for the work. What did a store clerk do anyway, besides show merchandise, take the customers' money, and make change? She wasn't sure. All she was sure of was that she must convince the Fallons she could do the job, whatever was required.

Ivy brushed her hair back into what she hoped was a sedate style, tucking in the wisps of natural curls that kept escaping from under her bonnet brim. Before leaving, she gave her appearance a final check. Satisfied, she nodded to her reflection. "There now. Off to slay the dragon!"

The image of Mrs. Fallon as a fire-breathing medieval monster restored Ivy's sense of humor. Garnering some of her old self-confidence, she walked briskly through the crisp, morning air to the center of town.

However, in sight of Fallon's Mercantile, her confidence drained away. Her mouth was suddenly dry, her palms clammy, her heart in her throat. For a frantic quarter of an hour, she paced back and forth on the sidewalk opposite the store.

Desperation finally overcame procrastination. Afraid someone else would apply and be hired, Ivy braced herself. Taking a long breath, she straightened her shoulders, and head held high, walked across the street. The sign was still in the window. But even at the door, Ivy experienced another sickening wave of reluctance. *I can, I will do it!* She rallied all her willpower, stretched out her hand to the door handle, turned it, and valiantly crossed the threshold.

The jangle of the bell announcing the entrance of a customer alerted Wilbur Fallon, who was standing behind the counter. Turning his head, he recognized Ivy, his steely eyes through the thick lenses of his glasses meeting hers in a cold stare.

Ivy found her voice. "Good day, Mr. Fallon. I understand you're looking for a clerk."

Ivy was never really sure why the Fallons hired her. Maybe the fact that, with the mill and the shoe factory providing better-paying jobs for women, few would work for the salary offered. Or maybe, sometime in the past, her father had done them a favor — bent an ordinance or eased a tax burden — and Mr. Fallon had not forgotten. There was another supposition Ivy tried not to consider but seemed probable. Since Mrs. Fallon made no effort to hide her dislike, maybe she got some twisted satisfaction in having Ivy work for them. Whatever the reason, she was hired. At least, she now had a weekly paycheck. And she soon discovered that she would be earning every penny of it.

When Mr. Fallon gave her the job, he told her that she was to report to Mrs. Fallon. From that day on, he never went out of his way to speak to Ivy, rarely met her eyes or acknowledged her presence. His wife, however, was a far different story.

Almost from the minute she removed the HELP WANTED sign from the window, Mrs. Fallon was rattling off a list of duties Ivy would be expected to perform. Hands on her hips, she gave Ivy an appraising look, from the bow at the neck of her lace jabot, over the trapunto embroidery on the lapels of her jacket, down to the hem of her flared skirt. "You're not going to any fancy tea party here, Miss Ellison," she said scornfully. "This is what *clerks* wear." She tossed her a coarse, brown cotton coverall, then pointed her to the broom and feather duster. "The floor has to be swept and all the counters dusted before we open the doors for business. Now get to it!"

Ivy bit back the retort that sprang to her mind at this unnecessary rudeness. That first day, Mrs. Fallon followed Ivy around, on her heels like a snapping turtle, talking constantly. She would jab a finger at a corner Ivy had missed, or run her fingertips along the edge of one of the display cases and show her a smidgen of dust. When closing time — six o'clock — finally came, Ivy was exhausted, her feet burning, her mind whirling with the myriad duties that would be part of her job.

Dazed with fatigue, Ivy wearily put on her hat and prepared to leave. Mrs. Fallon trailed her to the front door, keys jangling in one hand, waiting to lock up.

"Of course, we were looking for a clerk with some *experience*," she said pointedly. "So, we're hiring you only temporarily until we see how you do, you understand. And, of course, it will be a while before we let you wait on customers. Mr. Fallon is very particular how they're treated, you know. We take pride in the good will of this community."

Ivy resisted a quip, *which is at a very low ebb*. But she knew better than to jeopardize a position that was not only temporary but precarious. One false step, and she knew Mrs. Fallon would take great delight in firing her.

As the days went on, Ivy's natural ability, her quickness and energy more than exceeded any clerk's they could have possibly hired. Most of her duties were completed before midday. Mrs. Fallon was hard put to either fault or find other things for her to do to keep her busy until closing. Grudgingly she had to admit that Ivy could easily handle retail sales. However, to save face, she made the simplest procedures sound extremely difficult.

For one thing, Ivy was told to memorize the stock so that she could pull something from the shelf as soon as a customer inquired about it. As Mrs. Fallon had acidly informed Ivy and Allison, Fallon's Mercantile had indeed upgraded their merchandise considerably since the old days. Whereas the store had been known for hardware and sundries — a place where children came to buy licorice sticks or jawbreakers, a top or a kite — it now carried a large selection of yardage, trims, millinery supplies, as well as lace collars, gloves, stockings, hatpins and ornamental hair combs. All these items, Mrs. Fallon emphasized, must be learned by heart.

Ivy managed to look suitably impressed. Inwardly she determined to accept the challenge to master the inventory lest Mrs. Fallon have grounds to correct her or point out a mistake. Although the woman jealously guarded her own reign at the cash register, within weeks it was obvious that Ivy could do whatever was called for in any of the departments.

Unless the store was crowded and they were very busy, Mrs. Fallon assigned Ivy the most unpleasant tasks. The one Ivy hated most was taking stock up to the attic storage room at the back of the building. The area was reached by climbing a ladder, then pushing up a trapdoor in the ceiling. The ladder was wobbly, and Ivy always felt very insecure on it, trying to balance a stack of boxes in one hand while gripping the side of the ladder with the other. The unfinished loft was quite dark. Warped planks served for a floor, with excess stock stored in boxes shoved against the angled roofline.

New and uncertain, yet eager to do whatever she was told without complaining, Ivy fought her own fear of heights, the heart-pounding and mounting dizziness, as she inched up the thin spokes of the ladder. She clamped her teeth together, recalling Liselle's rule, "Don't look down and don't panic."

It seemed it was always at the end of a long day, near closing time, that Mrs. Fallon gave her this chore. It took all Ivy's willpower to do it. It also seemed to her that Mrs. Fallon's expression was one of sly satisfaction whenever Ivy emerged from the attic, disheveled, her face flushed and smudged with dust, and with spiderwebs caught in her hair. But no matter what orders she was given, Ivy refused to complain or protest. Keeping this job was important.

Day followed weary day, but Ivy doggedly

got up every morning and went off to work, knowing she would have to face Mr. Fallon's coldness, Mrs. Fallon's spitefulness, some of the customers' stares and intentional rudeness. Every day her pride was under assault. But her spirit remained unbroken.

When she first began waiting on customers, those who recognized her seemed embarrassed. But her pleasant manner and willingness to help soon overcame any initial awkwardness they found in having their former mayor's daughter waiting on them. Of course, Ivy knew there was plenty of buzzing behind her back, but it was something she had already worked through in her mind. In time, she paid little attention when curious glances or murmured comments came her way.

But something was happening inside of Ivy. She was changing. Little by little, a thin protective shell was forming, shielding her once vulnerable core. Whatever she had to put up with, Ivy told herself, was the price she must pay, not only for her lingering guilt over the switch with Allison, but for other wrongs as well. Putting up with Mrs. Fallon's mean-spirited attitude was hard. Bearing it with some grace was something else. Demeaning as this job sometimes was, at least it kept a roof over their heads and food on the table. Ivy had promised Daddy Dan that she would take care of her mother, and she intended to do just that.

Spring 1899

Spring came and Ivy hardly noticed. Her days were long and rigorous. At night, walking home from work, she was too tired to do more than mark that the blossoms on the trees she passed had turned to leafy green. On Sundays, her only day off, there was so much to do to catch up and get ready for the next week's work.

Saturday evening, Ivy sat down to write her weekly letter to Dan. It wasn't until she penned the date that she realized she had been working at the store for three months. Although the time might have passed quickly for her, she knew time for him had dragged. What to say in her letters was always the problem. Her days followed each other in a dreary pattern: go to work, come home, fix supper. Mercedes, who had been cooped up in the flat alone, was eager to chat. Ivy, bone-weary and longing to relax, nevertheless had to spend her evenings keeping her mother company.

With this monotonous routine, Ivy often

found it difficult to fill even a page with news that wouldn't remind her father too much of all he was missing in the outside world or would make him feel sad. She could imagine how eagerly he waited for these letters, how he must read them over and over. So she tried to make them as cheerful as possible, glossing over her own worries and concerns and making the smallest incidents amusing and interesting. Keeping up his spirits while he was in prison was the least she could do.

She owed Dan so much. She knew she could never give back what the Ellisons had given her all these years. Until she had been adopted by them, no one had ever really loved her . . . at least, no one she could re-member.

Ivy dipped her pen into the inkwell and began: "Dearest Daddy, It is getting to be spring here. I noticed when I was walking to work this morning that buds are on the dog-wood trees and tulips and daffodils are making the gardens along the way bright with color.

"You will be glad to know Mama is doing fine. She is sleeping better at night . . ."

Here, Ivy paused, caught between telling the truth and what she knew her father wanted to hear. If she told him her own concerns about Mercedes, he would just be upset. Besides, he couldn't do anything about the problem anyway.

Part of what she said was true. Mercedes did now sleep through the night. She was no longer getting up, pacing the floor, weeping. But the reason was far from reassuring. Taking laudanum at bedtime — the prescription that had been an emergency measure suggested by Dr. Miller after the arrest and trial — was now a habit Mercedes insisted on continuing.

How white and drawn her mother looked these days, Ivy thought. There was no color at all in her face. Though only forty-two, she looked years older.

Ivy bent again to her writing: "She is working on her needlepoint again and is generally more cheerful . . ."

Again Ivy paused, lifting her pen to ponder. It was only at *her* insistence that Mercedes would pick up the chair cover she was making and do a few rows of stitches. After awhile she would put it down with a sigh and stare vacantly out the window. More and more often Ivy would find an empty glass, smelling of wine, on the table beside her mother's chair, or would notice how quickly the laudanum bottle by the bedside was dwindling. Ivy felt so helpless.

It seemed that her mother had given up the fight against depression and despair, looking for an escape from her present circumstances.

It was only to Miss Fay that Ivy could speak these fears about her mother. She had come to rely more and more on Allison's Aunty, finding her a staunch ally even when the whole town of Brookdale seemingly turned against them after Daniel's disgrace. Ivy realized she had perhaps taken this dear friend for granted.

Since Allison was at the Art Institute, Ivy began to see Miss Fay more and more, stopping by after work or on Sunday afternoons when Mercedes was napping. At first, it was simply the comfort of having a cup of tea in the cozy kitchen, while Aunty shared Allison's letters with Ivy. Together they would delight over Allison's success, her happy reports of her interesting classes, her new friends.

But Ivy also found in Allison's Aunty a confidante she could trust. Mostly Miss Fay listened while Ivy poured out her heart, telling her about her mother's deteriorating condition. Ivy never came away empty-handed — physically, emotionally, or spiritually. Miss Fay always packed a basket of homemade jams, jellies, pastries, fruit, and other delicacies to tempt Mercedes's appetite. She also gave Ivy sound advice, the warmth of true caring, and the inspiration of her own faith. Most often she would simply say, "Pray, Ivy."

Of course, Ivy prayed. Too often these were "tossed-up" prayers that she suspected were largely ineffective. She remembered the Fortunatos crossing themselves hurriedly before they mounted the platform at the top of the tent before they did their trapeze act, and seeing Liselle's worn little Bible open on her dressing table before she went on the high wire. Maybe one had to have a consistent, devout relationship with God before one was worthy of being heard. Ivy, always conscious of the lie that overshadowed her life, felt it probably forever blocked her access to the Almighty.

Shrugging aside this fear, Ivy thought again of the woman who had been the only mother she had ever known. Sympathy, tenderness, and pity all mingled with concern for this once vivacious, interesting person, now a faded reflection of herself. All Ivy could do was try to be as devoted, as vigilant, as helpful as she could and hope for the best. But sometimes she felt like a blind person, stumbling along on a path she could not see.

What should she say in her letter to her father? "Allison will be coming home for the summer soon," she wrote. "She is doing very well, Miss Fay tells me. She's won some awards and another year's scholarship."

At least she could share the good news that continued to surround her very best friend.

Chapter Twenty

Ivy woke up early and lay quietly for a few minutes before getting up. These first moments of wakefulness were always the hardest for her. Another day awaited her at the store. Then she remembered. Today Allison would arrive home for her vacation. That delightful prospect would help her through the day. She had missed Allison. None of her other former classmates — the ones who had enjoyed the Ellisons' hospitality in the past — now seemed to remember she even existed.

Ivy tiptoed past her mother's bedroom out to the kitchen. She filled the kettle and put it on the stove. She needed that first cup of coffee. She hadn't slept well. Troubled thoughts had kept her tossing and turning all night. So many endless questions demanding answers she could not give. She hated leaving Mercedes alone all day, but what else could she do?

The kettle whistled, and Ivy poured the

boiling water into the small percolator. She had been working at Fallon's Mercantile for months now. Every single morning she had to gird herself for whatever grubby task Mrs. Fallon would find for her to do in addition to her usual duties. At least today was payday. Remembering how grudgingly Mrs. Fallon thrust her check at her, she cringed. Still, she knew she had to take it. Without that weekly check, pittance that it was, she couldn't meet the monthly rent on these few rooms, buy groceries, keep Mercedes even modestly comfortable.

Ivy finished her coffee and went to put on the outfit she had laid out the night before. The hands of the clock pointed to eight. She had to leave. It took her fifteen, sometimes twenty minutes to walk into town. Unless it was raining very hard or the weather was really bad, she never took the streetcar, and thus saved the fare.

Taking a final glance around the room, Ivy peeked into her mother's bedroom. Mercedes was still asleep. In an effort to wean her mother off the laudanum Ivy was afraid would become addictive, she had started reading aloud to Mercedes at night until her mother drifted off to sleep. It seemed to be working, thank God, and gradually Mercedes fell asleep naturally.

Ivy was also grateful that once the supply of fine wine brought over from the mayor's former residence had run out, Mercedes had never asked to replace it. Although they never discussed it, Ivy felt her mother had recognized the danger herself and had proved strong enough to resist the insidious habit.

Ivy left coffee on the back of the stove and bread sliced for toast, propped against the cup and saucer she had set on the table in their small kitchen. Now all she could do was pray that her mother would be all right. She would run home on her noon lunch hour to check. She hesitated a few minutes longer, then she put on her hat and coat and hurried downstairs.

Ivy made it a point to continue to wear her well-made clothes to work, for all Mrs. Fallon's sneering at the stylish suit she had worn her first day. Even though covered by the clerk's apron all day, her nice clothes gave her secret confidence. Although, according to Mrs. Fallon, she might have come down in the world and had to work like a drudge, she did not intend to look or dress like one.

Summer seemed to have arrived, Ivy noticed, as she walked to work. Allison was coming in on the noon train. Ivy wished she could be at the station to meet her, but of course that was out of the question. She would just have to wait until evening when she would join the Lunds' welcome-home dinner for Allison.

The workday seemed to creep by. To make the time pass more quickly, Ivy kept extra busy, rearranging stock, straightening displays. She couldn't help darting quick glances at the wall clock, to see if the hands had yet formed a straight line marking six o'clock.

Just as she was about to put the dust covers over the counters and go into the small cloak room at the back of the store to put on her hat, Mrs. Fallon spoke sharply. "Here, Ivy, take these boxes back and put them up in storage." She pointed to six or seven large cardboard cartons that Mr. Fallon had brought back from the freight depot.

Checking an inward groan, Ivy took a long breath. Mrs. Fallon always seemed to find something for her to do at the last minute, something that would delay her departure. Almost as if she waited like a spider, her beady black eyes alert, to see if Ivy made a move to leave before the official closing time.

Taking things up to storage meant mounting the ladder and doing what Ivy hated most! She stood for a full minute, clenching and unclenching her hands, trying to think of an excuse, some way to get out of it.

But Mrs. Fallon had gone back to work on the ledgers. Ivy had nothing to gain by protesting. It would just bring on a confrontation she could not afford.

Luck was with Ivy, however. When she carried the cartons to the back room, she found Mr. Fallon there, preparing to take some stock up to the attic storage himself. Seeing this was her chance, Ivy said, "Oh, Mr. Fallon, as long as you're going up, Mrs. Fallon wants these put away."

"Well, just put 'em down. I'll get 'em on my second trip," he grunted.

"Would you like me to hold the ladder while you go up, Mr. Fallon? I've noticed it's rather unsteady."

He grunted again, an affirmative grunt this time, and set the ladder beneath the trapdoor into the attic. His arms loaded, he began to climb, Ivy gripping the sides. Halfway up, he reached out an arm to shove the cover open, then proceeded. The ladder wobbled shakily in spite of all Ivy could do to steady it.

"One of these rungs is loose, Mr. Fallon," she called after him.

Another grunt was the reply.

Ivy hoped that meant he would fix it. It was dangerous enough without the added peril of a rung ready to break at any moment.

Presently his face appeared in the opening as he looked down from the storage room. "Want to hand up those cartons, one by one?"

Still holding the ladder with one hand, Ivy slowly lifted each of the cartons up to him, stepping on a lower rung, and taking care to avoid the damaged one.

In a few minutes Mr. Fallon descended and, without another word to Ivy, left through the back door. Quietly she gathered up her things and walked back through the store. As she passed by, she called, "Good evening, Mrs. Fallon," and went out the door. Outside, she gave a sigh of relief to have escaped this time without any problem and hurried down the street, anticipating her reunion with Allison.

At the gate of the white, frame house swung a small wooden sign, THE LUNDS, enclosed in a circle of painted blue morning glories, Allison's touch. Lights were already on behind the ruffled Priscilla curtains at the green shuttered windows. Ivy ran up the flagstone walk and onto the porch. The door opened as she reached the top step and, a second later, she and Allison were hugging each other and circling around in a little dance together.

"Come in! Come in, Ivy, I'm so glad to see you!"

"And you, Allison! It seems ages since last summer!"

"So much has happened. I have so much to tell you."

Arms around each other, the two went inside. Good smells emanated from the back of the house.

In the kitchen, Matthew was sitting in a rocker drawn up to the window, reading the paper. He looked up and waved as Ivy came in with Allison.

Fay greeted her with a smile. "How good to see you, Ivy. Everything's just about ready."

The table was covered with a light blue woven cloth and set with Fay's blue and white Danish stoneware. Soon a platter of golden-brown fried chicken, a bowl of fluffy potatoes, baked yams, and fresh salad were placed upon it. Iced tea was poured and served in tall, frosty glasses. Allison did most of the talking during the delicious meal because she had the most to tell. Her life in the city had given her a chance to attend concerts, visit museums, and the wonderful zoo, in addition to her work at the Art Institute and her fellow students and new friends there. These provided her with a wealth of interesting experiences to share.

After they finished their strawberry shortcake, Allison spoke up. "Now, Aunty, Ivy and I will clear away the dishes." Fay hesitated only a few seconds, then agreed. Matthew excused himself to smoke his pipe out on the back porch, and Fay went to put the finishing stitches on a dress that was due to be delivered the following day.

As soon as the two friends were alone, Allison squeezed Ivy's arm. "Oh Ivy, I have something so exciting, so wonderful to tell you, I can hardly believe it myself!"

Ivy saw the flushed face, the shining eyes, and held her breath. She almost guessed before Allison burst out, "I'm in love! And the most wonderful part of it is that he loves me, too."

Later, Ivy told herself, she should have known. She had never seen Allison so animated, so glowing. Something had happened to change her, to make her more of everything she already was — lovelier, more radiant, more open.

"Who is he?" Ivy begged. "Tell me all about it. Where did you meet? What is he like? What's his name?"

"I haven't even had a chance to tell Aunty yet. But she'll meet him soon. He's coming here the third week in June, when he has finished all his work at the Institute. You see, Ivy, he's an instructor there. I've taken several classes from him — that's how we met originally. But he's a fine artist in his own right, a well-known watercolorist. He's had one-man shows, actually. He's exhibited regularly in galleries — and oh, Ivy, he's the kindest, most intelligent, dearest man. I can't wait for you to meet him!"

Ivy tried to absorb this jumble of information, but finally she held up a hand in laughing protest. "Wait a minute! Slow down! You say he's an instructor at the Art Institute, one of your teachers? Then, he must be much older than you, Allison."

"No, not really. He's one of the youngest of the teaching staff. He's thirty-two, that's only thirteen years older. And we have so much in common. We never run out of things to talk about. And he's been so helpful and encouraging about my work. Oh, Ivy, I never in my life imagined, *dreamed* such a thing could happen to *me!*"

Impulsively Ivy hugged her. "Of course it

should. You deserve all the happiness anyone could possibly have, Allison."

They sat down on the high kitchen stools, dawdling over the dishes as they went on talking . . . mostly about this paragon, Roger Benson.

"Not done yet?" Fay's voice brought them back to the present. "I thought many hands made light work!" she teased. "I never knew you two not to make quick work of getting the dishes done."

Ivy glanced at the kitchen clock and jumped down from the stool. "Oh my, it's nearly nine o'clock. I'd better be on my way. I told Mother I wouldn't be late."

"How is your mother, Ivy?" asked Allison, her eyes mirroring her concern.

"Well, truthfully, she hasn't been herself since . . . well, since all the trouble. I don't think she'll ever really get over it. Not until Daddy comes out . . . comes home."

"Do give her my best, won't you?" Allison paused, then asked, "Is there anything you can think of that we could do to help?"

Ivy shook her head. "Thank you, but I don't really think so. She doesn't want to go out anywhere, and she discourages company coming in, so . . ." Ivy shrugged, then picked up her jacket and hat. "I really must go. Thank you for the marvelous supper. I should take cooking lessons from you, Miss Fay."

"Come any time, Ivy, cooking lessons or no!"

Allison walked out to the gate with Ivy. "I wish you didn't have to go. Wish you could sleep over like in the good old days."

"Well, we're all grown up now, aren't we?" Ivy replied half jokingly, half regretfully. "Anyway, you'll be here all summer. We'll have lots of time together."

But as it turned out, it didn't happen quite that way. Roger Benson arrived as promised the third week in June and stayed. On the pretext of wanting to do a collection of paintings of the area, he rented a room in a nearby guest house, but became almost a permanent member of the Lund household. Naturally it was with him, not with Ivy, that Allison spent most of her time.

Before he left in the middle of August to go back to St. Louis and prepare for the coming term at the Art Institute, he had won over both the Lunds and asked for and been given Allison's hand in marriage.

Ivy had tried to like Roger. She tried to see him through Allison's eyes. Knowing he was an instructor at the Art Institute, Ivy was surprised he was so youthful looking, with a boyish manner that made him seem much younger than his years. He was very affable and greeted her enthusiastically, saying how glad he was to meet her at last. "Allison's forever talking about her friend Ivy."

Ivy knew the resentment she felt toward him was only because of his proprietary attitude toward Allison, for while he was in Brookdale, he took over her friend's every free moment. They were always off on sketching jaunts or painting expeditions, Roger declaring it the prettiest country he had ever seen. He celebrated his thirty-third birthday while he was in Brookdale, and Miss Fay outdid herself with a magnificent coconut lemon layer cake in honor of the occasion.

Roger eventually departed, but Allison was soon packing up to return to St. Louis for her final semester at the Institute. Although a definite wedding date had not been set, Ivy knew her friend was already stepping into a new life, a new world Ivy could not possibly share. Roger had spoken of a trip to New England the following summer, a combination honeymoon and painting vacation for the two artists. Ivy knew when she said good-bye to her friend this time that she really was saying good-bye to what had been the closest bond either of them had ever known.

At the end of the summer, Ivy knew a soul-wrenching loneliness, a deeper one than even in the hospital when she had been told the Tarantinos were not coming back for her, or at the orphanage with its gray walls and endless corridors. This was a different kind of loneliness. Before, she had always had a stubborn determination that things were going to get better. But after Allison left, a heavy miasma of spirit dragged her down, so that just getting up in the morning became an effort.

Ivy struggled daily with fear, sadness, and bitterness. She envied Allison's romance. She had thought she knew what love was until she saw her friend with Roger. They were so absolutely absorbed in each other, so devoted. Had she loved Russ that way? She had *thought* she was in love with him, had thought he was the ideal beau of her dreams. Instead, he was selfish, shallow, self-centered — everything Allison had told her he was. Still, she had wept bitter tears over their broken engagement.

How did one recover from grief, hurt, loss? Ivy lost her father, her home, Russ — all in the span of a short time — these added to the losses Ivy had already suffered as a child.

Other people found solutions or escapes from pain. Some turned to God, others buried themselves in their work, lavished affection on pets or children, or moved to a new place, or found a new love.

None of these options seemed open to Ivy. She was trapped in Brookdale, with all the old ghosts of her father's disgrace, isolated by it, alienated from former friends, and bound by love and obligation to her mother.

Ivy remembered her father's words the last time she had seen him: "With God's help, we're all going to get through this, Ivy. I'm counting on you."

Ivy knew she couldn't let Daniel down. She couldn't run away. She owed him too much — owed them *both* too much. She had to see this through.

Chapter Twenty-One

Fall 1899

September came again and it nearly broke Ivy's heart with its beauty. Even though it had a certain melancholy, it was still her favorite time of year.

On these warm, sunny days Ivy walked over to the park to eat her lunch. The trees that dotted the sweep of grass — the gold, russet, crimson, and saffron of the leaves — painted a glorious picture against a clear, cloudless blue sky. This little interlude in her busy day restored and refreshed her. It also gave her time to think. Ivy had never spent much time alone before. Now with aloneness forced upon her, she discovered solitude didn't necessarily mean being lonely. She realized that she had sometimes been loneliest in a group of people — in a social gathering, at a party. At those times when she least expected it, she would be suddenly gripped with a feeling of being orphaned, like at the hospital when she realized that no one was coming for her, and on the station platform the day she was put on the Orphan Train.

Ivy could look at those times now, and sympathize with the little child she had been. They didn't reduce her to panic anymore. She no longer thrust the memories away, not daring to see and confront her feelings. Slowly she was getting to know and understand herself, changing, growing up.

One particularly lovely fall day, Ivy would have liked to linger in the sunshine, enjoy the beauty of Indian summer, but checking her watch she saw her lunch hour was nearly up. She knew better than to be late getting back. Mrs. Fallon would be quick to notice and reprimand her or even dock her pay.

Reluctantly she got up from the bench and walked down to the edge of the pond where she scattered the remains of her sandwich on the water for the ducks. Then, putting an uneaten apple back into her small reticule, she left the park.

Just as she turned down the street leading back to the store, she saw a tall, familiar figure striding down the sidewalk toward her. Baxter McNeil! Instinctively she wanted to wheel around and run in the opposite direction. But he was directly in her path. There was no way to avoid him unless she pointedly crossed the street.

Then she made a decision, and she stopped. She had just passed some women she recognized, all notorious busybodies, who never acknowledged her these days. As the mayor's daughter, Ivy knew she had often provided grist for Brookdale's gossip mill. Not only had her romance with Baxter been a topic, but also her courtship with Russell Trent and the subsequent broken engagement. Surely someone in the courthouse had seen her tirade the day of Dan's trial, too, and had passed on this juicy report. This time, Ivy refused to give them anything more to talk about.

She had not seen Baxter since that awful day. She was ashamed of her loss of control. At the time she was so full of pain she'd had to lash out, and he was the obvious target. Even her father had not held a grudge against Baxter. "He was only doing his job," Dan had said when Ivy had railed against his exposé of the mayor's office.

Now here he was, right in front of her. What was she going to do?

At about the same time Baxter saw her. He slowed, his face flushed. Obviously he, too, had dreaded this moment. Now it was inevitable. Neither of them could escape.

Baxter took off his hat, bowed slightly.

"Ivy," he murmured her name.

"Hello, Baxter."

Ivy swallowed, then lifted her chin a little. "Baxter, I owe you an apology."

"No, Ivy, it's I —"

"Baxter," she interrupted, "I was wrong to accuse you of lying. My father . . . well, I know differently now. You were just doing your job. You were right. My father admits that."

Baxter seemed distressed. "Please, Ivy, you needn't . . . I don't want you to . . ."

"I had to, Baxter. Now that I've said it, I feel better. You've been on my mind for a long time. I just didn't have the courage to . . ."

"Don't say anymore, Ivy. It isn't necessary, and I understand. I'm only sorry you were hurt."

"No one gets through life without being hurt at some time. I've done my share of hurting other people, too." She lowered her voice until it was almost a whisper. "I hurt *you*. I was thoughtless, unkind. And I'm sorry about that."

"Oh, Ivy. I never . . ."

"It's all right, really it is, Baxter. I must go now. I have to get back to work."

"Ivy, maybe this isn't the time or place, but would it be possible . . . maybe, for us to talk again? I'd like very much to see you."

"I don't think that would be a good idea, Baxter. I don't really have much time these days. I'm at the store six days a week until six o'clock, and I try to spend my evenings with my mother. She isn't well."

"I'm sorry, Ivy. Believe me, I'm very sorry."

"Well, I'm glad we had this chance to talk," she gave her lapel watch a quick glance and said, "I'll have to hurry now, or I'll be late getting back." With a nod she passed him and hurried down the street.

Not caring that curious eyes had witnessed their encounter, Baxter stood for a long time watching the slender, graceful figure of the girl he had never stopped loving.

Ivy found her heart was still thudding. The meeting with Baxter had been both unexpected and unnerving. She was glad it was over, glad, too, that she had met the challenge and triumphed over her own fear of facing him.

Later that evening, reliving their meeting, Ivy realized that seeing Baxter had touched something within her. Something she had buried deep, unwilling as she was to examine it. Now she brought it into the light. For once she had told the truth, asked forgiveness. It was remarkably freeing. Baxter, too, had had the courage and humility to do that. It didn't change the facts, nor had it made it any easier for Ivy to accept Daniel's guilt. No matter what his motives or intentions, he had acted illegally, and Baxter had reported it.

Ivy read somewhere that unless one confronts one's pain, it cannot be healed. It simmers beneath the surface, undermining one's happiness. Slowly her old burden had added weight. Could she never be free of it? Was it possible to get rid of guilt even if one had carried it for a long time? The more she thought about it, the more convinced she became. Whatever happened as a result, Ivy knew she would have to confess at last what she had done so long ago.

The Sunday following her chance encounter with Baxter McNeil, Ivy walked over to see Miss Fay.

"Oh, Ivy, you must have known I was thinking about you!" Allison's Aunty declared as she welcomed her. "Yesterday I got a letter from Allison with some surprising news. Wait till you hear! It seems Roger has accepted a position to fill a sudden vacancy on the teaching staff at an eastern school. He has to report immediately. So, what do you think? They want to be married right away so that she can go with him. I know it's a surprise. And they're only going to be here a few days, so there's no time for anything more than a small wedding."

Stunned at the suddenness of this news, Ivy followed Miss Fay into the kitchen. Since the woman's back was to Ivy as she put on the kettle to boil water for tea, she did not see the expression on Ivy's face as she said, "Of course, she wants you to be her maid of honor. I'll have to get busy on the dresses. So much to be done and so little time." Without turning around, Miss Fay got out cups and saucers from the cabinet. "Allison thought dusty rose would be a perfect color for you, dear."

Quickly Ivy tried to collect herself and enter into Miss Fay's enthusiastic plans. Aunty never guessed that the news of her friend's wedding sent a shaft of pain through Ivy's heart, remembering that only a year before they had been planning *her* wedding.

Ivy knew marrying Russell would have been all wrong. He could never have made her happy, nor she him. She could see that now. To be honest, Ivy had thought Russ "a good catch." Of course, she would have tried, would have put on a good show of it.

That's what she had always done, hadn't she? Tried to be what someone else wanted her to be? For Paulo, the best equestrian; for her adopted parents, someone they could take pride in; for Russ, the kind of wife an ambitious young banker needed.

Painful as it had been, it had taught her something. Choosing a person to love was not the best way of securing love for yourself. Love often happened when you were not searching for it, not trying to make it happen — like it had happened for Allison. She ought to be grateful things had turned out as they had.

That night the first rain of winter fell and Ivy knew it was the end of the lovely Indian summer. The sound of its pounding against the roof echoed strangely in her heart. Memories. The night her father had been killed. The night Bunty had hidden in the toolshed on his way to hop a freight train. The night before her accident the last week she was with the circus.

Involuntarily Ivy shivered. *Don't be so morbid,* she scolded herself, trying to shake her gloomy mood. But somehow Allison's happy news had cast a shadow over her. You could never tell what lay just down the road. A year ago *her* future had seemed as bright and exciting as Allison's did now.

Ivy remembered once, after the last performance, she pointed to the crystal ball and
asked Sophia, "Can you really see the future
in that?"

Her dark eyes had narrowed and she an-
swered, "Nobody can see into the future.
And if they could, they wouldn't want to."
She shook her head mournfully.

The answer hadn't satisfied Ivy then. She
had dreamed about a future that would be
all sunshine and happiness. Now the future
seemed veiled in unutterable darkness. If
Daniel Ellison served out the minimum sentence of five years, Ivy would be nearly
twenty-five years old when he got out. Five
years, a lifetime. And if he had to serve his
entire sentence of fifteen years — what did
that mean for *her?*

Ivy sat down on the edge of the couch, put
her head in her hands. She had no future
but to go on working at Fallon's, being her
mother's caretaker. Her youth, her possible
chance for another love, another kind of life,
were cut off, bound inexorably by the chains
of love and duty.

Enough of this! Ivy told herself firmly. She
stood up, went to the trunk disguised as a
table, got out pillows and blankets that were
folded inside, and began preparing her bed
on the cot.

The idea came to Ivy quite suddenly, as clearly and positively as if she heard an audible voice directing her. The day after Allison came home, Ivy went to see her. "I would have come sooner, but with working and all . . ."

"I know. I know," Allison said, giving her a hug. "But now that you're here, come in. We have so much to talk about. Aunty wants to measure you for your dress and . . ."

"That's one of the things I've come to talk about, Allison. I won't be able to be in the wedding . . ."

"Oh, no! Not be my bridesmaid, but why?"

"Fallon's Mercantile is open six days a week."

"But, surely, she'll give you time off for your best friend's wedding!"

"To attend the ceremony, but not enough time to be *in* it or for the reception."

"How mean!"

"Well, I guess I could have insisted, but they would have docked me, and besides they're so busy at this time of year, with inventory to be taken next week. Well . . . I simply couldn't."

"I'm so disappointed."

"I am, too, but that isn't all, Allison," Ivy said. "There's something else I need to talk to you about."

"Of course. Let's go into the kitchen. We'll have some tea."

"No. I mean, I have to talk to you privately. Could we take a walk? Down to the river, maybe?"

Noticing Ivy's expression, Allison asked, "Is something wrong, Ivy?"

"I hope not. That is, I hope it can be set straight."

Puzzled, Allison quickly agreed. "Just let me tell Aunty. She's in the sewing room."

In a few minutes Allison was back, slinging on one of Matthew's old sweaters that hung on the rack by the door. She tucked her arm into Ivy's and they went out into the garden, now mostly barren, all the bright blooms of summer faded.

Walking along the graveled path past the gazebo where they used to have their doll tea parties in the olden days, the two friends strolled through the gate and down the road toward the river.

"So, what was so important?" Allison prodded.

Now that the moment had come, Ivy felt a knot form in the pit of her stomach. How would Allison react to this long-held truth that had so affected her life? Would she be terribly angry? Would she find it impossible to forgive her? Whatever the outcome, it had to be told. Ivy had waited too long already. Was it also too late?

"Allison, I have a confession to make," Ivy began hesitantly. "I've done you a terrible wrong."

"What on earth? What do you mean?" Allison halted, staring at Ivy. "You're my best friend. You've always been."

"Wait until you hear what I have to tell you." Ivy bit her lower lip, struggling to continue. "Remember when we came here on the Orphan Train?"

"Of course. How could I forget that? But you never wanted to talk about it."

"I know. I tried not to remember. I wanted to start a whole new life, didn't want to be reminded of any of it. I've never told anyone about the circus, either. You remember, I made you promise not to tell?"

"And I never have, Ivy. But I never really understood why not. I thought it was such an interesting kind of experience. All of us on the train were fascinated."

"I guess I wanted to forget. It was too painful. Maybe I made it sound exciting, telling you kids about it, but believe me, it wasn't all wonderful. The man who trained me . . ." Ivy bit her lower lip. "It doesn't matter now. I thought once we were adopted, we'd start a whole new life. It would be like none of the bad things ever happened."

"I don't think you can ever completely erase the past, Ivy," Allison said softly. "Although, quite honestly, I was so young when I was taken to the foundling home I can't remember much at all. But I'm sure it's all in there somewhere. I've told Roger everything . . . at least as much as I can remember . . . and he says it may come out in my paintings. I was just seven or so when I was sent on the Orphan Train." She gave Ivy's arm a little squeeze. "And you were so sweet to me. Took care of me all those days."

Ivy shook her head impatiently. "That's just it, Allison. That's what I have to tell you. You might have *thought* I was nice, taking care of you and all, but I did something terrible. Something wrong and now . . ."

Allison stopped walking and faced her friend, frowning. "What on earth did you do?"

Ivy swallowed, the words still hard to speak. "You see, Allison, I thought going to the Ellisons was the best thing that ever happened to me."

"And it was, wasn't it, Ivy? Of course not what happened about the mayor, that was really awful, but the rest of it. I mean, all the time we were growing up, they both loved you very much and gave you everything possible to make you happy."

"That's just it, Allison." Ivy's voice trembled. "All that *should* have happened to *you* — it should have been *you!* You were supposed to go to the Ellisons, not *me.*"

"I don't know what you're talking about, Ivy."

"Remember? Just before the train came into Brookdale, we traded dresses?"

"Yes, that cute little plaid suit you were wearing and . . ."

"And I put on your flowered dress with the lace collar. It had *your* name, *Allison,* on the hem. So, don't you see? We went to the wrong families. I was to go to Miss Fay and you to the Ellisons. The woman, Mrs. Willoughby, who brought us out on the train got us mixed up. She looked at the name on the hem and thought it spelled *Ellison.* I was wearing *your* dress and I knew it, but I kept quiet . . ." Ivy flung out her hands in a hopeless gesture. "And so I've kept this secret all this time and —" Tears began to gush from Ivy's eyes, coursing down her cheeks. "Oh, Allison, I'm so sorry! Can you ever forgive me for what I did?"

Allison stood absolutely still, her face blank, her eyes wide with disbelief.

Ivy stumbled on with her explanation. "Don't you see? I traded *lives* with you, Allison. You would have had *everything* the Ellisons gave me — clothes, trips, education! I cheated you out of all that was supposed to be yours. If I'd spoken up and told the very day we arrived in Brookdale . . . I *should* have, but I was so afraid. I thought . . . oh, I'm not sure what was going through my mind. There's no excuse for what I did, but please, please, Allison, say you forgive me." Ivy put her hands over her face and began to sob.

The next thing she felt was Allison's arms going around her shaking shoulders, holding her, saying soothingly, "It's all right, Ivy. It's really all right. It doesn't matter now. It's all worked out. Don't cry anymore."

But it was a long time before Ivy's sobs became gulping breaths and finally stopped.

"Here," Allison said, handing her a handkerchief so Ivy could wipe her eyes and blow her nose.

"Do you hate me, Allison?" Ivy asked at last.

"Of course not, Ivy. It's pretty hard to

take this in all at once. So much comes back to me now. I remember the dress. But I really liked your little plaid suit. It had tiny shiny buttons, didn't it?" She smiled, then gave a little laugh. "Oh, it's so long ago, Ivy! How did you find out about the mistake?"

"Well, I could read. I was nine, even though I was small for my age. Mrs. Willoughby turned up the hem and read your name, 'Allison,' thinking it meant the child was to go to the *Ellisons*. She didn't realize we'd traded dresses." Ivy couldn't bring herself to add that she had also been afraid when she saw Miss Fay limping toward them. That would hurt Allison too much. It had been such a childish fear that there was no use bringing it up now. With Allison's next words, Ivy was grateful she hadn't.

"Oh Ivy, maybe it was all *meant* to be. I've had a wonderful life. Aunty couldn't have given me more love, more care, more devotion. I've always felt so lucky. And then Matthew came into our life, and he's been a marvelous father to me. So, dear Ivy, don't spend another minute worrying about it. It was a natural thing for a scared little girl to do. I understand. So there is nothing to forgive."

They embraced. After awhile Ivy's tears stopped. With their arms still around each other's waists, they walked slowly back toward the house. There was so much unsaid between them, but now Ivy knew those very things were understood. They felt closer than they ever had before. After all, there were unbreakable bonds of suffering they shared — the same loneliness, the same groping for security, the searching for a place to belong. Those same strong ties that had bound them as children still held. Now they were strengthened by the truth, by the release of an old secret.

After having carried her heavy burden for so long, Ivy felt enormous relief. Confession *was* good for the soul, she thought that night at home. Her prayers rose, unhindered, and she felt cleansed, fully forgiven. Her spirit was free. The tears came again, but these were different, like a spring thaw after a frozen winter. She wept at last for the frightened little girl she had been, the one who was forced to live by her wits, to avoid punishment, pain, the consequences of any childish mistake. The years of layers upon layers of guilt were finally washed away in the healing warmth of tears.

Calm now, Ivy realized there was one more thing she wanted to do for Allison. She went to the trunk that was pushed into a corner of the room, whipped off the fringed shawl that covered it, and opened the lid.

A smell of crushed rose petals and lavender scattered inside came into her nostrils. She brushed aside the dry leaves and lifted out a muslin-sheathed bundle. Placing it carefully over a chair, Ivy began to unfasten the hooks and eyes down the length of the garment bag. After folding back the protective cloth, the wedding dress Fay had made for her was revealed in all its pristine loveliness — the shimmering satin folds, the gossamer lace, the painstakingly tucked bodice, the chiffon ruffles.

Strangely enough, seeing it spread out in all its glory did not cause Ivy pangs of either sadness or regret. The dress seemed something out of another lifetime, not connected with her at all. She knew now that marrying Russ would have been a terrible mistake. Not all the fanfare nor luxurious trappings of an elegant wedding would have made up for the lack of real commitment and real love. She had learned so much since those days when she had floated on a cloud of euphoria, believing she had attained her heart's desire. But the dress still represented the ideal dream of true love, the real, if elusive, butterfly of happiness.

Because of such short notice and the fact

that she and Roger would leave right after the wedding to take the train, Allison planned to wear a traveling suit for the ceremony. But this would be so much more meaningful. With only a few alterations that Fay could easily make, it would be perfect for Allison. It was, after all, *her* creation. All of her own dreams, hopes and secret desires had gone into the design that Fay had turned into a beautiful reality.

Ivy replaced the cover over the dress. She lined one of the large boxes she had kept from their move with layers of tissue paper and placed the gown inside. It was only fair that this should be Allison's. In a way, it rightfully belonged to her anyway. Her artistic skill had created it, her beloved Aunty had fashioned it. That she should wear it on her wedding day was only appropriate.

In some symbolic way, Ivy would be giving back to her what she had taken away so long ago — the little flowered challis dress Ivy had coveted. Although neither of them knew about the name sewed on the inside hem when they traded, still the mix-up had occurred and they had gone to the wrong families, lived each other's lives. Would anything have been different if Ivy had spoken up as soon as she realized what had happened? She would never know. All she knew was that now was the time to wipe the slate clean. Allison's future was secure. She was marrying a man who adored her, understood and accepted her. Roger appreciated her talent and would see that it was developed, her goal of becoming a *real* artist fulfilled. In spite of Ivy's failure to speak up, things had worked out for Allison. Her childhood had been happy. No one could have asked for a more devoted mother, a more loving home. Maybe her life was what it had been designed to be, after all.

Chapter Twenty-Two

Mrs. Fallon had grudgingly consented to Ivy's request for time to attend the wedding, adding, "Of course, you won't expect to be paid for the time you're not here at work."

That meant at least an hour's less pay in Ivy's weekly check when every penny counted. In spite of that, she replied, "Of course. I understand that, Mrs. Fallon."

The morning of the wedding, Ivy reported to work in the dress Miss Fay had made and insisted on giving her even though she couldn't be Allison's attendant.

As soon as she arrived at the store, Ivy donned the clerk's overall apron, hoping to avoid any sarcastic comment from Mrs. Fallon. She should have known nothing escaped her employer's notice. She was soon the target of much irritated nagging as well as plenty of time-consuming extra tasks. Knowing her employer's motive, her particular brand of spitefulness, Ivy complied with every request with a pleasant, "Yes, ma'am," determined not to let Mrs. Fallon make her lose her temper, whatever she said or did!

But Ivy couldn't help glancing at the clock frequently, longing to be with Allison as she dressed in the beautiful gown for her noon wedding. She recalled Miss Fay's marriage, when she and Allison were still little girls, how they had promised to be each other's bridesmaid. Neither dream had come true. Ivy's wedding had never taken place, and now she must be content being merely a guest at the church instead of a member of the wedding.

About eleven-fifteen the bell above the door jangled, and a woman sporting a large hat, a feather boa, and a dress more suited to an afternoon tea than shopping, swished into the store. Ivy had never seen her before. But when Mrs. Fallon rushed forward to greet her, Ivy was curious. A new customer, certainly. Someone important? At least someone on whom Mrs. Fallon obviously wanted to make an impression.

Later, Ivy thought she should have been suspicious, when something unusual took place. Mrs. Fallon brought the woman over to where Ivy was setting out some handkerchief boxes. "Our *clerk* will be happy to help you select what you want, Mrs. Cates."

Then turning to Ivy, Mrs. Fallon said with a smirk, "Mrs. Cates has just moved to Brookdale, Miss Ellison. Her husband is the *new assistant cashier* at the Brookdale Savings and Loan."

For a minute, Ivy was jolted. Of course, Russ's replacement. Mrs. Fallon seemed to take malicious pleasure in the explicit introduction. Deliberately Ivy forced a pleasant smile, although her fingers gripped the edge of the counter.

"I want to see some gloves," the showy woman said imperiously.

"Any particular kind? Leather, kid, silk? Two- or three-button? Elbow length or —"

"Just show me what you have, something dressy," Mrs. Cates said peevishly.

There was no use explaining that there were several different styles to choose from depending upon the kind of outfit or occasion for which they would be worn. For all her fancy ensemble, Mrs. Cates did not seem to have knowledge of such subtleties of fashion. Ivy began bringing out various types of gloves, taking them out of their narrow boxes, and holding them up for her to see. Mrs. Cates was not only annoyingly slow but also inconsiderate, carelessly tossing gloves she discarded on the counter, picking up others, and generally mixing up the boxes in which the different pairs had come.

Ivy tried to keep track of all this while attempting to give the customer some suggestions and advice about which gloves might be suitable. In the meantime, the clock hands were inching toward eleven-thirty, at which time Ivy had planned to leave for the church. She also knew Mrs. Fallon was observing her from behind the cash register, watching for the slightest indication of irritation with the customer.

Mrs. Cates took a tediously long time in deciding between two pairs of dress gloves. Ivy, holding her impatience tightly in check, saw that it was now ten minutes till noon. Finally, Mrs. Cates flung down a pair of dove gray, three-button gloves with a sigh of exasperation, "Well, I suppose these will do. Wrap them up for me. I'll take them."

Quickly Ivy boxed the gloves, wrote out the sales ticket, and politely told Mrs. Cates she could pay at the register. Then hurriedly Ivy reassembled the discarded gloves and boxes on the counter and returned them to their places on the shelves. While Mrs. Fallon was ringing up Mrs. Cates's purchase, Ivy slipped from behind the counter and dashed into the small back room. There she put on the pretty hat Fay had trimmed for her with velvet roses on one side of the sweeping brim. She was just securing it with a pearl-headed hatpin when Mrs. Fallon stuck her head in the door and said sharply, "Don't forget! Mr. Fallon's gone over to Bridgeport to pick up some stock. I can't spare you more'n an hour."

"Yes, I know, Mrs. Fallon," Ivy replied evenly as she pulled on her gloves, picked up her small beaded bag, and went out the back door of the store.

Breathless from hurrying, Ivy could hear the organ music as she reached the church steps. Luckily, people in one of the back rows moved over to make room for her, giving her a seat on the aisle.

She had hardly time to remove her gloves, pick up the hymnal, and find the place of the marriage ritual in the prayer book before the organist struck the opening bars of the wedding march. There was a rustling and shuffling behind Ivy as people got to their feet. A low murmuring flowed toward her from the back of the church, the sound of awe and approval that sent a tingling all down her spine. The bride was coming. Ivy moved her head stiffly, turning her body slowly toward the aisle where she knew Allison would be passing.

On Matthew's arm, Allison, her golden

hair veiled in white tulle, moved gracefully forward to the altar where Roger was waiting. As she passed Ivy, she smiled.

Ivy felt a wave of tenderness and love, a rush of hope that Allison would be happy. The emotion was pure, for how could she wish anything else for someone as dear as Allison, someone she loved?

The ceremony itself was short. Listening to the vows spoken in clear, confident voices started a stinging sensation in Ivy's eyes. She blinked back the tears. Hearing those eternal promises being made, she found herself smiling, a reflection of Allison's smile as she turned from the altar on her new husband's arm. Roger, his boyish face flushed and beaming, gazed at his bride adoringly. The rising lump in Ivy's throat tightened.

As the couple started back down the aisle, Allison stopped at the front pew on the left and embraced her beloved Aunty. From her bouquet she drew a rose and handed it to Fay. Then they proceeded down the rest of the aisle until they came even with the pew where Ivy was sitting. Here Allison and her indulgent groom halted once more.

"Dear Ivy," Allison whispered as she hugged her. Then she drew out another rose and gave it to Ivy. Ivy's eyes were so misted she could hardly see Allison's face. But she was sure it was radiantly serene with a little smile lifting the corners of her mouth as though she were savoring a lovely secret.

Outside, in the sunlight, the couple was surrounded by well-wishers as they assembled for the photographer to take pictures. Ivy would have liked to linger and add her congratulations to the others, but she knew there was just enough time to get back to the store to avoid Mrs. Fallon's wrath.

Reluctantly she turned away from the joyful scene and started making her way through the crowd to the sidewalk. She had only gone a short distance when she heard her name called. She turned around to see Baxter hurrying to catch up with her.

"Ivy, you're not going to the reception?" he asked when he came alongside of her.

Regretfully, she shook her head. "I can't. Saturdays are too busy at the store. I couldn't get the time off."

Baxter started to say something, then seemed to think better of it. "I should really get back to the paper myself." He paused. "May I walk a way with you?"

Ivy smiled. A retort like "It's a free country" rushed into her mind, but she checked herself. That was something she might have said in the old, carefree days. But it sounded too flip for their tentative relationship, and it might hurt Baxter's feelings. Instead, she said, "Why not?"

He fell into step beside her and they walked along without saying anything for a minute. Then Baxter broke the silence. "Ivy, would it be possible for me to call on you some evening?"

"Oh, Baxter, I don't think so. We have only a small, one-bedroom flat, and it would be . . . well, rather difficult."

"Then, maybe, we could go for a drive some Sunday or . . ."

Ivy stopped walking and turned to face him. "Baxter, I know you're trying to be kind, but you don't have to. Things are so different now for me, for all of us. It would be foolish to think we could pick up where we left off."

"I'm not trying to do that, Ivy. Neither to be kind or to pick up where we left off. I realize things have changed — *you've* changed, *I've* changed, circumstances have changed. I'd like to start again in a new way. Couldn't we, Ivy?"

"I really don't know, Baxter."

"Will you at least think about it, Ivy? I'd very much like us to spend some time together. There are things I'd like to talk to you about . . . things I never got a chance to say before."

Suddenly Ivy realized the time. "Oh Baxter, I've got to go!" She walked briskly away from him. At the corner, she picked up her skirt and started to run.

"Ivy, wait!" she heard Baxter calling, but she couldn't turn back or stop now. Mrs. Fallon would be furious if she was very late getting back to the store. And Ivy could not afford to have her dock another hour's pay.

The store was full of customers when Ivy slipped back behind the counter. She caught Mrs. Fallon's accusatory glance, but the rest of the afternoon was too busy for any kind of confrontation. Besides, Ivy comforted herself, she had only been a few minutes late getting back.

That evening she regaled Mercedes with a full description of Allison's wedding. "It was beautiful, Mother, simple and lovely, just the way Allison wanted it." Ivy placed the single rose in a crystal bud vase, one of the few belongings they had been able to bring with them from the house on Front Street.

"What a shame you couldn't have been in it!"

After she helped Mercedes get settled in bed with a new novel from the library, Ivy brought her a cup of chamomile tea. Then she went to hang up her lovely new dress, wondering when she might ever have the opportunity to wear it again. She felt a tiny twinge of self-pity at losing her childhood friend, but that was quickly replaced by genuine happiness at Allison's "happy ending."

Thoughts of the wedding that day brought Baxter McNeil to mind. It had been strange and mildly disturbing to see him again. The memory stirred up all sorts of odd feelings and emotions. Baxter seemed different. All the old arrogance was gone. Ivy smiled, recalling how, fresh from college, he had sometimes lorded his superior knowledge over her, tried to impress her. Now a quiet confidence had taken its place. He seemed gentler, more thoughtful.

The fact that he wanted to see her gave Ivy pause. How could one ever go back? Not that he said he wanted to do that . . . in fact, hadn't he said he wanted them to have a new beginning? But that seemed impossible. They had too much history together — old hurts, promises broken, hidden truths, secrets. Ivy sighed.

She swathed her gorgeous new hat in tissue paper and put it away in a box on top of the shelf. She was emptying her handbag to transfer its contents to her everyday purse when she realized that her gloves were missing. She must have left them on the pew at the church, forgetting them in the tender moment when Allison had stopped by her pew. She would have to check with the church custodian to see if anyone had found them and turned them in.

The next day, Sunday, was unusually beautiful for the first week of December — warm and sunny with a clear crispness to the air. Thinking it would be invigorating for Mercedes to get outside, Ivy suggested they take a walk over to the park. It took some persuasion, but finally her mother agreed.

The trees were mostly bare, but the sun shone brightly on the sparkling surface of the pond. They strolled along the graveled paths, then sat down to rest on a bench near the pond where they could watch the children sailing toy boats and running about rolling hoops, shouting to one another. Ivy had brought a small bag of bread crumbs and it amused Mercedes to see the ducks, quacking loudly, circle to feed. Time passed pleasantly in quiet enjoyment of the peaceful scene.

Eventually the shadows lengthened over the grass and the sun began to fade. Little ripples moved across the glassy water of the pond as the wind rose. Mothers started calling to their children that it was time to go.

"I suppose we'd better go, too, Mama. I don't want you to get chilled sitting here," Ivy said.

But Mercedes shook her head. "Not yet, dear. I have something to say. Just sitting here today in the sunshine, I realize how much . . ." She laid a thin hand on Ivy's wrist. "Oh, Ivy, I've failed you."

Ivy looked shocked. "Don't say that! No such thing. You've been remarkable through all this."

"Don't humor me, Ivy. I have given in to melancholy and regret and recriminations — all useless. In the meantime, *you* have struggled on, mainly alone. And I'm sorry. I just want you to know I'm going to try." Her fingers tightened on Ivy's arm. "I've been a weak, foolish woman, Ivy, thinking I could blunt reality, blot out truth."

"Mother . . ." began Ivy, but Mercedes interrupted.

"No, Ivy. I think you *know* what I mean. And I promise . . . well, I will try. Believe me, I've done a lot of thinking lately, and I want things to be different from now on."

Ivy's heart swelled with thankfulness. Maybe her prayers really had been heard, were being answered. If her unspoken burden about Mercedes could be lifted . . . that nagging worry always just under the surface why, then, Ivy was sure she could stand anything. Even having to face Mrs. Fallon at work every day would be easier without that anxiety.

At last, reluctantly, they agreed to leave the park. A tired but tranquil Mercedes wanted only a light supper and early bedtime. To Ivy's great inner relief, she did not ask for any laudanum to sleep.

The next day as she walked through the chilly morning to work, Ivy felt more hopeful and optimistic than she had in months. She let herself into the store and saw that Mrs. Fallon was already there. Her cheerful greeting died on her lips at the sight of her employer's expression. Mrs. Fallon, arms crossed, mouth set, pinched nostrils quivering, stood in front of the counter by the cash register. What had happened to make her so angry this early in the day? She didn't have to wait long to find out.

"Well, Miss Ellison, I assume you are prepared to pay for the merchandise you took Saturday?"

Stunned, Ivy stared blankly at her. "I don't know what you mean, Mrs. Fallon."

"Oh, no? Don't play dumb with me. I'm

not stupid. Thought you could get away with it, didn't you? Thought I wouldn't check? Well, you're not as clever as you suppose. I found this empty box placed among the other boxes containing gloves. How do you explain that?"

She held out an empty glove box. Her hand was shaking so that the tissue paper trembled.

"I don't understand, Mrs. Fallon. The only gloves I sold on Saturday were to Mrs. Cates. I boxed those and you rang them up. I don't know about any others. The ones she didn't want I replaced in their boxes and returned to stock."

"So you *say!*" Mrs. Fallon's face twisted viciously. "There's a pair of cream doeskin, six-button gloves missing, Miss Ellison. Just the kind one might wear to a fancy wedding — the kind *you* went to Saturday!"

Ivy felt a sick disbelief at the implied accusation. She felt the rush of blood into her face. She tried to keep her voice even as she replied. "I wore my own gloves Saturday, Mrs. Fallon. Pale pink silk ones. They were purchased in St. Louis over a year ago. They have the tag of the store where I bought them inside."

Mrs. Fallon's mouth curled contemptuously. "Can you *show* them to me, Miss

Ellison, as proof?"

"Of course. But I shall have to . . ." Just as she spoke, she remembered — the discovery she had made when she emptied her purse. Her gloves were missing! Probably left at the church. Or dropped in all the excitement after the wedding. It hadn't seemed very important then. Now her honesty was being questioned. Of course, she could still check. But the building would be locked today. She would have to wait, see if they had been placed in the lost and found at the church.

As Ivy hesitated, a look of malicious satisfaction crossed Mrs. Fallon's face. "Just as I thought! You can't produce them, can you? Because the ones you wore Saturday were the ones you stole! Well, Miss Ellison, it goes without saying, we certainly cannot have an employee we can't trust. You can consider yourself dismissed. I'll take the price of the gloves off what money you have coming to you in your next paycheck. You're lucky I don't turn you in to the police! Like father, like daughter, I'd say."

Ivy stood rooted to the spot. *This can't be happening.* A wave of dizziness came over her. Ivy felt nauseated. The figure of Mrs. Fallon, quivering with fury, wavered in front of Ivy's eyes. *The woman actually be-*

lieves I stole a pair of gloves! Anger boiled up inside, ready to explode. An indignant denial sprang to Ivy's mind. That remark alluding to Daniel was the last straw. She refused to stoop to Mrs. Fallon's level. She had to get out of here. Without another word, she turned around and walked out the door she had just come in.

Holding herself ramrod stiff in shock-induced composure, Ivy went down the steps and started up the street. It wasn't until she was several blocks from the store that she fully reacted. Her hands were shaking, the palms sweaty. She felt a beading of cold perspiration on her forehead and upper lip. She felt bruised, as though Mrs. Fallon's words had flogged her so that her very skin felt sore.

Ivy stopped abruptly. She couldn't go back to the apartment. Not like this. To explain what happened to Mercedes could destroy all her newly made resolutions, send her back into a whirlpool of depression . . . perhaps even back to the wine and laudanum. So where could she go? Somewhere she could think all this through, try to get a handle on the situation.

Ivy had lost her job. That meant that their income was gone. No matter that the grounds for her dismissal were false. Ivy knew somehow she would be vindicated, but she did not know how. Not that she'd ever go back to that store to work. Not if Mrs. Fallon got down on her hands and knees and begged her. Not after what she had said about Daniel!

Ivy found herself walking toward the park, the place that over the last year and a half she had found a refuge. She tried to calm herself as she might soothe a child, repeating all the faith-building quotations she could remember, the ones Miss Fay had given her. She must be strong, she must see this for what it really was. Mrs. Fallon had been looking for a reason to fire her ever since she had been hired. Maybe she had protested Mr. Fallon's decision from the beginning. Maybe Ivy's very presence in the store was a bone of contention between the couple. Who knew what the motives were for such irrational behavior. *If I were ever going to steal anything, and I've had plenty of opportunity to, it certainly wouldn't be a pair of fancy gloves!* Ivy fumed.

Gradually she began to calm down. She was not sure how long she remained sitting on the bench at the park, staring out at the pond. She was hardly aware of other people who came and went — young mothers with babies in prams or with toddlers, pushing them on the swings and chatting with each other; older couples strolling in the winter sunshine; and later, boys and girls from the high school, cutting across the grassy knolls, homeward bound after the day's classes were over.

It was only when the sun went behind a cloud and the wind grew cool that Ivy realized she had spent most of the day out here. She got up from the bench, feeling stiff from having sat so long. While her body might have been immobile, her mind had been active, sorting out all the possibilities of what she should do next. The only thing that emerged from the day's swirl of ideas was that she had to find another job. And *soon,* before their meager bank account was completely gone.

On the way back to the apartment, Ivy bought an evening paper. Want ads might hold an answer. Even if it meant going as far as Pemberton to work, she was willing to do it. A possible problem loomed. Would Mrs. Fallon withhold a reference? If she did, how could Ivy account for the past several months she had spent gaining retail clerk experience?

That evening Ivy employed every shred of acting ability she had ever used in school plays. When she came home, she found

Mercedes not in her robe as she usually was, but dressed and waiting to greet her. She had set the table charmingly for the two of them, had shopped at the grocery store at the corner, and had baked a meat loaf and roasted potatoes for their dinner.

"See, I told you things were going to be different, didn't I?" She smiled at Ivy.

You just don't know how *different things* really *are,* Ivy thought. But she put a good face on it and managed to get through the evening without her mother suspecting a thing. It was a strain, however, when Ivy realized she might have to keep up this charade indefinitely. How long could she do it? She didn't know.

After Mercedes retired and the bedroom door was closed, Ivy took out the newspaper and started searching the help-wanted section. Nothing looked too promising. Of course, she could always do domestic work, if it came to that.

She had almost exhausted the list of available jobs and her own optimism when she heard a quiet knock at the door. Frowning, she wondered who it could be as she got up to open it.

"Baxter!" she gasped when she saw him standing on the threshold.

"Evening, Ivy. I hope you don't mind my

dropping by like this but you were in such a hurry the other day, you didn't hear me call after you to tell you that you dropped these." He held something out to her. Her pink silk gloves!

Ivy looked from Baxter to the gloves dangling from his outstretched hand. There they were — the gloves she had worn to Allison's wedding. Her proof! Her vindication that she was not a thief! The irony of it struck her suddenly, and Ivy began to laugh. Those missing scraps of silk had cost her her job. It was so ridiculous. Laughter bubbled up and would not quit until she was clinging helplessly to the door frame.

Baxter stared at her with a mixture of bewilderment and amusement. "What's so funny?" he asked at last as Ivy struggled to control herself.

"It's just that . . ." The scene with Mrs. Fallon began to look more comical than tragic, and she dissolved again into laughter. Finally she managed to beckon to Baxter. "Come in, and I'll tell you all about it."

Baxter stepped inside, looking almost too tall for the tiny, low-ceilinged parlor. Ivy motioned him to the one armchair. She sat down on the makeshift sofa opposite, smoothing the gloves on her lap. They were a little dirty from having fallen on the street. Then she told Baxter about the incident at the store.

His expression showed his disgust at how shabbily she had been treated. But Ivy held up her hand to stop his angry defense.

"Baxter, I'm certainly not going to try to explain to Mrs. Fallon how this happened. She's been looking for an excuse to fire me anyway. It doesn't matter what she *thinks* I took. After all the things she said, I would have quit anyway, except . . ." She sighed, "I'm out of a job."

"Well, you're in luck, Ivy. That is, if you'd be interested. I know there's an opening in Classified at the paper. You take in ads people want to place, help them write or re-write them to fit the requirements. It's not difficult, and I believe it pays fairly well." He added grimly, "Better, I imagine, than the Fallons paid you."

"Why, thank you, Baxter. I'll apply tomorrow." Ivy lowered her voice. "I haven't told Mother about the Fallon debacle yet. I didn't want to upset her. Now, I'll wait until I find out about this job." She paused. "It's very kind of you, Baxter."

"Naturally, I didn't know about the incident with Mrs. Fallon. I simply wanted to return your gloves." He halted. "No, that's not exactly true. I was glad of the excuse to come by, Ivy. I wanted to see you. Have a chance to talk."

Ivy smiled. "Would you like some cocoa?"

Baxter's face lit up. "That would be swell."

They talked for what seemed like hours. Little by little, the old misunderstandings, the hostility, the resentments and quarrels dissolved. Gradually they let down their defenses, took off their masks, were gentle with each other.

When at last Baxter rose to leave, he seemed hesitant. "I hope we can let bygones be bygones, Ivy. I'd like to be friends again."

"Of course, Baxter. And thanks . . . for everything."

The next day, Ivy left the apartment at the usual time, wanting to delay as long as possible telling Mercedes about the unpleasant incident with Mrs. Fallon and that she had been fired. If, as Baxter assured her, the job at the newspaper was still available and she got it, that would be time enough. The main thing was to find employment as quickly as possible, before their small store of money ran out.

Part 7

Free at Last

And the truth shall set you free.
John 8:32

Chapter Twenty-Three

At the *Brookdale Messenger*, Ivy was given an application form to fill out. She sat down and bent her head over the sheet, concentrating on filling in the blanks in her best handwriting. So many questions. They wanted to know a great deal about a prospective employee. It was all a little daunting. But this must be how the real, workaday world operated, a world from which she had been sheltered for years by the affluence of her adopted parents.

Ivy sighed. Well, now she had to face the fact that she must support herself and Mercedes for the foreseeable future . . . at least until Daddy got out of prison. She broke off the rest of that thought abruptly. Who knew what things would be like then? Dan Ellison had been given a sentence of five to fifteen years, with possible time off for good behavior. But what kind of job could *he* find then? Who would hire a fifty-five-year-old ex-convict when he was released? Suppressing a shudder, Ivy finished filling in the application.

As she put her pen back into her handbag, she noticed the store key at the bottom! Just a few weeks before, Mr. Fallon had given her an extra key to the front door, saying gruffly that in case of an emergency she should have one. At the time Ivy had felt gratified. At least, *he* must be satisfied with her work and considered her a trustworthy employee, no matter his wife's opinion.

Ivy took out the key, turned it over in her palm, staring down at it. She would have to return it. There was no alternative, though she recoiled at the thought of facing Mrs. Fallon again. All kinds of possibilities churned in her mind. Could she put it in an envelope and mail it back? But she had a paycheck coming. Should she keep the key until then? No, Mrs. Fallon would probably not send her check. She would make her come back and beg for it. Ivy shrank from a second ugly scene. There must be another way. Anything to avoid a face-to-face confrontation with the disagreeable woman. Ivy would just have to think of one.

Putting the key back in her purse, Ivy turned in her application to the personnel clerk and was told she would be contacted for an interview after the application was reviewed.

Leaving the newspaper building, Ivy walked down to the park. She always did her best thinking there. The wind was chilly, and Ivy bent her head against it, shivering a little. But it cleared her mind. By the time she had circled the duck pond twice, she had decided what she would do. She would place the key in an envelope and, after closing time, would slip it under the front door of the store. They would find it when they opened for business in the morning. But she would have to find some excuse to go out after supper.

Inadvertently, Mercedes herself provided one. That evening, when she mentioned she had finished her latest book, Ivy immediately offered to return it and select some new novels for her.

"Tonight?"

"The library is open this evening," Ivy assured her. "I shouldn't be long." She gathered her jacket and hat and the book, and left, having sealed the store key into a sturdy envelope and put it in her purse.

Outside, it was not yet dark, but the sky was an ominous grayish purple color. Ivy looked up anxiously, scanning the rain-threatening clouds. She would have to hurry.

A block away from the store, Ivy's anger churned again inside her. The closer she got to the building, the stronger the feelings of resentment and indignation grew. How dared that woman talk to her the way she had? How dared she accuse her of stealing? If she were a thief, there must have been dozens of times she could have stolen something from the store, something that never would have been missed — a package of pins, a spool of thread, even some hairpins, *even* a pair of gloves, if it came to that. It had simply never entered Ivy's mind. Why should it? Ivy thought of all the days she had unpacked boxes of new stock, marked it, put it away. It had never occurred to her to do anything dishonest. She had been working for the Fallons for almost a year, and Mrs. Fallon had never found any serious complaint with her work. Why now? And why over something so petty and without giving her a chance to offer a possible explanation?

Well, Ivy told herself, she was well out of it. With the possibility of a better job at the newspaper, as soon as she returned the key, she would be finished with the whole business.

It was all very well to come to these logical conclusions, but her emotions were a different thing entirely. At the corner across from the store, Ivy halted. All the injustice, humiliation, and spitefulness she had put up with as the Fallons' employee swept over her. Her chest felt tight, her stomach knotted painfully. She drew a deep breath and crossed the street. She took the envelope with the key inside from her handbag, went quickly up the steps, and bent down to wedge it through the small space between the double doors.

Just as she did, she saw something that caught her attention. Looking through the upper glass portion of the door, toward the very back of the store, she saw a wavering light. Ivy frowned. Curious, she peered closer and noticed that the door from the store into the storage room was open. The light seemed to be coming from there. That was strange. The Fallons always checked the back of the store first, before coming through to leave by the front door, locking it behind them as they closed for the night. Was someone still there? It was after seven-thirty — nearly eight o'clock. It was unlike the methodical couple to have closed the store and left a lamp burning in the back. They were unusually conscious of fire, having lost one store to fire in their early years as storekeepers. They were constantly reminding each other of that experience and careful about all the lamps in the store, keeping the wicks trimmed, the globes clean, wiping up oil spills.

Ivy hesitated. Her impulse was simply to push the envelope containing the key under the door and leave. But her conscience would not allow her that easy escape. Something about that dim light bothered her. Should she go in and check? What if it was a burglar who had somehow broken in through the back? And what if there was more than one? It would be foolhardy and dangerous for Ivy to let herself in the store and surprise them. What should she do? Much as she hated the thought, should she go by the Fallons' house to tell them a lamp had been left burning? Or would it be better to go to the police station?

Indecision paralyzed her. It was fast getting dark. The envelope with the key in it was still clutched in her hand. They had probably just left a lamp burning. She could simply go in and blow the lamp out, then leave. She'd have to make up her mind, and fast. The wind was blowing and it was now dark. Ivy still hadn't gotten to the library, and Mercedes would begin to worry if she didn't get home soon.

Yes, yes, the only thing to do was do what

was at hand. Ivy tore open the envelope, took the key, unlocked the door, and stepped inside. She closed it carefully behind her, the bell above jangling a little. The sound was startling in the silence of the empty store. If there were anyone in the storage room, a thief, it would have alerted him.

She stood for a moment, breathing deeply, straining to hear. Then she heard low moans. A cold eerie feeling gripped her. What was *that?* Then it came again. It was definitely the sound of a human voice. Another moan echoed hollowly. Slowly Ivy advanced toward the back of the store, her heart like a drumbeat in her ears.

At the door of the storage room, she saw a lamp sending out pale circles of light from where it had been placed on a wooden crate. Ivy stood still. The moans came again. Ivy took a step, her mouth dry with fear.

She swallowed, then called in a shaky voice, "Hello! Is anyone there?"

That was probably idiotic. What intruder would answer? But someone did. She heard a muffled groan, followed by an agonized voice. "Help!"

Ivy moved quickly toward the lamp. Its wick had burned low, the flame sputtering. She picked it up and held it high. An arc of light shed a flickering circle all around the room as she slowly turned. Then she saw the crumpled figure on the floor under the open trapdoor in the ceiling leading to the attic storage room. Over the prone body lay the ladder, pinning the person under it to the floor.

"Help, please," the voice came again, and Ivy ran over. It was *Mrs. Fallon.*

"Mrs. Fallon, it's me, Ivy. I came to return the store key and saw the light. I . . ." Ivy crouched down beside her.

"Oh, thank God," came a moan. "A rung in the ladder broke . . . I lost my balance and fell. The ladder toppled on top of me. I . . . I think I may have broken something . . ."

"Don't worry now. I'll try to help you."

"Oh, hurry. I've been lying here for hours. Wilbur's still in Bridgeport and I . . ."

Ivy wasn't sure what she could do. She had no idea how badly Mrs. Fallon was hurt. If she couldn't move, how was Ivy to get her up and out of there? The first thing Ivy had to do was reassure her that she was no longer alone and helpless, then go get help.

"Don't try to talk. I'll see if I can get this ladder off you first, then I'll go for help, get Dr. Miller," Ivy said breathlessly. She set down the oil lamp at a safe distance, but so it shed some light. Then she tugged at the ladder, trying to move it off the frantic woman. It was heavy, old, and splintery as Ivy remembered from times she herself had had to clamber up it, taking boxes to storage. At last she was able to pull it to one side of the injured woman. She pushed it out of the way with her foot, then bent over Mrs. Fallon again. Taking one of her hands, Ivy felt that it was icy. Mrs. Fallon might be in shock.

Mrs. Fallon's eyelids fluttered and she mumbled, "It's my ankle . . . it twisted under me as I fell. I heard something crack. I'm sure it's broken."

Quickly Ivy unbuttoned her jacket and put it over the injured woman. Scrambling to her feet, she unbuttoned the band of one of her petticoats, stepped out of it, folded it into a mound, and slipped it under Mrs. Fallon's head. Leaning down, she said, "Mrs. Fallon, I can't lift you myself, but I'll go get help. I'll come back as soon as possible. It's the only way . . . do you understand?"

"Yes." Mrs. Fallon tried to nod. Her face was chalky; she was obviously in great pain. "But, first . . ." Her bony hand reached out, encircling Ivy's wrist and with considerable effort, she gasped. "Ivy, I took another lamp up in the attic so I could see when I brought the boxes up. It's still there . . . been burning a long time. The wick must be dangerously low. You'll have to go up and get it or there might be . . . a fire . . ." She closed her eyes and moaned again.

Ivy's heart sank. The hated attic storage room. Her old fear of heights gripped her. All her old ploys to avoid going up there, even in the daytime, struck her. Now there was no way out. Nothing else to do but go. The burning lamp was a hazard. The possibility of fire was making Mrs. Fallon extremely agitated. Ivy would have to do it.

"All right. First I'd better get a blanket from stock and cover you better," she said, but Mrs. Fallon's eyes were closed again. Afraid that Mrs. Fallon might have slipped into a dangerous, even fatal, unconsciousness, Ivy knew she must hurry.

Running into the store, she grabbed a blanket off a shelf, and raced back. She placed it over Mrs. Fallon, tucking it around her body. Ivy's teeth were chattering, and she clenched her jaw. She could not waste any more time.

She slid the ladder over until it was under the trapdoor, slowly lifted it, and propped the top part against the open ledge. She saw the missing rung that had caused Mrs.

Fallon's fall. Feeling very insecure, she slowly mounted. Reaching the top, she squinted into the dark cavern of the attic. It was then Ivy also remembered that the loft had no real floor, only wooden planks placed across the yawning lower emptiness. She shuddered.

Leaving the unstable ladder, Ivy shifted onto her knees. Holding one of the studs on which the low rafters rested, she got shakily to her feet. From this vantage point, she could see the lamp. To her horror, she realized that it was set in one of the eaves clear across from where she stood. Here her courage almost failed her.

She would have to walk, step by step, across a board less than a foot wide to get to the lamp. The light from the lamp sent grotesque shadows wavering into the darkness. Not even when she had to learn a new trick for Paulo had she ever felt so afraid. But there was no escape. She had to do this. She would just put one foot down, then the other one, until she got across.

Trembling, Ivy remembered Liselle's warning: "Don't look down. Don't panic." Repeating that to herself, she placed one foot out, feeling the plank beneath her creak with her weight. She recalled one of the Flying Fortunatos telling her that when facing the possibility of falling, he curled himself into a ball to avoid serious injury. "Oh God, don't let me fall," Ivy prayed desperately. Then something from the psalmist's plea came into her frantic mind: "Oh God, an ever present help in time of trouble, help me!" If ever she needed divine help, it was *now*.

She was almost across. A few more careful steps, and she could reach the lamp. Then she would have to retrace her steps, this time carrying the sputtering oil lamp. With one arm she reached up, grasped hold of one of the cross posts to steady herself, and slowly leaned down to pick up the lamp. Her hands were sweaty and slipped a little on the base of the brass holder. She thought of Liselle and her parasol. If only the lamp were that light. Between gritted teeth, Ivy coached herself, "Don't look down. Put one foot in front of the other. Don't panic." Holding the lamp high, Ivy extended her other arm to balance herself and inched back along the creaking board to the trapdoor.

"Thank you, Lord. Thank you," she whispered as she shakily set down the lamp, turned herself around and carefully lowered her body, dangling her feet until they touched the top rung of the ladder. Firmly holding on with one hand, she took up the lamp once more, and began her slow descent.

One foot reached the bottom rung, and Ivy turned slightly, searching with the toe of her other shoe until it touched the floor. Shuddering with relief, she slowly placed both feet firmly on the floor. The flimsy ladder tilted forward and she gripped it, steadying it. She put the lamp on a crate nearby and hurried over to the injured woman.

Bending over her, Ivy said, "I'm back. Everything's safe, Mrs. Fallon. Now I have to go for help. I'll make it as fast as I can."

Mrs. Fallon's mouth twitched slightly and Ivy assumed she had heard and understood. She felt torn, hating to leave the woman in such a condition, but knowing she had to get medical aid.

Ivy blew out the smoking lamp that was burning hazardously low, then she ran back through the store, out the door, and up the street toward town. Where should she go? For the doctor first? Where did Dr. Miller live? She couldn't remember. Ivy kept running. She felt a sharp pain in her side but pressed on. She paused when she reached the center of town, seeing the courthouse and the city hall that faced the square across from the red brick *Brookdale Messenger* building.

There were lights on. Of course, they were getting out the morning edition. There would be people in there — printers, linotype operators, editorial staff members . . . Baxter! Why hadn't she thought of him before? Picking up her skirts with a last surge of energy, Ivy ran through the square, up the steps of the newspaper building, and into the lobby. Lights were on in the City Room. People wearing green eyeshades sat at their desks. She went to the door, searching frantically, then she saw him. At the same time he had raised his head and seen her. They moved simultaneously, he to his feet, Ivy forward.

"Oh, Baxter!" she gasped. "You've got to come with me. Something terrible's happened . . ."

"Ivy, what is it? Your mother?"

She shook her head, "No! Mrs. Fallon! We've got to get a doctor. She fell, and she's hurt. I left her at the store, but we have to hurry . . ."

The next hour was a blur of confusion, of voices, of movement. She heard Baxter shout to the copyboy to run over to Dr. Miller's house, tell him it was an emergency, and get the doctor to Fallon's Mercantile as quickly as possible. Then Baxter grabbed Ivy's arm and hurried with her back to the store.

Ivy stayed beside Mrs. Fallon, trying to reassure her, until a red-faced, hatless Dr. Miller blustered through the store to the back room, puffing in his haste and irritable for having left his dinner pudding uneaten. But when he saw the prone figure of Mrs. Fallon, he was all medical professionalism. He knelt down and examined her. She was conscious and able to answer the doctor's questions.

A few minutes later he got stiffly to his feet, pronouncing a possible fractured ankle, but no other serious injuries. He told Baxter to send for the ambulance to take her to the hospital. To Mrs. Fallon he said, "Since your husband's out of town, it would be best for you to be somewhere you'll be looked after properly for the next day or two. I'll go along and be at the hospital to meet you and see you settled."

He gave Ivy a brisk nod. "You can stay here, can't you, until the ambulance attendants arrive?"

"Yes, sir."

"Good. You did well to prevent her going into shock," he said, then bustled off.

"Ivy," Mrs. Fallon called in a weak voice

and Ivy went over to her. The woman moistened her dry lips with her tongue, then with considerable effort said, "Ivy, I was going to send you a note. I'm sorry . . . about the gloves . . . I mean, about accusing you . . ."

"Never mind about that now. I don't think you should talk, Mrs. Fallon."

"But I *have* to," she insisted. "It was all a mistake, Ivy. Mrs. Cates came in and told me . . . when she took the gloves she bought out of the box . . . there was another pair underneath . . . the gloves that were missing. It was just a mistake. Two pairs of gloves in the same box . . ."

Vindicated! How ironic that now it didn't seem to matter. Ivy felt neither satisfaction nor relief. She had not stolen the gloves. The fact was that it had simply been a mistake, her own perhaps, working too hastily in her desire to get to the wedding. But, at least, the matter had been cleared up. "It's all right, Mrs. Fallon."

The woman cleared her throat. "I just wanted you to know I'm sorry. And . . . thank you, Ivy." Her eyelids closed again.

Ivy remained beside her until the hospital attendants arrived with the stretcher, placed Mrs. Fallon on it, and carried her out to the waiting ambulance. Ivy was left with Baxter. He walked through the store with her, making sure everything was secure. Taking a final look around, they went out the front door and locked it.

Outside, Baxter gave the handle an extra twist, then satisfied, he said quietly, "You were very brave, Ivy."

"Oh, I'm not so sure of that, Baxter. I was scared to death."

"Yes, but you did it anyway. That's what real courage is, you know."

He surprised her by taking both her hands. When she winced slightly, he turned them over and examined them. Ivy's palms were stinging, scratched, and splintered from the rough wood of the ladder, the unsanded boards in the attic. "You hurt yourself!" he exclaimed.

She tried to withdraw her hands, but Baxter held them fast. He slowly raised them to his lips and kissed them. "Did I ever tell you, Ivy, how much I admire you?"

Embarrassed, Ivy shook her head and gently pulled her hands away. "Don't give me credit I don't deserve, Baxter. If you knew how much I disliked Mrs. Fallon, how I really felt . . ."

"That doesn't matter, Ivy. Don't you see that? It makes what you did even more admirable." He paused, then drew her hand through his arm. "You're tired, worn out.

411

We won't talk anymore. I'll take you home."

They went down the steps of the store. A light rain was falling. Suddenly Ivy realized that her jacket was still on Mrs. Fallon. Baxter noticed, too. Her thin shirtwaist would soon be soaked.

"Here, Ivy," Baxter said, taking off his own jacket and placing it gently over her shoulders. Together they ran through the rain. When he left her at her door, he urged, "Try to get some rest, Ivy. You deserve it."

To Ivy's great relief, Mercedes had gone to bed and fallen asleep. Grateful that her mother had not been concerned at her long absence, Ivy tiptoed out of the bedroom. She would explain everything tomorrow.

Although drained physically and emotionally, Ivy still found it hard to go right to sleep. Her mind kept reliving the events of the evening, their possible consequences. She thought of Mrs. Fallon pressing her hand and murmuring, "Thank you." It made Ivy uncomfortable that Mrs. Fallon now might feel some obligation, however reluctant. It didn't change the fact that she had accused her of stealing. Ivy closed her eyes wearily. She didn't want to think about Mrs. Fallon. It didn't matter. She would never work there again. She had to think about the future, the possible new job at the newspaper.

That possibility immediately brought Baxter to mind. He had been so wonderful tonight. Come to her aid without question, lending her strength and assistance she had really no right to expect from him. How could she show him how grateful she was? Before any satisfactory answer to that question came, Ivy was asleep.

Chapter Twenty-Four

The next morning, sunshine flooded the tiny parlor. Ivy stirred and nearly slipped off the narrow sofa bed. She shifted her position, then as she came fully awake, she was aware of movement in the kitchen, the whistling sound of a kettle, the clink of dishes. Ivy raised herself on her elbows just as Mercedes appeared in the arch of the doorway. She was dressed and smiling.

"Oh, good, dear, you're awake. You were sleeping so soundly, I hated to disturb you. But it's almost seven fifteen and I didn't want you to be late for work, so I made coffee. I'll bring it right in."

Glad to see that her mother was more her old self than she had been in a very long time, Ivy wondered how she would take the news about what had taken place over the last two days. Whatever the reaction, Ivy decided she had to tell her. She was done with secrecy, sick of telling lies.

Mercedes reappeared with a steaming

cup, handed it to Ivy, and stood watching her as she took a sip. "Is it all right? Not too hot?"

"It's fine, perfect." Ivy managed a smile. "Sit down, Mother." She patted the edge of the couch. "I have something to tell you." And the whole story poured out.

"Why, how could they accuse you of dishonesty?" Mercedes was indignant. "How could she treat you like that? She wouldn't have dared if . . ." she broke off. "And what a brave girl you were. That awful woman! And to think I slept through the entire episode! There you were in all that danger, and I never knew." She sighed, a pained expression on her face as she gazed at Ivy. "Oh, darling, how much I've let you bear alone."

"You didn't know. How could you? Besides, what could you have done?"

"I could have been stronger all along! Not been such an ostrich, not seeing what I didn't want to see. All this time I haven't borne my share of the burden. But from now on, things are going to be different. I promise you, Ivy."

"Oh, Mother . . ." Ivy put down the coffee cup and held out her arms and Mercedes went into them, their tears mingling.

Mercedes insisted that for the remainder of the day Ivy rest from her ordeal of the night before. About noon she put on her hat, took the shopping basket, declaring she was going to buy groceries and prepare a dinner for them that would be "fit for a queen."

Ivy took a leisurely bath, dressed, and was brushing her freshly washed hair when a knock came on the door. She went to answer it, wondering who it could be at this time of the day. When she opened it, there stood Baxter, holding a florist's pot of white hyacinths.

"For you," he said, handing her the plant.

"Why, thank you." Ivy buried her nose in the fragrant blooms. "Mmmm, delicious! Makes me know spring is coming."

Baxter looked skeptical. "They're forced, of course. But at least it's a promise of what's to come." He paused. "May I come in, Ivy? I'd like to talk to you."

"Of course, Baxter." Ivy stepped back and held the door wider for him. "Won't you sit down? Would you like a cup of coffee?"

"No, thanks." Instead of sitting, Baxter paced the tiny room, then turned and faced Ivy, his expression serious. "I've been up half the night thinking, and there are things we have to discuss."

"What things?"

"Important things. Us."

"Us?"

"I've spent a lot of time thinking about us. About what happened. About your no longer writing to me . . . about your engagement. Well, I *was* angry and hurt, I admit that. But if you think it had anything to do with . . ." Baxter flung out his hands in a pleading gesture. "I know you blame me for what happened to your father and . . ."

Ivy set down the hyacinth plant on the table, centering it carefully, and shook her head. "No, Baxter, I told you. I don't blame you anymore. It would have unraveled anyhow, whether you had discovered it or someone else. Besides, my father has admitted his mistakes and he's resigned to paying for them."

Baxter was silent, pondering all this for a moment. "I guess what I really came to say today was . . . I love you, Ivy. I've never stopped loving you. What I have to find out is . . . how do you feel about *me?* I mean, you *did* love me once. Is it over? Or could you . . . love me again?"

"Baxter, that's not the question, really. You see, there's a lot *you* don't know about *me.* There are things I never told you, never told anyone in Brookdale, except Allison . . . she knows. Not even Mother or Daddy Dan

417

know all my past. I wanted to forget, wanted to hide it, afraid people wouldn't accept me . . . wouldn't love me. Even coming here on the Orphan Train is something I wanted to forget."

"Ivy, do you think *any* of that matters to me? I don't care about what's happened in the past. I know you now, the person you are . . . and I love you just as you are."

"Wait, Baxter. Sit down. I want to tell you something that may make a difference in the way you feel about me. I've been living a lie all these years. I did something that changed my life and Allison's. I never told anyone until before Allison got married, then I told her. But, of course, then it was far too late to change anything, to undo any damage I'd done."

Baxter was frowning. "I'm not sure I want to hear this, Ivy. If it's in the past, isn't it best forgotten? I can't imagine your doing anything to hurt Allison. She's always been your best friend."

"Listen, Baxter. I need to tell you," Ivy said quietly. "Please."

They sat on the sofa, face to face, and Ivy began her long story . . . beginning with the little girl waking up in the middle of the night to learn that her father had been killed . . . to the relentless circus training . . . to the abandoned child in the hospital . . . to the decision made on the train . . .

"So, you see, Baxter, I'm not an admirable person at all . . . not what you thought, but a liar and a fraud."

Baxter reached for her hands, grasped them tightly. "Hush, Ivy, don't be so hard on yourself. You're talking about a child . . . eight or nine years old. No one can blame you for what you did. I certainly don't. And you *are* admirable. You're brave and resourceful and courageous. Just think of all you'd survived before you were even ten years old — the death of both parents, being put in the hands of a harsh taskmaster who then heartlessly abandoned you, and then put on a train to travel hundreds of miles to be adopted by strangers. Not many people would have had what it takes to survive all that, Ivy."

"Baxter, Mother and Daddy Dan don't even know about my trading dresses with Allison, coming into their home under false pretenses . . ."

"You made them so happy, Ivy. I *know* that for a fact. My own parents always said how changed the Ellisons both were after they adopted you. You have to take some pride in that." He squeezed her hands, leaned toward her. "Nobody can do anything about the past, Ivy. It's gone. We can plan for the future, but we can't guarantee it. All we have is the present. I love you, Ivy, I want to make up to you for everything you've been through. I want to marry you, Ivy. I promise to try to make you happier than you've ever been."

Ivy smiled. Dear Baxter, didn't he realize what she had learned through all this? That you can't arrange someone else's happiness? That each person has to grow, suffer, survive, and find her own happiness?

"Will you marry me, Ivy?" There was a long pause, then he asked her again, "Darling Ivy, will you?"

Ivy did not answer him right away. She felt tears crowd her eyes. "Oh, Baxter, I can't even think of marriage, of my own plans, now. I can't leave Mother, can't do anything until Daddy . . . well, he has at least four more years to serve in his sentence. I can't abandon them."

"I'm not asking you to do that, Ivy. I'm asking you to let me share these responsibilities *with* you. You've struggled alone so long, been so courageous. But you don't have to go it alone anymore . . . if you'll let me help. Together it will be so much easier. Scripture confirms that . . . remember? 'Two are better than one, for if they fall, one will lift up his companion.' Ecclesiastes 4:9." He grinned suddenly, his eyes mischievous, "I wasn't in Mrs. Gaynor's Sunday school class for nothing!"

Ivy had to laugh. "Oh, Baxter, you're incorrigible!"

"So, Ivy, what's the answer? Will you, at least, consider my proposal?"

Before she could reply, the parlor door opened and Mercedes entered.

Baxter got to his feet. "Good morning, Mrs. Ellison. I've just proposed to Ivy, so now I'll ask you for your daughter's hand in marriage."

Mercedes looked at Ivy, then back at Baxter, and smiled. "Nothing could make me happier, Baxter. Dan and I always thought you two would make a fine match. So I know if he were here, he would join with me in granting it with all our hearts."

Ivy was stunned. Things were happening too fast. Baxter and her mother were both beaming, looking at her expectantly. She thought of the long loneliness of her life, the secret fears. Then she considered what her life might be like if she gave Baxter the answer he wanted. Someone to be there for her, someone "to love and to cherish above all others." Someone to stand by her, to support and strengthen her in all that might lie ahead as Daniel came out of prison, as both her parents aged. A home, children . . .

For the first time she could remember, Ivy felt peace. She no longer needed to feel alone or afraid. Baxter was standing there, offering her everything she had yearned for, despaired of ever having. Slowly the excitement began, turned into certainty. Something wonderful was waiting for her, beyond anything she had ever imagined. All she had to do was accept it, say "yes."

"If you really want me to marry you, Bax—" She never finished, for Baxter stepped forward and was drawing her into his arms.

At last! All the years of fear of abandonment, the uncertainty, the insecurity, the possibility of not being loved for herself, were over. Love was powerful. It healed, renewed, made broken hearts whole. Perhaps it was possible, *really* true, what the Bible promised: "I will restore the years the locust hath eaten. . . ."

Ivy closed her eyes for Baxter's kiss.

The employees of Thorndike Press hope you have enjoyed this Large Print book. All our Large Print titles are designed for easy reading, and all our books are made to last. Other Thorndike Press Large Print books are available at your library, through selected bookstores, or directly from the publishers.

For more information about titles, please call:

(800) 223-1244
(800) 223-6121

To share your comments, please write:

Publisher
Thorndike Press
295 Kennedy Memorial Drive
Waterville, Maine 04901